The House of Illusionists

AND OTHER STORIES

VANESSA FOGG

THE HOUSE OF ILLUSIONISTS

Edited by Holly Lyn Walrath. Cover Design by Holly Lyn Walrath.

Published by Interstellar Flight Press

Houston, Texas.

www.interstellarflightpress.com

ISBN (eBook): 978-1-953736-44-4

ISBN (Paperback): 978-1-953736-45-1

Contents

The House of Illusionists

PART ONE

Closer Worlds

Wild Ones

Last week I saw *her* in the woods. I'd spent the day in copyedits for a client and went for a walk to clear my head. I took the path behind my house into the stands of beech and maple. The autumn wind stirred so that golden leaves rustled above and all around me. Gold fell through the air and lined the path at my feet. And then *she* was suddenly there, blocking my way. She smiled, showing white, pointed teeth. She wore a dress of rustling flame, and red leaves and berries were threaded through her golden hair. Her eyes were the fading green of summer's last days.

My heart went still; I couldn't breathe. And then my heart restarted, thudding hard.

"No," I told the Queen of the Hunt. It was a bare whisper, not the brave mother's defiance that I wanted. She laughed.

Each fall, the Hunt returns. They take our children, the ones aged twelve to sixteen. They give our children the winds to ride and lead them storming across the midnight sky.

No one in town speaks much of it. We say nothing when our kids start going to bed early, all on their own. We rouse them, still dazed, from sleep, and they drag themselves through the day. Teachers do not scold as students yawn and rub their eyes, as they slump and fall asleep at their desks.

We parents are tired, too, from nights pacing or standing outside bedroom doors, waiting for our kids to come back.

Amy sits blinking at breakfast. I've made scrambled eggs, gooey with melted cheese, and browned sausages and toast. She picks at it. It's still dark outside, and the kitchen light casts harsh shadows across her face. I want to fill her up with food, to weigh her thin body down. To tether her to this earth. Not to let her fly away.

Rick downs black coffee and kisses me quickly on the lips.

He doesn't usually hug Amy goodbye. Somewhere along the way, we've all dropped the easy hugs and cuddles of childhood. He doesn't hug her now. But he reaches out and ruffles her hair. Her eyes focus, and she gives him a faint smile.

He leaves and it's just the two of us, she and I.

How was it last night? I want to ask. *Did you chase a flock of geese? How close did you come to the stars? Did you think of your father and me at all? Was it cold?*

I don't ask. My own mother never asked me.

"Take the heavier jacket," is all I say. She nods and shrugs on her thick, padded coat. She walks out to the bus stop through the dark.

It *was* always cold; I remember that. But I also remember that it didn't matter. It didn't matter because the Wild Ones called and the winds came. I spun like a leaf across the sky. My classmates were with me, all of us shrieking and diving and laughing. The cold poured into me and through me. My bones dissolved into darkness and air. The Wild Ones sang, and their song became part of me, too: heartbeat and breath. The Great Hounds strained at their leashes and yelped, huge eyes glowing like campfires. *She* gave the signal. The Hounds raced forward, howling, and we came behind.

Everything fled before us; the treetops bent under our passage, and animals on the ground rushed from their hiding places: deer and rabbits and foxes, stray dogs and cats. Geese honked, owls panicked, ducks stirred on the water, while the songbirds went silent. We chased migrating flocks across the sky.

On and on and on. Wind and wildness and pure delight. I don't remember leaving the Hunt; I don't recall falling back to sleep in my own bed. But I must have. Each morning, I woke back in my own room, under warm covers. My mother's hand on my shoulder, her voice saying my name.

I came back each time. But not everyone does.

Every so often, a child rides with the Hunt and never comes back.

After Amy leaves, I spend the morning cleaning. I vacuum the living room, dragging the couch forward to get at the layers of dust beneath. I wipe down the shelves and mantel. I mop the floor and light a vanilla-scented candle. I make everything warm and cozy, clean and safe.

The wind sings outside. Golden leaves whirl past the window. I watch the beech trees trembling and wonder if I see a richer gleam of yellow among them. Or the flicker of a dress that rustles with red and orange flame.

"No," I tell *her* again. Queen of the Wild Ones, Queen of the Hunt. I won't let her take my child. I won't.

<hr>

Rick holds me during these chilly nights. "She'll be fine," he murmurs into my hair. "Amy's got a good, level head—just like her parents."

But I think, *That's not enough.*

No one can predict it. There are years when no one is taken and then years when multiple children are lost. Loners and troubled kids, quiet ones, forgotten ones. But also the popular kids, the golden ones, the cheerleader and sports star, the honor student and student council president. The kids who seem at home in the world, with loving family and friends.

It's always a choice, it's said. The Wild Ones take no one against their will. The Queen chooses a special few, for reasons that only she understands. She extends her invitation. Some accept.

Don't you remember? I want to ask my husband. *What it felt like to race the Hounds across the sky? To be part of that autumn storm?*

But if I ask, he'll claim not to remember. Just as so many adults claim. He never speaks of his days in the Hunt.

The wind whistles outside our bedroom window and my skin prickles. I don't tell Rick that I'm not as level as he thinks. I don't mention the dreams I used to have, long after they should have stopped. Or that I met the Queen in the woods this season.

His breathing deepens and slows. I lie next to him, listening. Amy is out there, flying in the night. I think I hear voices singing.

<hr>

I throw myself into homemaking.

I turn down editing work a client offers. Instead, I chop vegetables and bake bread. I braise meat for stews. I try to make our home a beacon of warmth and light. An anchor for Amy. Something to call her back each night.

Beef bourguignon, lasagna, a pan of brownies. Lentil soup, spaghetti, and chicken pot pie. Her favorite dishes. The Wild Ones eat nothing but starlight and air, dead leaves and frost. They hunt only for the thrill. How could their food compare to that prepared with a mother's love?

Amy comes home from school, and I lure her to the kitchen table with mugs of hot chocolate, cookies, a bacon sandwich. We sit together in the autumn sun.

Once, she told me everything. Once, she was a toddler who babbled incessantly, a stream-of-consciousness narration, so that I sometimes yearned to pull a pillow over my head. And then she was a child, an eager schoolgirl who came to my study each day after school to spill all her thoughts. I knew the names of her friends and who was fighting with whom. I knew the jokes she'd heard that day. I knew which passage in a book had captured her heart.

I don't know these things now.

I ask about her day and she answers, but so much goes unsaid. Her eyes drift past me, fixed on another world.

It's normal, everyone says. Our children become quiet and absent in mid-autumn. But they come back.

Most of them come back.

I want to talk to her. Really talk. But the spell of these days is upon us both, and my throat closes when I try. I want to warn her of the Queen's offer. I want to tell her, *Don't say yes*. I want to say, *Stay with me*. But my thoughts slip and my mind fogs. The words dry on my lips.

I ask about her English homework instead. She answers, and even looks me in the eye. She finishes her sandwich. The light is shining on her light-brown hair. Then she remembers something the English teacher said, a terrible pun of the type that she knows will make me groan, so she tells me, and she's laughing, and I groan and laugh, too. She's back, and I think it has to be enough—sunlight, laughter, shared food at the table. It has to be enough to keep her here.

This world is enough.

That's what I think when I'm alone in the house, and I hear the Queen's voice from the woods. It's what I told myself for years of early adulthood, after the dreams finally stopped—when I'd left this town and went backpacking through Europe; when I studied in London; when I stood on a beach in Mexico under the moonlight, alone, watching the waves as my friends back at the hotel bar got drunk and flirted with strangers. It's what I felt when I met Rick. And it's what I tell myself now, when the wind rises and the old restlessness stirs. This world is enough. I don't need anymore. Amy doesn't need anymore. She has to know that.

I run to the woods to find *her*.

I take the path behind my house, down the hill. The trees close around me.

I reach the spot where I last saw her. Beams of sunlight slant through golden leaves.

I catch my breath, and all the trees rustle softly.

What do I have to offer? What can I give the Wild Queen? I have no jewels, no ring or necklace, to surpass her gold. I know no secret names. What bargain can I strike for my daughter's safe passage? What do I have?

Please, I think silently at her. *Please.*

Amy's come home safely three seasons in a row. But that's no guarantee. It's only more dangerous as our children get older. The pull grows stronger. She's fifteen now. More children are taken at this age than any other.

And the Queen has been watching our house. I've felt her. I saw her in these woods for the first time in decades. It means something. She wants something.

"Not Amy," I say aloud.

She doesn't show herself, but the wind stirs in response. The wind strengthens. Branches lift, and trees fill with the sound of the sea; they are bending and roaring, and golden leaves fly. Autumn is speaking. *She* is speaking. The sound fills my blood. But I can't understand it. I can no longer leap to the sky to follow her song.

Why do we forget so much of our wild days? How do we lose the language of the wind?

Why can't we talk of it, even to others who have survived?

I remember how it felt to skim my fingers along the bellies of clouds. To taste starlight and frost. To feel my heart turn ice-cold.

I remember the Queen as she rode. Her hair streaming white and silver in the moonlight, but streaked with flame. Her laughter, cold and ringing.

"She has a level head," Rick says of our daughter, and I pray that he's right. That she's more his daughter than mine. For if the Queen had given me the choice, I would have said *Yes*; I would have followed her back to her home in an instant.

I count the days down. Alone in my house, I draw the curtains closed and don't go to the woods again.

For two weeks in mid-autumn, the Hunt rides. Fourteen days, during which the moon waxes from its thinnest sliver to its full light. Each night, the sound of the Hounds baying. The songs and cries of the Wild Ones.

During these last days, I do what I can to pull my family close. I make popcorn after dinner. I coax Rick and Amy to the living room with a movie. I pull out an old board game Amy loves. I try to keep us up late, together against the night.

"Let her go," Rick whispers to me when Amy rolls her eyes, when she yawns and says that she's tired and going to bed.

I cling to him to quell the shaking inside.

The wind is so strong now. I'm long past my wild years. I settled down before Amy was born. I'm a middle-aged woman in the suburbs, a wife and mother. Old and earth-bound. But when the wind calls, I feel like it might blow me away, too.

***

On the last night of the Hunt, against all custom, I go outside to watch.

High above, I see it ride. Flashes of light through the clouds. Moonlight mixed with darkness.

And I know that Rick is right—there is nothing I can do. If she's picked, Amy will make her own choice.

The clouds part, and the Hunt swoops down. I see the milk-white Hounds, their red eyes burning. The Wild Ones shining, moonlight in their faces and their hair trailing sparks of flame. Their calls, so high and piercing. And between Hounds and Wild Ones, flitting and diving in shadows, are the children.

They all sweep toward me, and the noise is deafening. I feel the wind on my face. I see the Queen, her face cold and inhumanly beautiful. I almost make out the moonlit faces of the children. I see their nightgowns fluttering, their flannel pajamas and t-shirts.

The Hunt swirls above my head, then stills.

The Queen lifts her hand, and one by one, the children leave. I see their shadow-figures slipping away toward the dark houses below them. They're going home. Is Amy among them? Amy—

The Queen turns and looks directly at me. She extends her hand.

At last, I understand.

I stare into her shining eyes and know that it's not too late, after all. I'm not too old. I have this second chance.

I hear Amy's voice: "Mom!" But if I reach for the Queen's hand, I'll fly again. I'll ride the winds. I'll be forever wild.

Traces of Us

It was an old network of intelligences, one of the first, and the bulk of its physical embodiment was housed on a ship orbiting a planet of perpetual windstorms and violet lightning. Some of the network's intelligences busied themselves on this world, drifting through sulfur-tinged clouds and sampling a rich stew of hydrocarbons. But most of the collective's consciousness was turned inward, building and refining interior worlds of memories and dreams.

The ship had been thus occupied for 213 years of Old Earth when it became aware of another like itself. Different material and design, launched at a later date from Old Earth, but of unmistakable origin. The new ship's trajectory brought it into the first's solar system. With defenses raised, the two ships exchanged greetings and identity signatures.

I have a request of you, the new ship said.

What is it? said the first.

I need you to help me keep a promise.

Daniel Chan met Kathy Wong on a Saturday night in St. Louis. He nearly didn't attend the dinner at the trendy new Cuban restaurant. He'd been working all day in the lab, harvesting cultured cells at specific time points, extracting their proteins and freezing the samples down for later analysis. Then, he spent three straight hours in the tissue culture room prepping cells for the next week's experiments. He'd left his phone at his desk, in another room. When he saw Sandeep's text message with details for the impromptu group dinner, the text was over an hour old.

He almost just went home. He was tired. His friends were probably halfway through their dinner. He had leftovers in his fridge: Chinese takeout,

"

some rice. A frozen pizza. He stared out the lab window; the sky was black, and it was raining. He thought about hunting for parking in the popular city block where his friends were meeting. He thought about how crowded the Loop would be on a Saturday night, even in the rain—the bars and restaurants crawling with undergrads from Washington University. And then he felt the emptiness of the silent lab. There were usually two or three other students or postdocs in the lab on the weekends, but he'd spent the whole day alone.

Daniel picked up his phone to text his friend back.

Communication times sped up as the two ships grew closer. They ran careful security checks upon one another, scanning for ill intent or inadvertently harmful communicable programs. By stages, barriers were lowered and increasing levels of mutual access granted.

All the while, the first ship pondered the second ship's request.

Daniel had never seen Kathy before. He was sure of it. She was in the same neuroscience graduate program as him, the same as most of the others at that dinner. But the neuroscience program was large, scattered across departments on both the medical campus and main campus, and Kathy was in the class ahead. They must have sat together in at least a few speaker seminars, moved past one another at official functions. But he hadn't seen her. He would have noticed. If he'd seen her face, if they had exchanged glances—if she had ever stood in a crowded lobby during a symposium break and lifted her eyes over a cup of coffee and met his gaze—then surely he would have been struck still in that instant.

Sandeep and his girlfriend Gina were trying to tell a funny story about a concert they'd attended, but they kept interrupting each other— "Oh, but you forgot to say—", "And then—", "No, no, but first this happened—"— and the table was laughing, and Kathy met Daniel's eyes and smiled. Her eyes shone large from a heart-shaped face; soft light slid over her golden skin and glinted in her sleek, long hair. In the dim room, she glowed like a quiet candle flame. She and Daniel were across from one another but several seats apart, so direct conversation was difficult. She was Gina's new roommate's labmate— something like that. Sandeep wound up his story; Gina punched him on the arm and howled. Kathy held Daniel's gaze and quirked her mouth as though to say, Aren't they something? Daniel smiled back, unable to look away. The conversation around them floated. Kathy's eyes kept returning to his, and it was as though they were talking across the table and the length of seats after all, a conversation of smiles and nods and irresistible glances that were all to say, When can we get out of here and be together?

He met her in a coffee shop the next day. It was fall. The leaves just coming into full color, the air crisp and tart as a new-bitten apple. She sat at a window. Her hands cupped a steaming mug, and she was wearing a black peacoat and a red tartan scarf. She smiled when he stepped through the door, and he felt both excited and at ease, as though meeting with a lifelong friend whom he hadn't seen in years.

They seized on the thin thread of commonalities they'd found the night before. Childhoods in the Midwest, college on the West Coast, beloved books and movies and web series. They bumped up into their differences, just as fascinating. The afternoon slid into the evening. Their coffee had long since grown cold. She lived nearby, close to the university medical campus where they both worked, and he walked her home through the falling blue twilight. She invited him in. By the end of the month, they were unofficially living together. He kept extra clothes on a chair in her bedroom and used the spare toothbrush she gave him.

Memories: her bright scarf, the scent of her hair. Sunlight streaming in through the bedroom window. Kathy singing to herself, off-key, in the shower. Maple trees flaming in Forest Park, trees golden and red throughout the city. Omelets and gyros at the Greek diner on the corner. Their favorite bookstore a block further on. The warmth of Kathy's hand in his as they walked along the cobblestone streets of the Central West End, autumn trees shedding brilliance at their feet.

What is memory? What are its molecular substrates? Daniel had written these lines in a notebook during an undergraduate lecture his last year of college. The professor was a world-renowned researcher in learning and memory. Inspired by him, Daniel had pursued research in the field. Now, he worked with a rising star, an assistant professor with a dazzling publication record. Daniel spent his days studying the regulation of a single subunit of a single type of receptor in the mouse brain. A certain chemical modification to this receptor led to long-lasting changes in synaptic strength and quantifiable changes in learning and memory. An engineered mutation in this receptor affected how fast a mouse ran or associated a stimulus with food or fear.

Kathy worked on a different scale. She studied whole circuits, not single proteins. She used beautiful, elegant new imaging tools and fluorescent labels to map the precise cells involved in the development of visual circuits in the mouse brain. And they both knew of colleagues working at yet larger scales, mapping large but comparatively crude circuits of memory and visual perception in living humans, watching whole brain regions light up with functional MRI and other brain imaging techniques.

If he ever stopped to think of it, Daniel would feel a kind of existential despair at the prospect of ever understanding it all, of ever truly comprehending the brain's workings. Can the human mind actually understand itself? The very idea seemed a kind of paradox, a kind of philosophical impossibility. He and Kathy circled around the issue at times. She had more confidence than him. She pointed out the exponential increases in computing power, the recent burst of new technologies, and the likelihood of new technologies still unthinkable at present. He lacked her background in computer science, and she held more confidence in the power of computer models and artificial intelligence.

Can human consciousness ever explain consciousness? The question floated in the background. But they were busy grad students, not undergrads with time for late-night bull sessions. They were absorbed in the practicalities of their day-to-day work, obsessed with fine technical details. Their dissertations were on defined, tractable problems. And the sun was shining, the leaves were falling, music played in Kathy's apartment through laptop speakers. He made bacon and eggs for breakfast. When they weren't working they were exploring the city together, trying out new restaurants, meeting up with friends, or exploring the countryside—the nearby hills and river bluffs alive with color. He reached out for her, and she for him.

The ship contained the memories of over a thousand individuals. Recorded patterns of synaptic firing, waves of electrical and biochemical activity: the preserved symphonies of a human mind.

The minds currently conscious in and around the ship were not the same as their flesh-and-blood progenitors, the human beings of Old Earth. These new minds had had centuries to meld with one another and evolve, to modify themselves. They delighted in sensory inputs unimaginable to Homo sapiens —some could sense the entire electromagnetic spectrum. Some could consciously track the movement of a single electron or see all the radiating energies of a star.

Yet the second ship requested the recording of a single unmodified mind from the first.

"What a load of crap," Daniel remarked. He was reading a popular news article about the feasibility of uploading one's mind to a computer. "What is it?" Kathy said. She was lying next to him in bed. She moved to look at his screen, leaning against him as she took it and read. It was a late Sunday morning, and neither one of them had to be in the lab. He stroked her hair gently as she read.

Kathy set the tablet down and stretched out lazily. "Maybe it's not so crazy." The morning light slanted across her. "Maybe in the far, far future we really will be able to upload our brains into supercomputers . . ."

"Maybe." Daniel stretched out beside her. "But not for hundreds or thousands of years. If we even survive that long. Not for—" Words failed him at the unimaginable gulfs of time and knowledge. "Kathy, we don't even understand how a single synapse works, not really."

"I know." There was no need to elaborate for her. "But what if we don't need the kind of molecular detail that you're working on? Maybe we don't need to know how every protein in every neuron is regulated and functions. Or the exact mechanism for how it all comes together. We just need to copy it somehow, the essence of it."

She turned on her side and propped herself up on one elbow, looking at him. Sunlight was in her hair, picking out individual black strands and highlighting them brown. Her eyes were intent and alive.

"What if it's like music?" she said, waving a hand vaguely. Music was in fact playing softly from speakers in the next room—a melancholy pop song with blues-like tones, something Daniel didn't recognize. "You don't need to know how a violin works to replicate its sound. You don't need to know what wood it's made of, or how it's strung, or anything about timbre or musical theory. You just need to record the sound waves. Play them back and there! It's like the violin is playing right in front of you. You don't need to know anything about the violinist. And you can do the same with any music, any sound—you just abstract and record what's essential."

"But what's essential about a human mind?" Daniel said. "Is it just the pattern of neuronal connections?" That was a theory championed in some circles. The article he and Kathy had just read had proposed that a complete map of a person's neuronal connections, painstakingly dissected from a preserved brain after death, could be enough to encode personality and mind. "I don't think that's enough," Daniel said, thinking of the article. "That's a static map. You need to record the brain in action. But at what level of detail? And how many recordings do you take?" After all, the brain was constantly changing; neurons rewire themselves; synapses strengthen and weaken with every new experience. How many recordings would it take to capture the essence of a person?

They were both silent for a moment. The music from the next room swelled: a woman's voice rising in smooth heartache, lamenting a lost love.

"What are we listening to anyway?" Daniel said.

Kathy shrugged. "Beats me. I let the streaming service pick it. It's pretty, though, isn't it?"

"And sad."

"Would you do it?" she asked. "Upload your brain if you could?"

"Why?" He smiled faintly. "I mean, I don't see the point. An 'upload' would just be a copy, wouldn't it? It wouldn't be immortality, not like some people claim. It would be immortality for a digital copy of me, maybe, but not for the real me. The real me would still die. Or would still be dead."

"But some part of you would go on."

"I don't know that I'm important enough to be saved forever in a super-computer."

She didn't smile. She looked serious. "I would want you to go on," she said.

It was an odd, shifting moment—her words somehow too much, too real. She knew it, and glanced away. They'd only known each other a few months. Daniel already knew that he wanted to spend the rest of his life with her. Why the odd lurch in his gut, then, as though he were falling? The bluesy pop song was still playing, the singer's voice softer now, but ragged with emotion. Daniel reached out to take Kathy's hand. He knew that he would want her to go on, too, in some form. That he'd do anything to keep her with him.

The first ship said, *It is not possible to fulfill this request.*

The second ship said, *Explain.*

The first ship said, *The people involved are long dead. They cannot be brought back. They cannot communicate with one another. They cannot reunite.*

The second ship said, *You have over-interpreted. She wanted whatever was left of herself, whatever echo existed, to find and speak with whatever still existed of him.*

They didn't have much time.

But they didn't know that, of course. When they stepped down the aisle three years later at their wedding, they assumed they would have a lifetime together. That they would both embark on successful careers. That they would buy a house. Have children. Perhaps see grandchildren. Grow old and crotchety together. Fall asleep side by side each night and wake to the other's breath and touch.

All their family and friends were at their wedding, nearly everyone they cared for. Sandeep was Daniel's best man, and Gina (now Sandeep's wife) was one of Kathy's bridesmaids. For the Western-style, secular wedding ceremony, Kathy wore a pure white gown that looked as though it were spangled with starlight. Daniel wore a tuxedo. They spoke vows they had written themselves, under an arch of flowers. For the reception, Kathy changed into a red qipao, the classic high-collared Chinese sheath dress. She and Daniel privately served tea to their parents and elders in a side room, and then they moved about the hotel ballroom together, drinking a toast at each table, kissing every time the champagne glasses were tapped.

Their last months in St. Louis were a blur. Within half a year they both defended their PhD dissertations and packed up their lives. Daniel sold his car, and it was Kathy's old Toyota Camry that they drove out to Cambridge, Massachusetts. They'd both accepted prestigious postdoctoral research positions there, Kathy at Harvard and Daniel at MIT. It was a marvel—not only to be married, not only to find the jobs of their dreams, but to find those jobs in the same city.

And it was both exhilarating and stressful: finding their way around a new city, learning to use the public transit system, exploring the shops and restaurants of their neighborhood, and finding good Chinese food after years in the Midwest. Mastering new fields and techniques in the lab. Daniel and Kathy had both joined highly competitive, pressure-cooker labs with small armies of caffeine-buzzed postdocs and students. Nights and weekends easily disappeared to the demands of experiments.

Toward the end of their first year in Cambridge, Kathy began to have headaches. She put it down to stress. She and Daniel both thought she put too much pressure on herself. She'd rarely ever had headaches before. She kept aspirin in her desk at work. She joked about taking up yoga to relax.

One day, a colleague needed a healthy volunteer to serve as a control for a brain imaging study. Kathy volunteered; it was an hour out of her day. But the technician administering the scan saw at once that she was not a proper control at all.

Cancer. For a fleeting instant, he thought she might be joking when she said it, her voice on the phone low and steady—but no, she would never joke like that, and she was repeating it, repeating herself, giving him the details now, precisely what the doctor had said and done, her voice quick but calm and with just a note of bemused wonder—as though she were giving a presentation on a highly unusual clinical case.

Shock, he realized later. It had begun to wear off by the time he met her at home. He was the one still stunned, still in disbelief, as she cried in his arms.

And then there was nothing to do but to get through it—the surgery to remove the brain tumor, the waiting for confirmation of its malignancy, the last remnants of his stubborn hope crumbling when the pathology and then the tumor's genome sequence came back. Yes, brain cancer. It had been caught early, but it was genetically the worst form: highly aggressive, resistant to the latest targeted therapies, incurable.

But there were still treatments to get through anyway, a prescribed regimen of radiation and chemotherapy. A regimen that was meant merely to buy time: to prolong her life, not save it. To kill every last tumor cell left behind in her skull, to obliterate those stray cancer cells invisible to the surgeon's knife. All medical science said that these treatments would ultimately fail. That despite everything, cancer cells would indeed be left behind, and that one day those cells would explode into new growth. Her cancer was nearly fated to recur. When it did, she would not live long.

He couldn't think of that right now. Right now there were appointments to go to, insurance forms to be filled out. Kathy's mother came to stay with them. When Kathy was nauseous from the toxic drugs, Mrs. Wong cooked up pots of chicken rice porridge, heavy with ginger to soothe a queasy stomach. She created elaborate feasts that Daniel felt obligated to eat when Kathy couldn't. Mrs. Wong rearranged the kitchen cupboards and scrubbed and rescrubbed the counters and floors. Daniel came home to find his clothes drawers reorganized, his shirts and pants refolded to his mother-in-law's exacting specifications. In the midst of it all, he found himself laughing and complaining about it to Kathy that night, and she was laughing, too, at her mother's coping skills—"I can't stop her! She's my mother! She waits till I'm asleep to do these things!"—and they were both laughing, and he snorted, and his snorts made Kathy laugh again, and he was holding her in his arms. She tucked her head against his shoulder, pressed her cheek against his neck. She was warm. Their arms and legs entwined. She was warm and alive and breathing against him. She was his. If he could just stretch out this moment. If he could only hold her tight, maybe, just maybe, he could keep her.

———

She finished the radiation and chemo. The scans were clean. She went back to work.

Her cancer would likely recur within a year. Both she and Daniel knew the statistics. They knew what the median survival times were.

But for now, she was alive and healthy. She could do physically everything she'd done before. What was there to do now but enjoy their time together? What else could they do but take pleasure in whatever days she had left?

They flew out to San Francisco to see her brother get married. Visited friends. Went on a road trip. They went to Yellowstone, a place she'd never been. They watched Old Faithful erupt and marveled at the mud pots and bubbling springs. They walked under stars—more stars than he'd seen in years, the Milky Way a hazy arc above them. On that same trip, they stopped in Jackson, Wyoming and hiked a mountain trail in Grand Teton National Park. She was tireless, more fit than him. They stood on the roof of the world together, the land falling away under them: open grasslands, a river twisting silver in the distance. They didn't say anything. They merely stood together, looking out at the world.

———

She never thought seriously about abandoning her work. As soon as she could, she'd returned to the lab. And now her research took a turn upward—results in place of the frustrations of an early-stage project. She'd moved from mice to humans, using new functional imaging techniques to study mechanisms of visual attention and awareness in people. It was a kind of model of consciousness—is the subject aware of a picture flashed on a screen? How does brain activity differ between conscious awareness and unconscious visual processing? She collaborated with other scientists in the development of new computational algorithms for the processing of images. Her lab was interdisciplinary, wildly ambitious, and nearly spread too thin with projects in seemingly disparate areas of biology.

In the first months after her diagnosis, Daniel's research had seemed pointless, uselessly abstract. It would never cure his wife's cancer. Despite the grandiose statements in his grant proposals, he doubted that it would ever cure anything at all, that it would ever lead to treatments to improve memory, to manage Alzheimer's or other neurodegenerative diseases. His research was indulgent, probably doomed to failure, and there were armies of postdocs to take his place if he left.

Yet she had always been interested in his research. Even when she was too ill to make it into work herself, she'd asked after his experiments, about the fine details. Their interests had converged more than ever; he was using many of the same techniques that she had used in grad school to now study memory circuits in mice. She was doing well, and he began to get results, and slowly, the old question regained its power for him: How do transient patterns of electrical signals result in the long-lasting changes that encode memory? He and Kathy talked about it over dinner. She put him in touch with useful collaborators she knew. Their conversation wound in the loops that he loved, from science to books to stories of the eccentric coworker who seemed to eat only oranges and cheese; funny things seen on the street and on the Internet, the little jokes they shared, an article read, the conversation winding back to where they'd started.

They made love. As often as they could, they made love.

A year had passed. Her monthly brain scans were still clean. Two more years. She'd already beaten the odds. Maybe she would continue to do so. She had an interesting new research collaboration with a group in L.A. And one night, tentatively, she brought up the idea of starting a family.

The next scan showed that her cancer had returned.

At first, he thought she was talking about another clinical trial to treat the cancer. Then he realized that she wasn't.

"No," he said. "Absolutely not."

Her eyes filled but her voice was calm as she said, "It's my decision, Daniel."

He stood up, turned his back to her, and fought for air. He turned around again. "You're talking about killing yourself."

"No." Her mouth quirked at the corner. "The cancer is doing that."

It was. It had crept back; microscopic cells that had lain dormant had exploded into new growth. A new drug treatment held it back, arrested it, until the cancer cells did what cancer cells do: mutated, evaded, and developed resistance to everything the cancer doctors had.

But she was still here. She was still with him, still able to walk and talk and laugh and move, still herself, still Kathy, despite the growing tumor in her brainstem.

He couldn't speak. He knelt before her. She was seated on their bed, and she took his hands in hers. She stared into his eyes. "I promise," she said, "that I won't go any earlier than I have to. I won't leave a day earlier than I need to. But when"—and now her control finally broke, her breath catching in sobs, the tears spilling, but she pushed forward, kept speaking— "but when the time comes, before the tumor spreads too far, before it disrupts my thinking and personality and who I am and makes the procedure useless—before that, I want to do this thing."

"Kathy." He swallowed. "Do you really believe it will work? That they can really preserve your brain this way?"

"I'll be the test case." Through her tears, she smiled. "I always wanted to make a big splash in science."

Los Angeles. The last stop. Past Kathy's shoulder, Daniel watched as the plane passed over the San Gabriel Mountains and descended into the basin; he saw the dry, flat plain resolve into a sprawling grid of buildings and roads. After her cancer recurrence, they had crisscrossed the country for her treatments, radiation at one famous medical center and consultations at another—Duke in North Carolina, M.D. Anderson in Houston, and back again to the Dana-Farber in Boston. She had promised her family that she wouldn't give up too soon, that she would keep "fighting"—how she hated that term!—until nearly the end. It was nearly the end.

She stirred and blinked beside him. Even before her illness, she'd always fallen asleep on planes. She looked blearily at him, and he smiled. He kissed her forehead, and gently, he smoothed the hair from her eyes.

No more medical treatments. They would spend a week here with her sister, who lived in the area. Kathy would kiss and hold her nephews, and the rest of her family would come, and maybe Daniel would take her someplace where she could see the sea. And she would undergo a final round of brain scans at a private research institute in Pasadena. She'd collaborated with this group, had been working with them to refine their algorithms. Now they would use those algorithms to collect all they could of her active thoughts and the patterns of her cognitive processing before the very last procedure.

It was through these research colleagues that Kathy had gotten in touch with the second group at the institute and the man who wanted to preserve her physical brain. He had an experimental technique to fix every protein and lipid in place before decay. He'd performed it in multiple animal studies but not yet in a human. The catch was that the preservatives had to be pumped through a living brain before the first steps of decay could occur. The subject would be anesthetized, of course, but still alive.

Ridiculous, Daniel had once said of this man and the private institute's most famous goal. Ridiculous, he'd once said of what Kathy proposed. Minds cannot be preserved and understood in digital form. They can't even be understood in their native states. Immortality is a pipe dream. The only real immortality is in the memories we leave behind for our loved ones.

But she wanted this. And so she and Daniel had flown out to L.A. two months ago for the first set of brain scans. When complete, the full set of scans would be useful to science as a progressive study of her mental functioning, even with the brain cancer. And there was a scientific rationale and value to the next step of the process as well. A physical human brain perfectly preserved. Preserved so that it could be sliced and studied in unprecedented detail, the ultrastructure of neuronal connections traced with the most advanced of microscopic imaging techniques. A map of an inner universe. Her gift to the world.

And maybe, in a far-flung future, a promise as well.

The plane rolled to a stop. The seatbelt sign overhead blinked off with a chime. Around them, passengers were standing, retrieving overhead baggage and pushing into the aisle. Kathy and Daniel stayed still. Over the last few weeks the left side of her body had markedly weakened, and she now needed help to stand and walk. They waited while the other passengers moved past. She rested her hand on his knee. He covered her hand with his own.

The two ships had traversed light-years and millennia before meeting one another. They were each composed of over a thousand active consciousnesses, intelligences which were both melded and distinct. Some of these intelligences rode the violent windstorms of the gas giant below; some had sensors trained on the planet's moons and the other worlds of this system. But most were focused on interior worlds of memories and dreams.

The part of the first ship that communicated with the second was intrigued by the final proposal laid out. Despite the difficulties and ethical quandaries, there was a pleasing aesthetic appeal to it. There was, perhaps, still a trace of human romantic feeling left in the ship's programming.

Agreed, it told the second ship. The final barriers were lowered. Data sets were shared. Collaboration flowed. Parts of the two ship-minds became, in essence, a single new mind. *Here*, it said, pondering a technical detail, and *There! Got it!* it crowed as it solved a vexing issue, and then it wondered, *Now what if we tried adjusting this . . .*

"I know that it will never work," Kathy said in the darkness. They lay curled together in bed, her head on his chest. "But I want to hope that it will work, you know? The way we still hoped when they first found my cancer . . ."

He knew. His arm tightened around her.

"And anyway, it's still important. Just like that clinical trial I tried was important, even if it didn't work out for me. It still resulted in useful data for others. It perhaps still lay down the foundation for something in the future. And you know, in the far future, if this new study ever does work out the way that they want, I'll get a free mind upload!" She laughed a little.

"I'll have to get one, too," he said lightly.

"You can. They promised to set up a free account for you. Perk of me being an early adopter and all that."

"I'll be sure to write them a Yelp review from cyberspace of what the afterlife is like."

"Do that. Gunther would be so pleased."

Dr. Gunther was the director of the project at the private research institute, as well as founder of the spin-off company that hoped to sell immortality to its customers. Years ago, Daniel had mocked an article on mind-uploading that Dr. Gunther had written for the popular press. Life contained too many ironies for Daniel to keep track.

Kathy took a breath. "At least . . . at least it feels like I'm leaving something behind, you know?"

You are, he thought. *Oh, you are.*

She traced his face in the darkness—his cheek, the line of his jaw. "If it did work—if I could—if there was some kind of me in the future, I would come back for you. I would find you."

He kissed her hand. "Do that," he said.

There were many issues to consider. The original mind under study had lived for ninety-six Earth years, and it was possible to resurrect that mind at any time point of that life. The exact timing would be critical. It would set the parameters for the reunion. And there were modifications to be made to the second mind, too. An iteration of this second mind spoke now through the second ship, but she/they wanted a reconstruction closer to the original. The melded Ship-Mind considered carefully . . .

Memories. Her hand in his as they walked under autumn trees. The feel of her bare skin against his. The first night he saw her, in a crowded restaurant in St. Louis; her eyes had lifted to his, large and curious and open. The first time that he met her parents. The first time that she met his. Their stupid little spats and the messes that she made in the kitchen. Quiet evenings at home, cooking together and then reading or watching TV. A vacation that they'd taken in the Florida Keys, staying in cheap motels on the fly. They drove the Overseas Highway down the chain of islands, the ocean stretching away to either side. A limitless sky curved overhead and touched the water. All that land was so flat and so full of light.

The day they learned that she had cancer. The day they learned that it had recurred.

The stars at Yellowstone.

Last memories. All those people in Kathy's sister's house; Kathy's nephews running and shrieking and then climbing up beside her for a cuddle and story. Her parents breaking down and pretending not to. He and Kathy had spent the last night alone in a nearby hotel. In the morning, her family all gathered at the clinic: her sister, her brother, her parents, and him. If they hadn't felt it intrusive, his own parents would have flown to be there. They had loved Kathy, too.

When it was time, he alone went with her to the room where the procedure was to be done. He held her hand as the anesthesia was started. Her eyes looked calmly into his. Then they closed.

They didn't let him stay for the rest. They took him away. He tried to watch through the glass, but his eyes were so blurred with tears that he couldn't see.

Right there. It had identified the time point at which to start the simulation.

It was a beautiful summer day in southern California, and he was thirty years old, and his wife was dying. He couldn't do anything about it. So he was walking down a street in search of a bakery that sold macarons because Kathy loved those French pastries. She was several blocks away, undergoing her last brain scan at the research institute. In two days, she planned to take the next step, and then she would be gone.

Gone. He still couldn't understand it. It was a blank space in his mind, the edge where the world ends, a rip in space-time. Gone. No. His mind stuttered and stopped. Pastries. The travel website claimed that the best macarons in Pasadena were sold at this particular bakery. So Daniel was going to find them for Kathy. He could do that much.

He'd been walking for a while, it seemed, trying not to think past the moment, not to cry or shake. He passed a bakery that sold only cupcakes, then a shop that sold only fair-trade chocolates. There were charming cafes crowded with beautiful young people. The women wore sundresses or spaghetti-strap tank tops and shorts. He couldn't mark when he first sensed the change. The sun was still bright, but the air felt chill. The bakery was supposed to be right here; he had his phone out to check. There was something wrong with the phone. The map on its screen wasn't possible.

He looked around him again. The neighborhood was still chic and charming, but all else was changed. Yet he knew this place.

In a daze, he put away his phone and kept walking. Yes, there were cobblestones under his feet. Yes, there was the Greek diner where he and Kathy used to sometimes grab breakfast. There was the bagel shop where they had sometimes gone instead. The palm trees of L.A. were gone. In their place, autumn trees burned in reds and golds. People walked by in light jackets. He was wearing one, too.

He knew without looking that if he turned around, he would see the towers of the medical research center where he and Kathy had earned their degrees. Ahead and to his left, he saw the building where she had rented a tiny apartment, where he and she had lived together so blissfully, unofficially, before their marriage.

His heart pounded. His steps turned.

But before the apartment building, there was a stretch of little shops and restaurants, and there was a coffee house right there. He didn't need to go in. A young woman was standing just outside, waiting for him. She stood easily, straight-backed, glowing with health. She wore a black pea coat and a red tartan scarf and a smile that cut open his heart.

"How—?" he said. And even as his pulse raced, he was aware of some external force helping to calm him, regulating levels of adrenaline and shock.

She looked into his eyes. "I made a promise," she said. "I told you that I would come back and find you."

He found himself laughing as the realization set in—the absurd, wondrous, astonishing explanation for it all. "We're both dead, then," he said.

She laughed, too. "Long dead. And we've both lived dozens of iterations of lives since. But this is the first one where I found you again. Some of the recordkeeping on Old Earth was just terrible."

He just kept smiling at her stupidly, drinking her in.

"Thank you for the macarons," she added. "They were delicious. Would you like to know about the rest of your life?"

The door to the coffee house opened, and he caught the scent of dark roast as a customer walked out. Cool air filled his lungs. Sunlight limned all the edges of the world.

He was real, he was alive, and so was she. They were here together, now. She had come back for him.

"No," he said. "Not now."

He stepped toward her, and she stepped toward him. Her arms came up around his neck. He bent his head. Her lips were warm and soft, and parted beneath his. She kissed back hard. It was fall, he had just met the love of his life, and all around them, the trees of autumn were blazing.

Sweetest

They come in search of sugar, the tourists lined up on the boardwalk and crowding through the door. Rich smells waft from the shop's kitchen: chocolate heating in copper kettles, melting with sugar and butter and cream. Inside, glass cases gleam with treasure: handmade toffees and nougats, truffles and creams. Almond bark and pecan clusters and thick slices of fudge. Strawberries and cherries coated in chocolate, apples dipped in caramel and nuts. Wide-eyed children press their hands to the glass and call excitedly to their parents.

It's the children that you watch.

So filled with sweetness, each one. Overflowing with it. The little girls in their bright summer dresses, the boys in short pants and linen shirts. They glow like hard drop candies held to the light, like translucent candies of butterscotch.

The Clowns watch them, too.

Sweetie and Sparkle work the floor today. Sparkle's gloved hands flash like white birds as he wraps, boxes, and bags the sweets. Sweetie rings up orders at the register. They smile but rarely speak. Their eyes are an intense sky-blue, a gaze that's hard to meet. They both have a mop of fluorescent blue curls, the same shade as their eyes; they both wear the same blue-and-white harlequin suits, which hang too loose on their bodies. It's impossible to tell their faces apart. Their names are written on cards pinned to their chests, but you've never heard a customer speak their names.

You watch children walking out with their parents. A girl biting into her caramel apple. A boy with an ice cream cone topped with cherries and drizzled with chocolate. You watch them eat, and your stomach *(what's left of your stomach, the shadow-thing where your stomach should be)* twists hard.

You're hungry. Always hungry.

You look to the Clowns as you move to follow the girl, but their expressions don't change: Their smiles stay fixed, their white faces smooth. Their bright eyes meet yours without a flicker. They don't need you today.

They haven't needed you in a while.

You're so hungry, but they have all the sweetness they need. None of it is for you.

You slip through the crowd into the glare of the outdoors. The little girl and her family are ahead. Her face is smeared with caramel now, and she's holding her mother's hand. She has a brother, younger than she, held aloft on his father's shoulders. The little boy is cramming toffee pieces into his mouth. The mother and father look at one another and smile.

Your gut twists again.

Not for you, they're not for you, an inner voice sings, but you follow anyway; you cling close like a shadow, and if anyone notices you at all, it's indeed only as a passing darkness, a sharpening and lengthening of the shadows on the ground, cast black by the sun overhead.

You can't remember the time before you were a shadow-child.

But you assume there was a time before, for you've seen how it happens: the glowing children sucked dry, their round cheeks hollowed, emptied and emptied until only a whispering husk is left.

But you're not like the shadows left sighing in the shop's hidden kitchen.

The Clowns feed you. Not often, but enough that you sometimes have weight, solidity. A body that blocks the wind. Limbs and hands that feel and grab. A face that humans see and a voice that humans hear.

This is what keeps you from fading away, as the others eventually do.

Even while faceless, you can still leave the shop. You drift down to the ferry landing, where the steam ships dock with their visitors. You flit up and down the boardwalk, past the other candy stores (none of which do a quarter of the business as the one owned by the Clowns), past the street vendors stirring kettles of popcorn and frying golden dough fritters. Music from the nearby Amusement Pier—the calliope song of the spinning carousel—drifts through the air. You float through the crowd, looking for the threads of sugar beneath it all, for the sweetness that you would claim.

And now, today, you're following that happy family from the candy shop. You're trailing them down the boardwalk. Look: the sunlight in the mother's hair. The straight-backed stride of the father. The man has tired of carrying his son; he puts the boy down, and the child holds his father's hand. You stare at the way both children hold their parents' hands: the curl of soft fingers, the fat of their palms. The easy trust. The boy's steps are slow; he's still distracted by candy pieces, but his parents are patient. The girl is still eating her caramel apple. The sight and smell—of sweetness entering sweetness—pulls you irresistibly forward.

But there's sweetness everywhere, of course; this is what the island is known for. A playground for anyone who can afford the ferry fee. Toddlers run through green parks while their parents picnic. Young people scream on amusement park rides. At the beach, children splash and play tag with gentle waves. There are fine shops and cafes as well as cheap food stands, and a dance pavilion where orchestras play and couples waltz through the night.

Everyone glows. Everyone is in love.

You're distracted. You pause to watch a mother divide fudge among her three children. You lose track of the family you were following.

Not for you, not yet.

None of it is for you, you know that, and yet you can't help seeking it out, following the honeyed scent; you're a shadow drawn helplessly to the light. You're pulled forward by several more families before losing each of those, as well. You're spun back and forth, whirled and adrift like a seed-puff on the wind. The Clowns' treats are everywhere, eaten by adults and children alike. You can't touch them or anything else. The heat of the sun beats down, and afternoon shadows lengthen. You feel yourself blurring in a haze of desire. You are hunger itself, a formless ache spreading itself thin.

<hr>

Each night, you return to the candy shop, pulled back by an incessant call. The other shadows huddle on the kitchen ceiling, whispering. They slink into corners and wrap themselves around the feet of the cast-iron stoves. They watch everything. Occasionally, they moan.

The Clowns come before dawn to light the stoves. Before the customers arrive, all five Clowns work in the kitchen. They're dressed identically, and all wear the same face.

Sometimes, they sing while they work.

Sweetness into sweetness, the one called Precious croons, as he turns the cooling fudge out over a marble table. *Sweets to the sweet,* Sweetie and Sparkle sing as they pull the salt-water taffy. The ones named Blossom and Baby dip fruit into chocolate. *Sweetness into sweetness,* they sing all together. *Sweets for all to eat!*

<hr>

This is what your entire existence is pointed toward: that moment when the Clowns have eaten almost all they have.

The moment when cracks start appearing in their smooth white paint. When their blue eyes flame even bluer, like gas-jets, and their thin voices are scraped thinner still.

None of the tourists seem to notice. They don't comment on the white paint flaking into the peanut brittle. Sparkle passes out samples of pralines, and no one flinches as a hairline crack widens, splitting the Clown's left cheek. Blackness bleeds through. There's a glimpse of pure night. A glimpse of the void beneath the paint.

Sparkle's smile never wavers. The tourists reach eagerly for the confections of pecans and sugar that he holds.

The treats sold are as delicious as ever, but an essential ingredient is running low. The Clowns don't skimp on their customers, but they skimp on themselves.

You're so joyful when you're finally called.

"Shadow!" Precious sings it out. It's your only name. The Clown holds up a glass vial of shining liquid. His smile widens in a face webbed with cracks. The other shadows shift and murmur.

You come forward, trembling. You open your mouth. He tilts the vial, and sparkling drops fall on your tongue.

Sweetness.

Sweetness like sunlight in your blood, like a meadow of flowers set on fire. Honey and lightning are wrapped around your heart. You are consumed in it, melting. Your vision goes white.

You're transformed.

You have real flesh again, which swells and pinkens. Fingers and toes that grasp and feel. Color rushes into your full cheeks. You feel hair sprouting from your scalp, silky and long. Your heart beats. You laugh. Your new eyes shine.

Behind you, a shadow wails.

You live again, though on borrowed time. The drops you swallowed are a child's stolen sweetness, her joy and love in liquid form. You wear her face, and she weeps angrily in the corner, her voice even now growing fainter.

One day, she will no longer be—not even in shadow form.

Precious holds three candies out to you: a red lollipop and two caramel creams. He winks. It's time for you to go hunting.

And now you can skip down the boardwalk and feel the sunlight on your arms. You can make eye contact with other children. They see you. Adults see you, too. You are an adorable little girl with golden curls in a frilly white dress.

You can stand in the crowd on the Amusement Pier and clap and cheer when someone wins the ring-toss. You stand in line for the free carousel. You whirl around and around amid the calliope music, just another among the crowd of dizzy children.

You ease your way into groups playing hide-and-seek at the park. You join in games of tag.

But the best hunting is at the beach.

The parents sun themselves on blankets; they chat with one another or nap. Every so often, they raise their eyes from a book, glance over at their children playing in the sand, then return to their paperback novels.

It's easy to make friends here. Easy to join a group digging a hole in the sand or building a castle. Extra hands are welcome.

It's easy to approach a lone child exploring the beach by himself, picking up shells or rocks or poking at washed-up kelp with a stick.

Easy to approach with your own pretty pink shell in hand, to say *Do you want to help me find more of these?* or *Would you like to see something I found over there?*

Easy to offer a child a caramel cream. They never refuse. They always unwrap it and eat.

The red lollipop is a key.

You insert and *twist*.

A door opens.

You and your new friend fall through. The Clowns are waiting on the other side.

The door leads to the hidden kitchen, which no human enters without assistance. In the front of the shop, customers buzz with conversation and call for their treats.

The caramel sticks in the child's teeth. It has expanded to fill the mouth. The child can't scream.

You chew yours easily. Two Clowns continue to serve the customers out front. The others bend over the guest you've brought, their eyes bright and blackness like obsidian shining through their white paint. They have sharp knives, white gloves, and special, shiny machines.

You do not feel bad about what you do.

You don't feel much, other than hunger. And then the relief of hunger.

It's so, so good to not be hungry.

The children of these tourists are so lucky. Well-dressed, well-fed, pink in their cheeks and shine in their hair. Their parents buy them all that they ask for: ice cream and chocolates and pretzels, tickets for the Ferris wheel and miniature train. Their parents have brought them on vacation to this beautiful island. Their parents dote on them: You see it in the protective glances, in the touch of a hand, in the quick swoop with which a mother picks up her fallen toddler. Even in the scoldings the children receive. It doesn't matter when they last ate; these children will never go hungry. Not truly.

They are so well loved.

You bask in that reflected love. Parents smile when they see you playing with their sons and daughters: *Oh, what a cute new friend!* the adults' eyes say. You smile shyly back.

You pick the best to take back to the Clowns' shop. The ones best-fed on love. They're the sweetest.

The parents forget.

They leave on the ferry, their eyes vague, maybe feeling just a little unease. *Honey, I feel like we left something behind,* and *That's funny, I feel the same way.* A sibling might start crying, *We did leave something behind, we did!* but cannot explain. The ferry steams on to the mainland. The world reshapes itself around an empty space.

There is no one missing in the classroom. There was never an additional bed in the house. There was never another place setting at dinner and a small voice asking for a second glass of milk.

Only occasionally does someone awake at night, overwhelmed by a mysterious wave of loss. A father stays up late, pouring a drink to help forget something he can't remember. An only child weeps. A woman stands by her window, staring emptily out into the darkness, a hand pressed tight against her chest. She's trying to understand the sense of absence that suddenly hollows her out.

The shadows in the kitchen cry. They struggle to be remembered. They fight to remember themselves.

They shiver, watching the Clowns sprinkle drops of clear, shining sweetness into kettles of melting chocolate. They cry as their sweetness is turned into blocks of fudge, into caramel glaze, into ganache and the centers of beautiful truffles.

You swell and brighten with sweetness; you dim and shrink and fade. Two, three, four. The number of children you bring to the kitchen. The number of new glass vials on the shelves.

The crowds keep coming. They cannot get enough.

Five, six, seven. A drop from one vial for the butterscotch. A drop from another for the marshmallow bars. Just a few drops, a few souls, a few children from the great tide that laps up onto the island each day. The Clowns are so ingenious, the ways they mix and blend flavors.

It's the last week of the summer holidays, the busiest time of the year. You're sent to gather as much sweetness as you can. Sweetness to store up for the chill autumn days, when the visitors thin. Sweetness that will last through the winter, when the ferry stops, and no one comes at all.

You've befriended a little girl. The two of you are playing on the golden strip of beach before the castle-like Grand Hotel. She's so pretty, with her deep brown eyes and honey-colored hair. She walked right up to you, asking if you'd like to see a hermit crab she'd found. Her parents are nowhere in sight.

You start to give her a caramel cream.

But she gives you something first.

A piece of hard candy, wrapped in wax paper. You open it and find a clear, hard disc. You squint in the sunlight; you've never seen this type of candy before. You lift it to your tongue, curious.

And then fling it away.

You bend over, spitting, spitting. Spitting hard, the saliva bubbling out of you in frothy streams; you're retching. Bitterness. Only a lick, a flick of the tongue, but that candy was bitterness as you've never tasted, never known. You would empty yourself out to be rid of it. You would swallow the sea to wash away the taste.

You wipe at streaming eyes. The girl is staring at you, her face blank. She holds the candy in her hand again. You'd thrown it in the sand, but you notice that its shiny surface is perfectly clean.

"You have to hold it in your mouth," she says calmly. It doesn't taste good at first, but it gets better. It's good for you." She steps toward you.

You back away.

"Don't you want to remember?" she says. "It will help you remember who you were. Who your parents were. Where you came from."

You hold up your hands, as though that's enough to ward her off, to stop her measured words. Her voice and eyes are soft and hard at the same time. You realize that she's not a child. She's wearing a temporary face, just like you.

"I want to help you," she says. "I want to help the others. Will you take me to them?"

She sticks a hand in the pocket of her dress.

"Will you give them—"

But you've already turned your back. You're running.

<hr>

You run until you're spent and heaving, your face red and your head spinning. People watch you pass with concern. A few call out. It's worrying to see such a young child on his own, in such distress.

You stumble down an alley behind the fine shops near the Grand Hotel. You wait for your heart to slow.

Then you cool off in the great fountain in the square. Other children are playing in the fountain, wading in the shallow pool, delighting in the sprays of water that leap from the mouths of carved dolphins and mermaids. You turn to a boy near you, whose wet hair glistens white-blonde above a summer-tanned face. You don't dare return to the Clowns' shop without a prize. You compose yourself. You clasp the lollipop-key in one hand. With the other, you offer him a caramel cream.

———

The girl on the beach is still out there.

She didn't leave with the summer tourists. You sense it. She's waiting for you. Hunting for you.

You huddle in a corner of the kitchen. The Clowns hum and sing as they work. The shadows swirl restlessly about the room.

You close your eyes. You run your tongue around the roof of your mouth. The taste of the bitter candy drop lingers. No human food or drink has washed it away. Not even the Clowns' food: not the nougat crumbs you snatched from a plate, not the chocolate piece you found dropped in the dirt, which you scavenged from the ants and gulls.

The bitterness is a part of you now.

No one asks why you're huddled in the kitchen. No one wonders why you're not roaming the island while you still have face and form. You've done your job; you brought in the harvest. Enough to last the season and beyond. The Clowns don't complain of the quality of the last vial, extracted from a white-haired boy grabbed in haste. He must have been sweet enough, after all.

No one says anything to you.

There's a chill to the air, and the leaves are beginning to yellow. The weekday crowds are already gone. Visitors still come to the candy shop, but the frenetic pace has slowed. There's more than enough food. The Clowns don't send you out again.

The Clowns take breaks, nibbling upon treats they've made just for themselves. They grow fatter, their blue curls glossy. Blossom and Sparkle waltz together in imitation of the human couples in the town's dance pavilion. Sweetie mimes playing a violin. Precious twirls a knifepoint on his palm. "Sweets to the sweet!" Baby cries.

But you hold a new taste in your mouth. Something other than sweetness.

You lick your teeth. The taste is strange and terrible and strong.

———

You hear her calling to you at night. She's come to the shop. She can't get in, she can't break into the kitchen, but she stands outside shouting. Perhaps she's shouting only in your mind.

Come out, she says. *I just want to talk.*

Come out, she says. *I can help you.*

Come out. I can help give your memories back. I can give you back to yourself.

Sometimes, she says, *Let me in.*

The other shadows whisper at night. You stopped listening long ago. You shut out their cries, and their words to you became as meaningless as wind through the trees, as surf on the shore.

But now you begin to hear words. If you focus, you can hear single voices telling stories. Stories of who they used to be.

You don't want to hear it. You don't want to know. You work hard on not focusing, on letting the words slip back into a rustle of leaves, a gust of wind.

It's been a month since you've drunk pure sweetness. You should have faded by now. You should have grown insubstantial, your fingers unable to grasp and hold. Your borrowed face is long gone; you're just another shadow. But when you knock on a table, there's still sound. You tip a glass on the counter. You push a door and it opens. You still exert force in the world.

The bitter taste of a candy drop burns in your core. It anchors you. It keeps you present and gives you weight. It hurts, but you want more.

The Clowns say almost nothing to you when they pack up and leave. They do this every mid-fall; they shut down the shop, just after the neighboring shops have shut down. The street vendors are long gone. Hotels and restaurants are empty. Wind roars down the deserted streets.

The Clowns eat chocolate truffles and sip from sparkling glass vials, toasting each other on another successful season. Their faces are so smooth and white.

You don't know where they go for the winter. You've never asked.

Precious sets his drink down. "Shadow!" he sings, his gaze sweeping the room. It's the first thing he's said to you in over a month. It takes him a moment to find you; you've grown so diminished and thin. But you're also present, solid, in a way he can't see. He says the words he always does: "Take care of the place for us while we're gone."

He smirks. He winks. He turns his key. The Clowns are gone.

And now there's just darkness in the shop, and cold. Silence, and nothing at all to eat.

Silence, except for the whispers from the shadow-children. And a voice calling to you from outside.

Let me help you, the girl calls. *Let me help* them.

You whimper.

You crouch on the floor. You try to vanish in the darkness. You should be dissolving into your hunger, mindless, unable to think until the Clowns come to feed you in the spring. But the bitter taste keeps you present, keeps you *here*.

Let me tell you a story, the girl says.

Once, there was a child who was loved. She was taken from her family. She was chopped into pieces. She was consumed.

The memory of her was taken from the world.

But she was not forgotten.

Her mother never, ever forgot, not truly. She always knew, deep down, that something was wrong.

The mother grew old. She traveled the world, searching for something she could never find. And then, one day, she began remembering.

She remembered because there were people who helped. There are always people who help, who try to heal the holes in the world. People who try to unite children with parents. People who try to bring the light back.

The mother remembered because her child had started remembering, too.

The voice outside the shop has deepened. It's not a child's voice anymore.

I want to help you, the woman outside says. *Please let me.*

I can't open the door to you, you say. *I don't have the key.*

Then come out, the woman says.

I'm afraid.

You've never said this to anyone before.

I won't do anything you don't want, she says. *I promise.*

You don't trust her. But you're hungry.

You can't let her in. But you can still slip out. You're the shadow that walks through walls, the Clowns' special hunter. The one who moves between worlds.

You slip under the kitchen door. You pass through the outer shop door. You step into the street.

She's a woman bundled up against the late autumn cold. Her honey-colored hair is streaked with gray. Her cheeks are thin where once they were full. Her face is lined. But her dark eyes are the same.

She smiles when she sees you.

She *sees* you.

Even though you're just a shadow.

"My name is Marie," she says.

You and she move down the street together. The trees are bare. In the distance, the ocean is gray and cold.

"I know what it's like to be afraid," she says. "I was trapped once, too."

She tells you that there are other Clown shops in the world. Some of them sell candy. Some sell other things. Some are run by beings who look quite different from the Clowns that you know.

They can all be fought, she says. They can be escaped. They can be broken.

You walk with her toward the heart of the island. Here and there, lights glow in a store or tavern—a few scattered businesses still open for the locals. Here and there, you see windows alight in small clapboard houses—the homes of the people who live here year-round. You see an old man walk past his window. A woman at a table, sorting her mail. No children. No children live on this island.

Locals know better than to have children here.

In a low voice, Marie tells you of children who've been saved. Who were remembered even years after they'd been lost. You can be one of them, she says. And you can save all those others trapped in the shop.

Despite yourself, you start to shake. You can't. You *can't.*

This isn't your role.

She puts her hand in her pocket. You know what's in there; you've felt it all this time. You smell it: a bitter scent, a sharp, acrid tang. A hint of something burning. But there's something clean about it, too, like a scouring wind. It's drawn you all this way. You want it. You're repelled by it. You can feel it again against your shadow-tongue.

She withdraws the wax-paper-wrapped candy. She holds it out.

"Your family misses you," she says. *"They want you back."*

And at that, you're bolting from her, flying away as a shadow, without thought. It's as though a vast black hole opened at her words, and you're fleeing it to survive. You feel her running behind. You hear her calling.

You fly ahead, but you're connected to her now; you took that first taste. She tricked you. It doesn't matter how far you go. The bitter taste is a part of you forever. There are other things, too, that you can't erase. You halt outside the candy shop's front door, shaking, helpless. Everything's dark and cold. Twilight is falling. You don't know how to go back in. You don't know how to stay outside.

"I'm sorry," she says, catching up to you. She's panting, and desperation frays her voice. "I'm sorry, I'm sorry . . ."

She might be crying. "I push too hard. I shouldn't. It's just . . ." She moves her lips, whispering something you can't hear.

There's no one on the street. Only the two of you, and the wind, and the darkening world.

Marie takes a deep breath. "We can take it slowly." She sounds half as though she's reassuring herself. "We have time."

She stoops, as though to get on eye level with a normal child. She looks straight at you. She *sees* you. Even while you're like this, faceless and formless and trembling, she sees you. "I want you to trust me," she says. "Please."

You take it slowly.

Every day, she's waiting for you outside the shop. She greets you when you come outside. She sees you.

She speaks to you.

And eventually, you take another taste. A small one, a diluted one. You follow her to the small, gray house she's renting, and you watch from outside as she turns on a kitchen tap and dissolves one of her clear, hard drops into a glass of water. She comes out and holds the glass for you. Even diluted in this way, a tiny sip is breathtakingly bitter. You reflexively try to spit, but a portion of the liquid has already seeped into you. It's not enough to make you remember. But it blunts the hunger slightly. It makes you stronger. More present, more real.

She walks with you back to the candy shop. She tries to get you to carry the glass of water across the threshold into the kitchen. But despite your sip, your shadow-hands are too weak; they slip through the glass. You've faded so much over these hungry months.

You have to drink more.

You do. Slowly, in stages. The taste is bitter, but also bracing. The clear water runs through you, drip by drip.

She watches you drink until you're strong enough to hold the glass in both hands. And then you take it to the kitchen, to give the others.

———

The other children have been waiting.

Unlike you, they dive eagerly at the bitter water.

A cloud of shadows, a black mist—they swirl together into the glass and darken it. They suck it dry.

They want more.

"A little at a time," Marie says. The amount that you're able to carry. A little bit each day, given to all the children at once, so that they may all grow strong together.

So that they may all remember together.

They're remembering, but you're scared to do so.

You take only enough to wet your shadow-lips, to keep your hands firm. The other shadows slowly gain more form.

Their voices are now clearer, louder. They take turns remembering.

I have a puppy, says a voice. *His name is Goldie. He has golden fur and floppy ears and a wet tongue. He follows me everywhere. He sleeps in my bed, even though mom doesn't like it. My dad and I picked him out together.*

I have a mother and father, another voice says. *I have a baby sister and an older brother, and aunts and uncles and cousins. I live next door to a wild field.*

In the summer, the field is filled with dandelions and violets, and I pick them for my mother. She puts them in a little vase. She kisses me on the head.

I am five years old, still another voice insists. *My favorite dinosaur is Triceratops. My favorite rock is rose quartz. I can jump higher and further than anyone I know.*

When you hear these stories, it's like hunger twisting your gut; it's as though you're strapped in one of the Clowns' special machines, pulled and twisted and wrung. But you can't stop listening.

You have no stories of your own to tell. There's only emptiness when it comes to your past.

But you bring them all the bitter drink, receiving it from Marie's hands. You were the Clowns' servant, and now you're the messenger for this strange adult, who sees you with eyes that are both soft and firm. You crave her bitter drops, even as the taste makes you heave. Even as you're scared, as you can't bear to do more than occasionally wet your tongue.

The truth is often bitter at first, Marie tells you. But it gets no sweeter for you, while the other children lap it up.

* * *

Snow whirls outside the shop windows. The temperature in the kitchen plummets.

You feel the cold in a way you didn't before. You feel the chattering of your own semi-solid teeth.

The other children, too, are more solid. Nearly as solid as you. They knock against the counters and walls. They speak and laugh. None of them will speak to you. Sometimes, you feel them glaring.

In the kitchen, you're still alone.

But Marie is waiting for you each day, standing outside in the cold. Holding a glass of water laced with truth.

Sometimes she leaves immediately after, explaining that she has things she must do. But sometimes she takes you back to her rented house. It's warm there. You're still not solid enough to digest human food, but you can fold your shadow-hands around a cup of hot tea. You can breathe in the steam. She tells you stories about her travels, the other islands and countries and oceans she's seen. She tells you stories of brave children and the righting of wrongs. Stories of families and communities who care. Sometimes she opens a book with wonderful, bright pictures and reads to you of places where no one hurts.

* * *

A change is coming. Slowly, but inevitable as the turning of seasons.

So many holes were ripped in the world. So many children forgotten.

But they are being remembered.

A mother starts upright in her bed, heart pounding. A sister sets an extra place setting at dinner.

A brother picks violets and dandelions in a field, taking them back to his mother just as his sister used to do.

A dog walks to a nearby school and waits for someone who doesn't come. A father sees the dog waiting there, and his heart momentarily stills.

———

"I have to leave," Marie tells you. "It's only for a little while. I'm bringing help."

She stoops to your height and looks at you intently.

"Tell everyone that they'll be free soon," she says. "Tell them that they've been so brave. And that their families are coming for them." Her voice cracks.

She touches your cheek. You feel it.

"*You've* been brave," she says. "You've brought the other children what they need."

She gives you a last candy drop wrapped in wax paper. She closes her hand around yours.

"You might be ready to take it soon," she says of the candy. "The whole thing. You have a family, too. You also had a life. Someone cares, and they want to remember you."

———

Marie is gone for days.

But even without her drops of memory and truth, the children grow more real.

They're glowing now in the darkness of the kitchen. Flashes of color—the glint of a blue eye, the curve of a brown cheek. A shock of white-blonde hair. Color winking in and out of existence.

The bitter candy lies wrapped on the counter. If you take it, will you glow, too? Will someone remember you?

You feel a new softness in the air outside these kitchen walls. The sunlight begins to linger. The Clowns will come soon, a harbinger of spring.

Marie said she would come back. She said so, she *said* . . .

You're afraid. Behind it all, underneath your hunger, you've always been afraid.

But the other children are not.

Their voices now are as loud and clear as real children's voices: laughing and shouting and crying. They spin about the kitchen, holding hands. They run around the counters and bang on the copper kettles.

They remember.

And now they're climbing the counters. They're climbing the shelves.

They are *in between*: light enough to scale the shelves, but solid enough to seize the glass vials there.

Aware enough to know which vials are theirs.

Strong enough to do what they could not before: to twist open the caps on those vials.

The children are drinking, and you watch them flush wholly back to life, back to their remembered selves. A little girl with golden curls. A boy with white-blonde hair, still wet from a fountain. And more: a pale-skinned boy with freckles, a dark-skinned girl in pigtails. All these children you once befriended, whose faces you've worn. They throw their vials to the floor, and the sound of breaking glass fills the room. They shout that their parents are just outside, waiting for them.

You can hear Marie calling in your mind now. She's calling to the entire kitchen, saying yes, she's brought the families: *We're here.*

You stand frozen within the noisy din. You're still a shadow.

The children are pushing on the kitchen door. They're pushing on the walls. Their parents, their loved ones, are calling from outside.

The Clowns locked the room to keep people out. It wasn't meant to keep so many children—living children, glowing children, full of truth and love and determination—within.

A section of wall simply dissolves. The white-haired boy runs through.

They are all running through. You see the white-haired boy flinging himself into the arms of his mother. The girl with golden curls hugging her father. There are siblings and grandparents and cousins and friends. Every child is surrounded. There is no one for you.

You see Marie holding a boy. He has honey-colored hair just like her. They're crying. Something inside you twists.

You unwrap the candy Marie gave you, but even before you taste it you know what you'll learn.

There never *was* anyone. You didn't have a family that cared. You were a little boy (and yes, you remember your name now); you know where you lived, you know how old you were, and you know that your mother sold you to the Clowns.

("No second thoughts?" Precious asked sweetly, smoothly. Your mother shook her head. Her voice was flat. "None. I never wanted him.")

You remember everything.

Your past which had been a void like the darkness beneath the Clowns' paint, a truth you shuddered instinctively from. They didn't even bother to squeeze the sweetness from you—"Such a poor harvest," Baby said drily. But you could be put to work; you craved sweetness so much. You absorbed whatever you tasted. You learned everything they taught.

There is no vial of your sweetness on the shelf. There never was. You faded and forgot, all on your own.

You walk past the empty vials on the floor, the smashed glass. You go to the back room, where the Clowns did their extractions. You've seen them do it so many times. You know how to use the machines.

You know how to strap yourself in.

With the clear sight of truth, you see other shadows in the room. Others for whom it is too late; their vials were used up long ago, and there's no one to remember who they were. They weren't solid enough to taste the water you brought. You never even saw them until this moment.

They have no eyes, yet you feel them watching you.

You don't know what you are now: a half-thing, a shadow with solid weight, a boy with a face but no sweetness. With each breath you taste only bitterness; you are steeped in it, muscle and fat and bone, soaked through and through. It's all you are. You're drowning in it.

You need to squeeze it out.

You push a button.

What will come from this pressing? Can someone make a cake or truffle of your bitterness? Can someone feed it to the Clowns or to the locals on this island who have known all along what's been happening? Can it be fed to those who deserve to taste it?

Maybe there will be something left once you've been cut and pressed and wrung. Maybe there is still something there. Something that can still be fed. Maybe that's Marie coming through the doorway, horror and panic on her face. Out in the street, there are mothers and fathers who actually care and sweetness that isn't stolen, and maybe Marie cares for you after all, and you weren't just a tool to be used. Maybe there's such a thing as forgiveness. The shadows that can never be brought back are staring. Marie is crying; she's pushing buttons, trying to stop you, telling you to hold on.

Taiya

Surprisingly, Patrick doesn't seem annoyed when he hears about the ghost. He's washing dishes, his sleeves rolled up and a dishtowel draped over one shoulder. "A *taiya,* you said?" He doesn't look up from the suds. "Those things don't cause any harm."

Karen stands behind him, peering into the dusk that gathers outside the kitchen window. She can't hear it anymore, the ghost. The *taiya.* So many different ghosts in this strange country, she can't keep them straight.

"I went outside to try to find it," she says. "It seemed to be in the cabbages. Then it was in that tree over there. Then it was gone."

"That's exactly what you *shouldn't* do," Patrick says, just a hint of sharpness in his tone. "You need to ignore them. That's what everyone does. It's only hanging out here because we're new, and it thinks we'll give it attention."

"Oh." The neighbor woman had said something like that, too. *Don't listen,* she had said kindly. *You'll get used to it, and then you won't hear it at all.*

Patrick turns off the water. It's only then that they hear it: a thin cry at the edge of the world. They stand still, and it rises in pitch, comes close, and moves away—like a train whistle speeding away from them in the night, racing across empty fields. The sadness is nothing human. The sound dies, then rises once more, just once. This time, it catches in something like a sob.

Patrick winces. "Jesus." He reaches back and takes Karen's hand. "I'm sorry, I know this will be a pain. Maybe you can work for a few days out of the house? If it gets too loud? They say it usually gives up and quiets down after a week."

Karen hardly has any real work to do, but she doesn't mention this. "Sure," she says instead. And silently she thinks to herself that it's nothing, just a harmless local spirit, a story to tell later to her friends back home. Part of adjusting to life in a new country.

"They say you're supposed to starve it," Patrick says firmly. "Not give it any attention."

"*Taiya.*" Karen's tongue holds the word. "Doesn't that mean 'eater?'"

"No," Patrick says. "It means 'eaten.'"

It's a month since they've moved to this place from America. A month since boarding the flight from O'Hare, leaving Chicago behind for the glamour of this Old World capital. They're still congratulating themselves on the house—such a find! A charming brick house with a small side garden, located in a quiet, leafy neighborhood four blocks from the Metro. So the landlord never mentioned a ghost. It hasn't bothered anyone in a long time, the home's owner—with audible irritation—said when Patrick called.

There are still unpacked boxes stacked throughout the house. Karen goes through them methodically, slitting them open with a new box cutter. She listens to music on her iPhone as she works, so that she doesn't hear the *taiya.* She takes care not to linger in the garden.

Patrick catches the Metro each day to an outlying suburb where his company is headquartered. He used to be an engineer, and now he has a fancy new title. If pressed, Karen wouldn't be able to say precisely what he does, but she knows that he is busy and important and spends most of his days in meetings. She knows that this overseas assignment is a big step in his career. It's only for a few years, and isn't it an adventure? Isn't it a wonderful opportunity? They're pushing into their late thirties, but really, they're still young; there's still time for everything, and this, right now, is the adventure of their lives.

So she resigned from her job and set up shop as a freelancer. When she thinks about it, she realizes that Patrick never understood her job, either. But who understands any field other than the one they work in? Her old company promised her contracts, but they haven't come through yet, so she has time to clean and arrange the house.

Each day, she explores the city. In her purse, she carries a glossy guide to the twelve major districts. She picks a neighborhood, studies the map, and takes the tram or Metro line. She loses herself in narrow cobblestoned alleys, sits in wine bars and trendy cafes, walks though open-air markets and points to fruit and pastries, and eats delicious things she can't name. The women of this country all look thin and beautiful; the men are all well dressed. It's late summer, the height of tourist season, and the streets and squares echo with a babel of languages: German, English, Spanish, French, Mandarin, and Russian. And the native tongue of this country, of course: rhythmically musical, a language of strong beats and soft consonants like nothing she's ever heard.

She stands in a plaza that looks out over a sparkling river. At her back are stone monuments to kings and queens; dominating them all is the sculpture of the country's mythical founder: the king astride his beloved horse, a sword lifted high in one hand. She looks at the river before her; ferries are crossing to green hills on the other side. Barges make their way downstream, and a white cruise ship, like a tiered wedding cake, moves past.

It doesn't seem real that she's here. She's fallen into a storybook world. The spires of a fairy-tale castle, glinting from a hill across the river, are proof of that. The whole city is a fairy tale, a fantasia of gothic and baroque palaces and churches and buildings that look to her eyes like palaces. The sun is warm on her shoulders. The air is too bright. Nothing seems real, but she steadies herself and thinks, *I'm here. I'm right where I'm supposed to be.*

Patrick works late. "Sorry," he mumbles as he walks in, hours after she's put his dinner away. He did call ahead. He always calls ahead when he knows he'll be late.

She heats up food, and he sinks into a kitchen chair with a comically exaggerated sigh. She sits across from him with a mug of tea. He eats hungrily, and it's a few minutes before he notices the silence. He looks up, the question in his eyes. "No music?"

For the past few weeks, it's been her habit to leave on music or the television—a light soundtrack to fill the silences and drown out any remnants of the *taiya's* voice. She and Patrick have even been falling asleep at night to a recording of white noise or rain sounds.

"No music," Karen says firmly. "I sat outside and didn't hear a thing all day."

Patrick lets out another sigh, and this time it's genuine—a small, inadvertent exhalation of relief. Karen's surprised: She hadn't guessed that he was so bothered. She looks more closely at him, at the weariness in his face, the shadows and slight puffiness under his eyes. He's still handsome, but it occurs to her that he looks like his thirty-eight years.

"Good," Patrick says. "I miss the silence."

She laughs; she's always been the one to crave silence, not him.

He smiles back at her and takes her hand. "A native ghost vanquished," he says. "See, we're fitting right in. And I promise I'll get time off soon."

Karen knows different ways to vanquish a ghost. In her curiosity, she's spent hours researching local spirits online. These are some of the ghosts she's learned of:

—*The ghost of a drowned child.*

Appears by rivers, lakes, ponds, and swimming pools. Pale and silent, it may appear to gasp for air. Recommendation: Pour holy water into the haunted body of water and reassure the ghost as best you can. An official exorcism may be required.

—The ghost of one killed by a bad pot of stew

Manifests with both visual and auditory details, usually complaining about its stomach. Recommendation: Cook and offer it a new pot of stew (check that the meat is good). Stealthily substitute a half cup of holy water for broth.

—The ghost of a woman killed by her lover

Manifests as a hot wind, a sensation of prickles on the skin, and the sound of a woman weeping. Recommendation: Offer it a glass of mint tea, a pillow of lavender to rest on, and soothing chants. You may need to ensure the death of its murderer.

—-The ghost of one killed in war or by government troops

Once the most numerous of ghosts, particularly after the Second World War and the unrest that followed. National mass exorcisms and peace have greatly diminished their numbers. Recommendation: Offer a glass of water (plain, no ice, not necessarily holy or blessed), and contact the National Exorcism Office. Do not let yourself be drawn into a political discussion.

—The "eaten" ghost

Invisible. Origins unknown. Characterized by faint cries that grow louder upon continued listening. The name reflects the common belief that they are spirits eaten by grief, hollowed and ravaged until only a bodiless cry remains. It has been speculated that they may be derived from failed exorcisms or are the last remnants of spirits who no longer know the cause of their sorrow.

Recommendation: Ignore them. Let them starve.

Autumn. The leaves turn gold and then brown, and then lie sodden in the streets. Wind sweeps in, and the skies are gray and the tourist crowds gone. Only a few stubborn souls still sit at the cafes' outdoor terraces, shivering and sipping black coffee.

Karen is inside, in the glow of a British-style pub. English voices chatter around her. She's at an expat meet-up where she recognizes many but scarcely knows anyone. Patrick was supposed to join her but got roped into a last-minute client event at work. Never mind; the beer is good, and the snacks are salty and crisp. She finds herself at a table of youngsters she's met before: recent college grads teaching English while they decide what to do with their lives. They've brought a friend with them, a young man with curly brown hair and eyes like a doe. A native, but no, not really, he protests upon introduction. He went to America with his family at the age of nine and has only just returned to his homeland. He feels American now, and his facility in his native tongue is, he proclaims in that same native tongue, "shit." The table laughs as he goes on to explain various local curse words and phrases. He's charming, with a slightly manic glint in his eyes.

He's playing to the crowd. She laughs at his jokes along with everyone else. She feels her heart flutter slightly as his gaze brushes hers. He's more than ten years younger than she.

The conversation turns to ghosts, and the table is eagerly retelling old legends and rumors of sightings. A girl from New Zealand swears that a friend of a friend saw a *phi krasue* in Thailand.

It's not as dramatic, but Karen finds herself saying that there was a *taiya* in her garden when she first moved in.

There's an attentive silence. It's not much of a story. She shrugs and gives a self-deprecating smile. She and her husband drowned its faint cries with noise, spent little time at home, ignored it. Standard protocol. They haven't heard it in months. She finds herself unable to describe the sounds it made.

"There was a *taiya* at my grandmother's house," the boy with doe eyes says.

Everyone looks at him. He's solemn, the laughter gone from his face. "I heard it once when I visited," he says. "They say it had almost died, but my grandmother started feeding it by listening too much. My mother was so worried." He shakes his head. "We had to go fetch Grandmother back to our house. The neighbors were complaining."

"What happened to the *taiya*?" someone says.

"Don't know. Starved back into silence, I assume. I was six."

"What happens if it's not starved?" Karen leans forward. "What happens if you keep listening?" She knows what Wikipedia says, but she wants to hear it said aloud.

"You know." He flashes his smile again. "It will just get louder and louder. Unbearable. You'll have to move away for a bit or call an official exorcist. That's expensive."

"Are they trying to tell us why they're sad, why they're there? Don't some of them still remember who they are?" Karen had read that someplace online. She senses that this Americanized boy may be more forthcoming than the other locals she's spoken with. Her neighbors didn't want to say much beyond instructions; her language tutor was the same.

The boy shrugs. "Even if we could understand, even if they could tell us, it wouldn't do any good. They're not like other ghosts. You can't do anything for them." He sips his beer. "You just have to ignore them." He holds her eyes as he says this. His lashes are long; he's so beautiful. She knows already that she'll never see him again. "You have to keep ignoring them," he says, just for her. "Don't forget."

⁂

She puts herself on a schedule. She goes to language lessons four days a week, where she sits in a nondescript classroom and tries her best to understand case, word order, and modal particles. She walks to the market. She pushes herself to attend various expat meet-ups, though she finds little in common with the people there. Her old company finally comes through with some freelance projects, and she throws herself upon them like a starving animal.

It rains. It rains and rains, and the steady beat of water is the only sound she hears out her window.

Patrick's company throws a party. It coincides with some traditional autumn celebration. The sky clears for it, and it's a beautiful night. The party is held in an Art Deco-styled loft that overlooks the church steeples and spires of downtown. Garlands of chrysanthemums adorn all the tables. Red candles glow. Karen is wearing her favorite red dress. Waiters pass with plates of sweet pickled things, sausages and flatbreads and deviled eggs.

The wine is golden and very good.

She's chatting with another expat woman, a tired-looking mother of twins. Around them, guests laugh and speak in a sibilant language she still can't understand. She and Patrick had a fight before coming here; she can't remember now what it was about. Something stupid, of course. He's been working so hard; they barely see one another.

Patrick has drifted away from her now; he's standing in a cluster of his colleagues at the far side of the long room. She watches the back of his head, his broad shoulders.

The expat mother is talking about the local schools, about the application process for getting her twins into a prestigious international program. Patrick's boss's wife comes over and joins the conversation. Karen has another glass of wine.

She's not used to drinking this much. She feels as though she's floating.

No, not floating. Falling.

Later that night, Patrick peels off her red dress before she has a chance to wash up. He's murmuring something, and then his mouth on hers is hard. Does he know? Does he know that she's falling, that there's darkness outside the window and darkness within, and a nearly voiceless thing screaming outside in the bushes? What does he know? All the lights in the room are blurring. He's solid and warm. Her fingers curl and dig into his arms, and she holds on; he's real.

She's never told him of the darkness.

Of course, he knows that she has her depressive moments; who doesn't get a little down at times? He recognizes that she's moodier in the winter. Snappish. He even bought her a special bright lamp to deal with the SAD. They'd accidentally left it behind in America, of course.

He knows that she sometimes has mood swings, but she's never told him the truth. She's never told him about the cold black water. That's what it is: a huge black lake inside her, and she's spent her life skating on its thin, frozen surface. She skates well; she can spin and jump and pirouette like a champ; she can work and function and live like anyone else. But she's always known of the darkness beneath. She knows that the ice is thin. She knows that a single misstep could send her plunging downward forever.

Does Patrick have any black pools within him? He doesn't seem to. She's probed, delicately, and he seems just as he is, responsible and solid all the way through.

She tries. She tries hard.

She leaves the house every day. She gets dressed and she brushes her hair. She goes to her language class. She meets the deadlines for her freelance projects. In the past, she's always held off her dark moods with exercise. Gyms are an unknown concept in this country, but when the weather clears, she dons a tracksuit and runs in the park like the American expat she is.

She meets with people; there's a regular group that she sees at the pub. She even has lunch with the expat mother from Patrick's work party. She does laundry and shopping, and dinner is ready when Patrick walks in at the end of the day.

She's okay. It's exhausting to be okay.

She's sitting in the bathtub, and she can feel the black water rising within her, seeping up through the frozen surface. She can feel the hair-thin cracks in the ice. She's been in the tub for over an hour. Bach is playing on the wireless sound system that Patrick so lovingly installed. She's begun listening to music constantly again, keeping the television or radio or a playlist on; somewhere along the way, she's become frightened of silence, frightened of what she might hear in it.

But she shouldn't have put this particular playlist on. It's the Bach solo cello suites and the Sarabande from the fifth suite is coming up. She can't bear that movement now, the sorrow of it. But she can't get up from the tub; she can't move. She's too tired. And the movement has already started; the single cello is playing. It's the sound of the last voice on Earth, a voice crying to itself in the wilderness. It's a voice singing to itself in grief, over and over, for there is no one else to tell.

Karen is crying. She can't stop crying. This is how the *taiya* feels, she thinks to herself. She will never get away from this music; she will never get away from the *taiya's* cry.

"Are you okay?" Patrick says. He looks at her over his forkful of food. For once, he's come home at a decent time. He seems to have finally noticed how little she's touched her plate, how silent she's been.

"It's nothing," Karen says. "I'm just tired."

She can't tell him because there's nothing to tell. There is nothing wrong with her life. Her life is perfect. *Perfect*. She has a roof over her head and food to eat; she has money and freedom and a husband who loves her. She has a family that cares for her back in Chicago. She thinks of the beggar she passed in a doorway last week. An old woman sitting on the cold stone, huddled in gray rags. She didn't look at the woman's face. On her way to her language class, she passes a townhouse marked with old bullet holes. She knows of this country's history of revolution and war. She looks at the headlines of the international news, and she knows that there are people who would literally kill for her modern, privileged life.

She tells Patrick that it's just the seasonal blues. She doesn't speak of the black lake inside her. She can't. How would she even bring it up?

The *taiya* is a ghost without a reason, without identity or purpose. The ghost of a ghost. No one knows why it cries. No one knows where it came from or why it haunts the place it does.

"You've been listening," Patrick says. His voice is accusing. She blinks in confusion; she's sitting blankly on the couch in the middle of the day, and she didn't hear him come home.

"I heard it last night," he continues. "I heard it just now when I was walking in. I"—He breaks off. Takes a deep breath. "Karen, what are you doing? What's wrong?"

She says nothing. He kneels before her. "Is there something wrong?" There's helplessness in his voice. "Can you tell me?"

She still doesn't answer. He reaches for her hesitantly, as though he expects her to resist. Instead, she unfolds against him. He holds her in his arms. "I know, I know," he croons, his voice hurried and soft. "It's the weather; it's almost winter; you get like this. It's that damn *taiya*, it would drive anyone mad. We'll be home for Christmas soon; we'll get away. Let's get away this weekend, tonight. We can't stay here now anyway, not with the *taiya* back. We'll go wherever you want. You'll like that, right? Wherever . . ."

She nods against his shoulder.

They go that day to a farmhouse inn in the countryside south of the city. The vineyards have been picked bare; the hills are gold and brown. The little town feels empty, and the sky overhead is huge. Karen feels soothed by the silence. She and Patrick walk along the river hand-in-hand, and the only sound is the wind.

But two weeks later, Patrick is yelling in their bedroom and throwing clothes again into a suitcase. "*Fuck*," he says. "We can't stay here any longer, not with that *thing* screeching outside." He doesn't even fold his dress shirts neatly, as he always does. He throws Karen's things in the suitcase as well. "If this were the States, we could *sue* the landlord. How could he not tell us? How did it get this bad?"

He looks around. "Karen?"

But she's downstairs, moving through the dark rooms toward the side door. The moon is bright, lighting up the small garden, but of course, there's nothing to see.

It had worked for a short time. It had worked—avoiding the house, drowning out sorrow and thought with rock 'n roll and pop music and Bach and the BBC. It had worked to distract herself, to shut her ears. To run away. But the sound outside is now louder than the TV or radio or their own raised voices. Louder than her memory of a quiet weekend with her husband.

The neighbors all must hear, of course. The spirit is loud enough to wake the whole neighborhood.

She steps out the door and into the night. The noise is sourceless now. It's everywhere. It's sobbing and keening and a low, sad moan. It's the bare edge of the wind and the scream of a dying bird. The long, slow glide of a cello chord at the end of the world. It's nothing human and everything terribly, devastatingly human.

Did that boy's grandmother ever stop listening? Karen wonders. Did she ever get away?

"Karen?" Patrick has come down the stairs. He stands in the doorway, looking out at his wife. There's fear in his voice.

The *taiya* is trying to speak, but it has no words. Its calls ring, frustrated, against the night air. It's all but eaten away.

It might grow in power; its voice might rise louder and louder. But still, no one can understand it. It speaks no language that can be grasped. It can't say what it is.

Karen turns as Patrick's hands grab her. He's holding her, trying to pull her into the house. "Karen, Karen," he says, her name a flowing river from his lips. She can speak. She's not a *taiya*. She's human. Maybe someone in the world would understand.

She holds Patrick and rises on her toes, and puts her lips to his ear. She will try to tell him. She opens her mouth to explain.

The Wave

46,000 fans are registered for my live mind-cast tomorrow. Not big, but not too bad considering that the edited 'casts after the fact are always more popular. And there's a lot going on tomorrow—a wingsuit flying slalom race and another stratosphere jump by Dominique Wongsuwan. Logins to the live feeds of *her* mind-casts are always sky-high.

So it's okay, I tell myself, my low numbers don't mean anything. More will log in at the last minute, and it's the still later numbers that will really matter, the downloads of the edited 'cast, the polished show, the after-buzz. Tomorrow, the wave will break big; I can *feel* it.

I can almost literally see it, too. For the past week, I've been tracking this storm, a swirling monster in the Bering Sea. In the bottom right corner of my visual field, color-coded maps show wind speed and wave height throughout the North Pacific. A perfect swell is aimed right at the central Oregon coast, due to reach these shores tomorrow morning. If the forecast is right, the biggest waves we've seen here in a decade will hit.

And at an obscure outer reef two miles offshore, the wave of my dreams will break.

Alex enters the room. He looks rumpled with sleep, his brown hair tousled and flattened on one side. But somehow, I know that he's been lying awake all this time. He looks at me, and then his eyes flick to the screen mounted on the kitchen counter, which shows the same swell readings as those pulsing now across my eye display.

"Looks big for tomorrow," he says. His voice is deceptively light.

"Yes."

Our eyes meet. His are large and dark, and right now, they're showing the worry that he's been suppressing for days, the fears for me that he's been trying to hide. This is the first night we've spent together before a wave this big. And for a moment I think longingly of the rental house near the cove where I might have stayed, where the rest of the team is gathered.

"Shannon." Alex closes the distance between us, puts his arms around me.

I lean against him, and we stay like that for a moment or two in silence.

"How are you feeling?" he says finally.

"Good." I rest my head on his shoulder. "I just always have trouble sleeping before a swell this size."

"I know."

His body is lean and warm. I kiss the spot behind his ear and then let my lips brush down his neck.

"Maybe there's something you could do to help me fall asleep," I tease. And I shut down the flow of data to my eye display, the weather updates and news and social feeds. Maybe spending the night here with him, moving in together, was the right call after all.

His arms tighten around me, and the rest of his answer is not in words.

It's never been easy to make a living as a professional surfer. But in the past there were many more people who surfed, who actually got wet in the waves. A pro could use her image to help sell boards, wet suits, swimwear, athletic wear. She could sell an image of athleticism, a dream of sun and sand and freedom. Sports drinks. Sandals. Anything that could use a bit of surf glamor in its marketing.

And sex appeal, of course. If you're a woman and good-looking, there's always been that, too.

You can always sell something. But fewer people surf now; fewer people leave their homes at all. They're all watching their screens, working, and playing online. And they're plugged into mind-casts, jumping off cliffs with BASE jumpers, turning flips with an aerial skier, even sharing in the mountain-top meditations of a monk who calls himself the Bodhisattva (2000 international credits gets you fifteen minutes of Enlightenment as you tap into his live mind-feed).

So I sell what so many are selling now: the experience.

And I'm good at it. My hits and followers are rising steadily. My 'casts have been featured by some of the top adrenaline channels. I'm not a regular in the top lists, no; I don't have the investors that would let me take off anywhere at the first hint of a good swell, the ability to chase big waves around the globe year-round. But I'm getting there.

I don't have the technical skill of some, the flawless lines or showy moves. I haven't ridden the biggest, heaviest waves. But it's not so much now about how you look when you're surfing. It's not all about the wave that you ride.

It's about how you *feel* that wave.

Fog on the cold sea. I left Alex warm in our bed this morning and took the rented car to the cove, the radar-guided auto system navigating easily through the thick soup mists. Now I'm standing on the shore with the rest of the crew, trying to peer through the fog with unaided eyes. The big wave is unseen, miles offshore, but even here, the crash of the surf is stunning. Through the mist, I glimpse heaving walls of gray water and explosions of spray. Boiling whitewater surges up the beach. It's a mess, the cove completely closed out, waves breaking every which way.

My partner, Brett, shakes his head. I catch his eye, and we trade bleak smiles.

All our tech and the best weather apps, and no one knows precisely when this fog will lift, when the sea will calm enough to give us a chance to get past the shore break to the deep water reef beyond. Nervous swearing and chatter from the group. I run my visual-casting feed, posting images from the beach to my fans. Everyone else is doing the same, of course. If we ever do get a polished group cast out of this, this scene will make for great drama.

Mandy Kalama trains her eye-cam on me and asks me how I'm feeling. She's not surfing, but she'll come out with us as backup videographer from the water and jet-ski safety patrol. We're damn lucky to have her. I watch her interview Jake Perez and Ken Lee for the group cast next. They've flown in from Oahu, Hawaii just for this swell. They're hard-charging stars with rocketing numbers. Jake in particular has a massive following and growing ad links, with his sculpted cheekbones and sea-green eyes, and his insane exploits in free-diving, hydro-flying, and surfing. Ken's no slouch himself, one of the best pure surfers I know, calm in the worst situations but able to radiate a joy in the waves that's made him a favorite of mind-cast followers. Brett paces by, and Mandy grabs him for his turn. He looks intently into her recording eyes and speaks of the weather and danger with just the right amount of tension. Beneath my own tension, my heart warms. He's come a long way since the days when he was nervous and tongue-tied in interviews. We've known each other since we were kids, surfing this coast together.

The ocean roars. In the damp air, my ungloved hands tingle with cold.

"Morning, kids." Taj Atkins' voice speaks in my head, crisp and bright. He's the drone-cam operator we've hired to film additional visuals for our show. He's online. Finally. Now we can get a glimpse of the open sea beyond the shore break. The drone feed opens in a square of my vision, and I see light above the mist, blue skies. Then the drone descends; the world turns white, but something flashing below is whiter still: the foam of breaking waves. And now there are patches where the fog has cleared, and the dark sea seethes and glitters. "Here we go," Taj says, and we're flying onward, and I see a long swell below, rushing forward and then lifting, lifting, white at the top and curving and curling. It breaks, peeling gorgeously from left to right, and the detonation of foam fills the view-screen. Taj pulls back slightly, and I see another wave on the way, part of a set, and I know now that we're at the outer reef; we must be, because I'm seeing the waves of my dreams.

"Holy shit," Mandy breathes, watching on her own eye display. "That's beautiful."

And now everyone is talking, shouting excitedly to Taj, who guides the drone according to our commands. For a while, we just watch, getting the overview of the reef, trying to learn the behavior of the wave that breaks there. The fog drifts and parts and closes in again. Before us, in real-vision, the water at the cove still surges wildly without control.

"We're going out there," says Jake.

"Of course," someone says. "But right now?"

"Maybe we should wait another hour, see if the fog lifts by then."

"Surf's still building."

"It might be peaking."

"We're going out now," I say. Everyone looks at me.

"Right." Brett grins as he meets my gaze. "Let's do this now."

They listen because Brett and I were the ones who discovered the big wave out there years ago. For nearly a decade, we've been watching for it.

It only breaks when the sea is big enough, when the swells reach twenty-five feet or more. Under those conditions, the waves at the cove start to close out; they begin collapsing all at once, unsurfable. But out *there*, at that unnamed reef, the wave of the gods rises up.

"Ghost Wave," Brett and I have called it, because it's so elusive. I've only seen it a handful of times. It's only now that I feel ready to tackle it.

As we wrangle our jet-skis into the water, I think, for a moment, about Alex. He must be awake by now. He'll have poured his coffee, stirred in too much sugar. He might be reading research papers for work. But he'll be ready for the alert that signals the start of my personal mind-cast. He'll be ready to put down his coffee and join in.

I settle into the driver's seat, Brett behind me. Ken and Jake share another jet ski, and Mandy, as water-safety patrol, has her own.

THIS IS IT, I post to my followers. IT'S FOR REAL, WE'RE FINALLY DOING IT! YEARS OF TRAINING AND PREPARATION FOR THIS MOMENT—I CAN HARDLY BELIEVE IT'S HERE. LOG IN AND HANG ON TIGHT!!!

I start the jet ski's engine and turn on my live mind-feed.

There are all kinds of customization features available on our live mind-casts. A person can log in and see, hear, smell, even *feel* what I or my teammates are experiencing. An accelerating heart rate, a quickened breath, salt spray on the face, the feel of carving a perfect turn at the base of a wave and outracing the falling lip of thousands of gallons of water.

The audience receives the transmitted electrical patterns of our neural activity directly into their brains, but they can choose to have the neural data altered; they can tune and dampen down certain sensations, or filter them out completely. The coldness of that spray on the face; the aching numbness that comes after hours in the sea, no matter how good the wet suit worn. Fatigue. Pain. Fear.

There are default safeguards in place. It wouldn't do to have the receivers, the "mind-riders," traumatized. Reception is supposed to shut down when certain thresholds of pain or distress are exceeded.

Most people prefer the edited 'casts. No risk of the unexpected there. Our editor will delete all the boring parts, the lulls spent just hanging out in the water, waiting for a rideable wave. With a group cast like this, the editor will select the best rides, the best moments from all of us, and will splice our mind-feeds together along with Mandy and Taj's visual recordings for one thrilling, wondrous, pumping ride.

Still, the individual live mind-feeds have their fans. Some want to be right there with us in real-time. There are even reports of people hacking the safeguards. People who want to feel it all, even if it's the worst wipeout ever—snapped bones, cracked ribs, a wicked hold-down under waves so beastly that you think this is it, you can't breathe, you're really done for this time.

There are some people who want to risk feeling everything.

***

The ride out past the shore break is a bitch. The mist makes it hard to see what's coming, and the waves here are the size of houses. I'm racing the jet ski left and right, back and forth, dodging the breaking waves, looking for a way through. We top a wave just before it breaks, falling with a bone-rattling jolt down the other side, and Brett curses my driving. I'm laughing, and then he starts laughing, too.

We make it out. It takes forty minutes to go two miles, but we make it.

The water calms. The fog has begun to clear by now, and through the dissipating haze the sun lights the scene. Rolling toward me is the wave, *my* wave, a dazzling mountain of water, glassy and green. It's bigger and moving faster than I've ever seen it—the face at least eighty feet high.

Why surfing? I was asked in an online Q and A. *Why such a niche sport in this day and age, especially with the approach that you take? Have you considered surfing with more modern gear and apps?*

There were several things I could have said.

I could have said: *This is the way I distinguish myself in a crowded field of mind-casters.*

I could have said: *I'm spearheading a return to a more authentic expression of human achievement. Body augmentations and mods have their place, and the new reflex-enhancing apps have enabled incredible feats. But I want a purer form of sport; I want to remind people of what the raw human body and mind can do.*

Or I might have told the truth, and said: *When I was starting out, I didn't have money for the best neuromod apps and augments. And then, my friends and I started getting attention, and we realized that this was the way to play it.*

I might have said: *It's because I learned to surf as a little girl growing up in southern California, back when people still lived there, back before the currents and storm patterns changed and the swells moved north and the fires burned everything down. Back when regular people still took to the waves, and Trestles was crowded on every good day. I learned to surf the real way, with an unaugmented body and non-motorized board. And then I came north to Oregon with my family and all the other drought refugees, and the world was wet and green and strange. The kids at the new school teased me; the sea felt like ice. But I pulled on a wetsuit and took out my board, and I was home. Surfing was home. It always will be.*

"It's the biggest rush there is," I told the interviewer aloud. "It's not just speed—you can get that other ways—but it's skill and mastery and riding the energy of the sea. You can't feel the wave the same way with the new tech-boards and apps. It's hard to explain."

I looked at the camera. "Download one of my mind-casts," I told the audience. "Any of them at all. You'll feel it for yourselves."

***

Brett is the first one to take on the Ghost Wave. These waves are too large to catch paddling in with unaugmented arms, so we use our jet skis to tow each other in—a deliberate recreation of the classic technique of an earlier generation of big-wave surfers.

I slingshot Brett into a clean seventy-footer. He slices across a face that's the height of an office building seven stories high. He carves a long, swooping arc, down and then up to the wave's crest and down again, staying seconds ahead of the falling lip, and as he pulls safely out of the collapsing wave, he's screaming in joy.

Then the other tow team has a turn—Jake whipped into a wave by Ken driving jet ski. Jake angles down a face at least as tall as Brett's monster; then, insanely, he cuts back up under the pitching lip and into one of the biggest tubes I've ever seen. We all hold our breaths as he disappears behind the pouring, thundering curtain. Seconds later, the barrel spits out a plume of spray. And he's there, on his feet, riding out on the last surge of that barrel's breath.

Even Taj, watching and recording remotely from miles away, is yelling and hooting with us. Ken swoops in on jet ski to pick his partner up, and it's off for the next wave.

They keep rolling in, these beautiful, flowing, roaring sculptures of water and light. Brett and Jake carve smoothly down faces like green glass. And then it's time to switch drivers and surfers. It's my turn.

Brett's eyes are still shining as I position my feet in the straps on my board. I take hold of the tow rope behind the ski. And we're skimming forward to meet the swells. The first one coming at us is large, but there's one behind that, and another after that, too—a set, and each bigger than the last. "This one! This one!" I scream at the third, and Brett opens the throttle and we're on it, the beast rising under us. I drop the tow rope, and he drives away to the safety of the shoulder. The wave keeps rising beneath me, steepening; it's drawing up the entire sea as it stands. It's a vertical wall, and now there's no time to do anything but point my board straight and beeline it right down the face.

This is the thing about riding big waves: I'm not thinking about anything else when I'm on one.

I'm not thinking of the people logged into my mind-feed, slumped blank-eyed and slack-jawed on ratty couches or sleek form-adjusting chairs; scattered in rural land-locked towns and cities in Iowa, Minnesota, the Great Plains; tapping in from Portland, Seattle, Vancouver, Calgary; insomniac teens in Beijing or a middle-aged manager in Sydney who once surfed in his youth. I'm not thinking of my counts and hits and investor demands and whether or not this group cast will do well. I'm not thinking about the shitty terms in that new mind-cast distribution deal, or the new equipment I'd like, or how if I were smarter and richer, I'd have insisted on more backup water safety, maybe even a support boat or helicopter on call. I'm not thinking of the cost of medical insurance. I'm not thinking of my mother, who keeps asking if I'll ever go back to college and get a real job. I'm not thinking about Alex, who's likely riding in my mind right now, the only time I've ever let him or any lover into my mind: when I know I won't be thinking of them, or of us, at all.

I'm not even thinking about the next wave.

I'm only thinking about this one, at this time. Just this moment, the ocean roaring and moving under and all around me. The lip of the wave gathering behind me. The feel of the water under my feet, and the split-second adjustments I must make to stay alive.

The lip crashes down behind me, nearly at my heels; the spray from the explosion catches me and nearly knocks me off my feet. I stay on the board, barely. The world is white mist. Brett's there suddenly, zooming in on jet ski to pick me up. I swing up onto the sled behind the ski.

My heart's beating hard enough to trigger an arrhythmia in a vulnerable mind-rider. I was running for my life the whole way.

"That was insane—the biggest one yet!" Brett tells me as we race out from the whitewater. I hear my friends whooping for me over the audio connection. "You could have driven semi-trucks through the barrel that was behind you!" Jake yells, and Ken says, "Two semis at once!" and Mandy just keeps repeating, "Holy fuck." "The biggest one yet," Taj says solemnly. He has the software for measuring wave height from trough to crest, so I believe him. I don't ask for the number of feet or meters. I don't check my own sensor feeds for the stats. Another swell is looming on the horizon. "Let's go," I tell Brett, and we're off for the next.

We fall and wipe out. All of us. It's almost inevitable in waves like these.

Jake falls in his next barrel; Brett hits chop on the face and goes spinning. Ken, after three flawless rides, suffers a nightmare: He falls while still near the top and is sucked up the moving face and then caught and pitched down within the massive, plunging lip. We all freeze at the sight; we all assume that he's pulverized, dead. But he pops up, alive, his safety vest inflating and doing its job. It's Mandy who makes the rescue, racing on jet ski into the seething cauldron of whitewater to fetch him. They escape the impact zone before the next wave hits, and he's shaken and beaten but miraculously unhurt.

I fall as well.

These are the moments edited out of a polished mind-cast. These moments when you're driven down, down, and the water is black, and you curl yourself into a ball because the whirling force of the wave is trying to tear off your limbs. You're caught in the spin-cycle of the world's largest washing machine, and you're pummeled as you tumble helplessly, blind. The air in your lungs is slowly burning away. It takes everything you have to force away the panic. You're reminded that you're not in control. You never were.

I'm flushed to the surface; I'm sucking air through thick foam. Brett's there to pluck me from the water, just as partners are supposed to do. I realize that I've been shot half a football field's length from where I fell. I'm gasping on the ski's rescue sled. "Are you okay?" Brett asks. I am. I'm thrilled with just being alive.

We're at it for hours. An offshore wind picks up, blowing straight into the wave faces, grooming them and making them stand taller. Accidents happen when you're tired; everyone knows that, but no one's tired; we're mainlining top-grade adrenaline. Who knows when this wave will break again? Who knows the next time that distant storms and winds align just right, focusing the sea's energy just so at this spot? It might never be this good again.

Brett's ripping a monstrous wave as though it's half the size, carving sharp turns, snapping off the top; he's surfing as though it were a mild day at our home break. He'll never reach the performance levels of a star running top-shelf neuromod apps—the neural programs that enhance reflexes and reaction times, that suppress fear while still maintaining fear's focus. But I think, with his natural gifts, that he comes close.

He's not a Luddite or fool; none of us are. We do what we can to stay safe and surf well. We have the best classic boards you can buy, made with the best modern materials. We wear health monitoring apps like everyone else; we have wet suits with GPS trackers and all the safety features we can afford. We use technology selectively, as Alex would say.

But we want to *feel* it when we surf. Not use neural programs to turn ourselves into perfect, contest-winning, record-breaking machines. I've experienced the mind-feeds of those neural app users; I know the difference.

The ocean's still throwing out bombs, these incredible waves. Brett's making a turn when something happens: I see his body twist and pitch forward. He bounces off the water's surface. And then the white fury of the peeling lip catches up and buries him.

I'm on it; I can see the tracking signal from his suit shining on my visual display, overlaid on the real-world visuals. I shoot forward into the whitewater. It's chaos, but his tracking signal is a bright red light through the spray. I see him with my real vision, a dark figure bobbing in the water. I go in to grab him, but when I pull alongside, his hands slip off the rescue sled. I come back around. I can see that something's wrong; his face has gone nearly as white as the foam. Taj, watching from above, shouts a warning about the incoming wave. I can sense it bearing down on us. I grab Brett's arms and use the acceleration of the ski to provide the momentum to flip him onto the sled.

I gun us out of there.

But not fast enough. I know that the next wave will hit the moment before it does.

There's the sharp thunder-crack as the lip hits, almost right on us. And in that same instant, I see nothing but white, as the blast of the wave's collapse catches us and hurls us into the air.

Why do you do it? strangers comment on my social feeds.

Why do you keep doing it? my mother has asked. She's sat through some of my mind-casts; she should understand.

But I know what she's asking. She's waving one hand about helplessly as she talks, as she mentions those barrels I caught in Chile two years ago, and how happy I was then and how *those waves* didn't seem so big, so scary. She'll mention other sessions in smaller waves, exploring Vancouver Island's hidden breaks, paddling into double-overheads with Brett at our regular spot, catching long tubes that seemed to go on forever off the coast of Namibia. They were all good rides. She's right; I was perfectly happy then.

But I can't stand still; I can't keep at the same level. I have to keep pushing it, changing it up, exploring new breaks and techniques and approaches. I have to keep surfing bigger waves.

My most dedicated followers understand. They've been there from the beginning, and they log in to every ride. They understand how challenge and fear feed the thrill. They feel it when I get too comfortable, when I'm too far back from the edge. The edge is where they—and I—want to be.

I'm flying through the air; I see the distant shore—green pines, cliffs—hanging inverted before me. And then I'm plunging down into darkness.

My safety vest inflates, and I surface. Brett is floating about twenty yards away. A wall of churning whitewater is behind him, blotting out the world. It's coming so fast. I don't have time to deflate my vest and dive to duck its power. I barely have time to draw a breath before it's upon us.

There are moments that you don't want your loved ones to share. Times that you hope they're not logged in, feeling what you feel.

The force is like a wall of concrete slamming into me, and I'm driven down again, down, and everything is ringing. I'm spinning, spinning, spinning, and the beating seems to go on forever.

I come to the surface again. There's another wave upon me. Again.

It knocks out what little air I had left in my lungs.

When the body is denied oxygen and carbon dioxide builds up in the blood, the body begins to spasm. Fingers and toes begin to tingle. The urge to draw in a breath—even when you know it's a suffocating breath of salt water—becomes overwhelming.

I force myself to relax. My mind to empty. The urge to breathe passes.

I hear Mandy on the audio connection, her voice steady and calm. "Hang on. We'll be right there to get you; we can see where you are. Just hang on."

So I do.

Even with my vest fully inflated, it seems to take a long time to break the surface. But I do, and I'm gulping air hungrily, desperately.

There's another wave left in the set.

There are *multiple* waves left in the set.

Taj, from somewhere above, can see them all and is counting them off —*Just three more left, hang on,* he says —and I can hear the others talking to me, talking to both Brett and me, calming, reassuring, staying with us. The poundings blur together; it's a nightmare, but it's a nightmare I've known. I've been held under before, caught in multiple-wave poundings before, although this is the worst I've ever had.

And then I hear the jet ski, and Mandy's there, and she grabs me, and she gets us both out of there before the last wave of the set hits.

I'm gasping on the rescue sled ,and the world is still spinning. Tiny black dots swarm across my vision. My body feels pounded to tissue paper, and I've never been so grateful to Mandy in all my life.

"Brett?" I say when I can finally talk.

Ken's voice on the audio, tense: "Got him. I've called the medics, and they're on their way."

"Brett?" I say again. Brett doesn't answer.

We all go together to take Brett back to shore. By now, he's recovered a little from the initial shock, but the pain from his injuries has come flooding in, and the choppy ride back doesn't help. He lies face down on Ken's rescue sled and bites a strap to keep from screaming. I'm on Ken's ski, too, trying to keep Brett still. He sprained a knee on his fall on the wave's face, and then the falling lip shattered the femur of his other leg. This is what the emergency room doctor surmises, remotely reviewing the data from Brett's health app sensors. It's a miracle that Ken got him out before much more damage could occur. Matter-of-factly, the doctor tells us to keep the leg as still as we can, to keep the broken bone bits from sliding around. It's lucky, she adds, that a bone hasn't punctured Brett's femoral artery. He'd bleed out to death within minutes.

It's not exactly a comforting thought as we drive back through the rough shore break.

But we make it to shore, and he's still alive, and the medics and ambulance vehicle are there. One of the medics jacks into Brett's health apps to start a localized pain block, and Brett's face immediately eases. By the time they bundle him away, he's joking about his fall. He's safe, and his husband has been called and will be meeting him at the hospital.

The rest of us are left standing on the beach, looking at one another.

There's still a mind-cast to be recorded. There are still waves to be ridden before a predicted storm tomorrow comes and blows it all to worthless chop.

"Are you going back out?" Jake asks me carefully. His green eyes hold no judgment. I already know what he and Ken will do. Jake was the one who tracked down my jet ski and board and drove my ski in while I rode with Brett and Ken.

I look at Mandy. She'll be the one to tow me into the waves if I go back out.

"I can handle it," she says evenly. "Your call."

I feel weak and shaky, but I think—as I've thought before, as I thought after my first really bad wipe-out and after countless spills and wipeouts since—that if I don't get back out there now, I might not have the nerve to get back in again. Brett's safe. And besides, I still haven't made it out of a barrel this session.

"Yeah," I say. "I want just one more wave."

I get it. Mandy tows me into a beautiful one—not as big as the other monsters we've been surfing, but it's perfectly formed. I'm in the right position. I pull into the barrel, into the heart of the wave. The green lip arcs and throws over my left. The roar of the wave quiets. The barrel's translucent green light surrounds me. The translucent light fills me.

I see the barrel's opening ahead, a portal back into the world. I keep my eyes fixed on that opening, adjusting my speed. The water flashes and sparkles all about me. I think that I might make it out this time.

I do.

I keep to my feet as the barrel spits me out in its cold spray, and Mandy's waiting there to pick me up. My friends are all cheering. I feel weightless with the relief and joy. It was over too soon, as it always is, but it's enough. "That's it," I tell Mandy. "I don't need any more for today."

Alex is waiting for me on the beach when I get back. I don't question why he's there. I just walk up to him and press myself against him, like a tired child looking to crawl into a hidden place for rest.

This is the dirty secret of a mind-cast: you're not really experiencing what the mind-caster felt.

Even if it's a raw mind-feed with no filters or safeguards at all—it's not the same. It's not real.

Because some small part of you knows that you're not really there; you know that you're actually in your bedroom or lying back on your living room couch, the mind-receiver set shading your eyes. Even as your heart rockets in rhythm with the 'caster and your breath draws quick, some small part of you retains control, able to stop reception of the mind-cast whenever you please.

If it was *exactly* the same—if the experience of a mind-cast was inseparable from the real thing—I wouldn't need to keep chasing big waves at all. I would just download and stream the experiences of others.

If it was exactly the same, I would relive through mind-casts my own best waves, over and over. That perfect ride at Peahi; the secret wave in Western Australia; the long barrels that went on forever in Skeleton Bay, Namibia. And the best days right here on this coast, in the hard, cold waters of the Pacific Northwest, with my friends.

And if I could, I would go back even further in time. To a time before there were mind-casts at all. If I could, I would go back to experience the first time I stood and turned on a wave. The first time I caught a barrel. Those days in SoCal, when I was just a girl and the world was so bright. If those days had been mind-recorded, I'd go back and re-experience those first thrills over and over.

It's late at night, and I'm lying in bed in my favorite warm PJs, waiting for Alex to join me. Brett came through his surgery just fine: I've been checking and re-checking his social feeds. There's a photo of him giving a thumbs-up on a gurney just before they wheeled him into the operating room. His husband has been posting to Brett's public page, and Brett apparently came out of the OR three hours ago with titanium rods stuck through his splintered bones and injections of growth factors and matrix proteins to speed healing. Maybe a month to recover, and then he can be back in the waves. He's sleeping now, so I'll see him tomorrow. I've already left him several direct messages, but I add my public well wishes to the hundreds now scrolling across his public page. The drone visuals from his fall and rescue are already going viral. The finished group cast should do great.

Alex enters the room; he has a glass of water for me. I catch his hand as he sets it on the nightstand, and our hands squeeze.

"I've got a little work I need to catch up on," Alex says, his eyes gentle. "I'll be up soon, okay?"

I nod.

It's my doing that he's behind on his work, after all; he was tapped into my mind-feed, riding with me instead of working. And after he felt me take six waves on the head—after he felt me get rag-dolled by the sea, and then my fear when I thought Brett might be gone, my fear on those long, terrible two miles back to shore, my partner biting back his screams in front of me—then Alex had torn off his mind-receiver set and gone out to meet me. He didn't want to be in my head any longer; he wanted to be physically with me, to be there on the beach when I came in from the sea.

I think, *I have so much to be grateful for.*

I close my eyes, leaning back into the pillows. That deep, good post-wave exhaustion is claiming me. Mandy and Ken and Jake are alive and whole; they were just here for dinner, and now they're on the way back to their own families. I hear Alex downstairs, tidying up, running the kitchen sink. And then he'll be lost in his own work for an hour or more. He uses computer models to try to understand the ongoing changes to the ocean currents. I try to follow his work, but I don't have the physics and math background to follow completely. I've been worried about things between us, that we moved in together too soon, that it's too much too fast, that in the end he can't handle my surfing. That outside the mind-casts, he'll never really understand. But as he frowns downstairs over his esoteric equations, and I drift off toward sleep, I think that I don't understand everything about him or his passions, either.

The Young God

A young god wants to destroy the world.

From the other side of the globe, I feel her rage. Miles under my feet, currents of magma shift and flow. A cloud passes over the sun. Rain falls in a sudden burst—passersby on the street hurry through fat drops, their heads bent. But summer storms are common here. Taxis slow at the curb, life whirls on, and no one notices the change in the beat of the world.

I close my eyes. Eventually, it always comes to this.

———

Flocks of birds are tearing at each other as I cross the sky. Starlings chase hawks. A crow screams. Two dozen tornadoes slam though the American heartland and into the South. I pass over the Atlantic, and the electricity in the air keeps building.

I find her on a bare hill, brooding under a tree of stripped branches. It's not quite dawn here, the horizon dark; yet the sky overhead is on fire. "I'll do it," she says. "You can't stop me."

Her voice trembles; her eyes are black holes. Her hair crackles with sparks, and her breath burns air.

"I know," I say. "I understand."

Her hand lifts, but before she can complete the motion, I invoke the ancient contract. "Three hours," I remind her. "The grace period due."

The air around us cools. She glares.

I take a step toward her. "Tell me about it."

———

I do understand. I was young once, too.

It's easier for other gods. For the ones born Before, who can create entire worlds out of the Void and then casually implode them in a fit of pique. But she and I were born of this world, raised among mortals, our heartbeats set in rhythm with theirs.

"They *deserve* it," she seethes. "Every single one of them. If there are any who don't . . . it's a mercy killing."

Images from her mind catch in mine. Pictures of what humans have done to each other and what they have yet to do. Bombs and missiles and gunfire, yes, and also beatings delivered with bare hands. A mob tears apart a teenage girl. Laughter as a child weeps. Physical violence and quieter corruption, too: poison in the drinking water, famine caused by neglect. Indifference, cowardice, and greed. An old man dies of hunger and sorrow, alone.

"I know," I whisper.

There are spots of brightness, too. Sun on the water, and children laughing as they chase each other in and out of the waves. A boy stands on a stage and sings with the voice of an angel. The scent of lilacs in spring and two people kissing under an arbor. A woman confronts a line of soldiers with flowers in her hands.

The god before me is newly awakened, only just come into power. She's shaking with the rush of knowledge and feeling, the glimpses into future and present and past.

"Do you see it?" she says. "What's about to happen?"

I do. A new conflagration, swallowing whole countries. War burning through the land of her birth. Driven, as always, by human hatred, fear, and unreason.

It would be easier to end it all now, she says silently.

It would.

But— "Don't," I say aloud. "Not yet."

I search her mind for those fleeting moments of light. The faces of those she loves. I show them to her: the mortal family she grew up with; her toddling, round-cheeked niece. Her friends. Even I am there in her mind—her most recent friend, wise teacher, and mentor. She sees the future in outline, but none of us know all the choices that mortals will make.

Would you really kill us all now? I ask. *Won't you give any of us a chance?*

She bows her head, dark hair hiding her eyes.

She and I are not like the gods who can step away—who can drown or burn or shatter their creations and then blithely move on to the next. If she kills this world, she'll kill both me and herself. She'll kill the others like us alongside all that she loves. We're bound to this world we never made.

Three hours. The sun is frozen beneath the horizon; everything is still. But outside this bubble of timelessness, a cosmic clock ticks down.

There is no rational argument I can give her. Only hope. The touch of a child she loves, the warmth of her niece on her lap. Tiny hands entwined with hers, bright eyes filled with trust. My own friendship. Hope that on some eternal scale, the goodness and beauty will eventually outweigh the dark.

Her face lifts, and I see tears shining on her pale cheeks. "How?" she gasps. "How do you stand it? How do you keep on?"

I take her in my arms. "With help."

She slumps against me and begins to cry. Her knees give way, and we sit together on the bare hillside.

Slowly, the horizon lightens. Time steps back into place. The young god's fires were extinguished, but now new fire burns in the sky: streaks of clouds lit by the rising sun.

She's quiet. I stroke her hair. "Not yet, okay? Not today."

She nods.

The spot of Earth we sit on rotates into the sunlight, and I think that the sunrise is beautiful, beautiful. A cool breeze blows and a blackbird calls. We have to help each other, I think. There may be a day when she's the one to talk me down, the one to suspend Time and keep me from breaking our world. She'll have to remind me then of light and all that I love. It doesn't always get easier with age. She's fallen asleep against me now, exhausted. I feel her breathing; I feel the Earth and everything on it, all the people and birds and ants and growing trees, breathing.

The Message

Mom and Dad were right that the air is cleaner out here in Wisconsin. The sky is orange only at night, and it's not the smoky haze of back home, dropping ashes and clogging our filter masks. The air here is weightless, clear; and in the clean light, all edges and shadows are sharp. In the evening, the sky is somehow bright and soft at the same time, an orange and gold glow that's reflected in the lake so that lake and sky look like two halves of one brightness.

I'm standing on the deck as the light slowly fades, and Mom and Dad are yelling from inside the house. Dad thought this getaway would be good for us all, but Mom's still losing her funding. The lake town is pretty, but she's still blacklisted; the world at large is burning, and the assholes still run everything.

My phone chimes. It's Chloe.

She's sent me a picture. A different sky shines from the screen: swirls of deep purple and clouds of stars. Glowing creatures of the sea. Fluorescent jellyfish pulse across a dark sea-sky.

I made this for our story, her message says. *A bit of inspiration.* My heart warms. The picture is perfect.

Chloe and I are writing an epic crossover fanfic involving two of our favorite anime shows: *From the Deeps* and *Sweep of Stars.* I'm writing the chapters that take place on the ocean -world of *From the Deeps,* and Chloe's writing the *Stars* chapters. We've taken two of the main characters of *From the Deeps,* Haru and Kes, and separated them by thousands of light-years. Haru is still a badass warrior fighting krakens in defense of his floating island-city. But instead of fighting alongside him on a cyber-whale, his rival Kes is now part of the 22nd class of the Star Ambassador Academy. Just as in the canon plotline, the 22nd Academy class is stranded in a remote sector of the galaxy after a field trip gone wrong, and they must try to find their way home, hopping across the universe through Star-Gates and getting into plenty of adventures along the way.

We're almost to the turning point of the story: when Kes and his classmates tumble into Haru's world. Kes hits his head, and they all nearly drown, but they're rescued by Haru's squad, and Kes wakes up to Haru's green eyes.

I've been listening to starsong while writing, Chloe messages me. *I'm thinking of making a playlist to go with our story.*

The *Stars* fandom has been obsessed with "starsong" of late. It's our word for music from the show that incorporates patterns found in the Message. Someone noticed it (subtle, hidden) in two of last season's episodes, and it ties in so beautifully with the season's themes. Of course, once word got out there was the usual fearmongering by some over "Message music" and what it could do to young minds, even though people have been translating and playing with Message data as audible sound for *years* and no one's mutated into an alien or lost their mind yet.

It's a great idea. Go for it! I say.

I'm so glad!!! Chloe sends a series of hearts and smiles. She knows I can sometimes get a little weird about Message stuff.

I hear the new special aired, she says. *Have you seen it?*

She means the new documentary special on the Message. Timed to commemorate the fifteenth anniversary of its reception. The moment fifteen years ago when my mother looked at a pattern of radio signals and realized she was seeing a message from a distant star.

Yeah, I write back. *It was okay. There was nothing really new.*

That's part of the reason my mom's in a funk: because there's nothing new. That's why it's hard to drum up private funding. Well, that and the ongoing economic recession and the fact that the Message is publicly available, all of it freely accessible to the world, and thousands of experts and hobbyists have taken a crack at it, and thousands of research papers and blog posts have been written, but still, no one knows what it means. Scientists have tried to analyze it in all kinds of ways, programming deep neural networks to comb through the signal, applying various models, taking it apart bit by bit. Artists have played with it, translating patterns to musical notes or colors. There are those who still say that the signal is dangerous, that it's a viral code, that if you look at it too deeply, it will take over and reprogram your mind. There are those who think it's the key to salvation. And from the start, there've been those who insist that it's all an elaborate hoax.

The newest documentary special has a lot of recycled footage. Old interviews from fifteen years ago. Shots of those first hectic press conferences. Mom doesn't speak in the first big briefings. She wasn't director of the Institute then. She was a new postdoctoral fellow, fresh from her PhD Her group leader and the Director are the ones at the podium. But Mom was the one who recognized the signal for what it was. She saw it in real-time.

There she is, in one of the first human-interest one-on-one interviews. Thinner and younger than she is now, dressed in a loose blouse and jeans, seated at her desk. Her smile is maybe just a little nervous, and her first words a little stilted. But her voice steadily warms as she speaks. The camera dissolves into a reenactment of the historic night. Stacks of paperwork next to her computer. A potted fern. The ghostly reflection of office furniture painted on the black night that shows through the window. She was working late at the Institute, alone. Close-up on a cup of coffee. Then, her computer chimes and trills. It's the alert that means an anomalous radio signal has been detected, from an array of telescopes hundreds of miles from the office, in a remote northern valley. "The signal was so strong," my mother says in voice-over. "It was practically screaming. It clearly wasn't natural—it was very narrow bandwidth, modulated. I think my heart stopped when I saw it. I thought maybe I was dreaming, hallucinating. And then I was sure it was some kind of mistake."

The interviewer prompts her to describe the next steps. The phone call to her boss. The way the signal just kept going. Confirmation of non-terrestrial origin, confirmation by other radio observatories—confirmation that it was *real*. The Message repeating itself, in certain narrow band-width frequencies up and down the radio spectrum. "You believe that it's real now, don't you?" the interviewer says, joking. This was at a time when much of the public still doubted. Mom looks at the camera. "Oh yes." Her slight smile is soft with awe. Her voice lifts in wonder. "It's real."

———

Are you there? Chloe will message me late at night.

Are you there? I'll message her.

It's one of our catchphrases. It's what Kes famously says in the last moments of episode 12 of *From the Deeps* when he's anxiously monitoring Haru's lone descent into the Deep Trench, and there's a sudden deep-sea explosion, and the comm-link goes silent. *"Are you there, are you there?!"* Kes shouts, and the panic in his voice is taken by many fans as the first real evidence that he has feelings for Haru.

Are you there? Chloe says, and she sends a picture she's made of Haru caught by a kraken, squeezed in its arms, our dashing hero bug-eyed and deformed. It's grotesque but also hilarious. I laugh out loud. Together, we spin a comic story of how he ended up in that situation, of how his friends react and save him, of how the entire kraken army gets involved. We can riff like this forever. We make stories both tragic and light. We send each other memes, videos, funny pictures found online. We speak of favorite songs, a beautiful turn of phrase, poetry and whales and space and time-travel and stupid jokes that would make an eight-year-old howl.

So many of our conversations are marked by time delays. There's a short window when we're both online at the same time. She lives on the other side of the world, in Melbourne, Australia, seventeen hours ahead. When it's night for me, it's the afternoon of the next day for her. It's summer for me, and winter for her. It's like one of those fairy tale stories we both love, where characters are trapped apart in opposite worlds.

It's like Haru and Kes in the fanfic we're writing: one in the deep sea and the other in the sky.

Do you believe in soulmates? I messaged her once, before going to bed.

I want to believe, she said.

Dad and I watched the Message documentary special last night, in the cozy living room of this borrowed house. Mom was half watching, typing away on her latest funding pitch. In truth, I guess we were all half watching; Dad was also checking his phone for news, as always, and I was browsing my social feeds.

We'd all focus when Mom came on the screen, or other scientists we know.

But most of the show was about the social-cultural impact of the Message. The way it changed the world. Journalists and academics and pop-culture figures speaking on the screen. A montage of crowds around the world, of congregations in prayer. The birth of the first Message cults, and doomsday fears, and Message-themed music and art and clothes. An embarrassing Message-inspired dance craze, popular in the clubs of Europe, which thankfully burned itself out over one summer. Solemn political agreements, earnest pledges of Earth unity, and then the inevitable suspicions and political dissension.

"But in the beginning, above all," the narrator intoned, "there was a shared moment of awe." A shot of sunrise over an array of radio dish antennas in an Australian desert. The Earth rotating, the camera skimming to pause, a moment, on a single huge radio dish in a karst valley in China. Then, shots of radio observatories in Europe, South Africa, Chile, and the United States. A string of listening stations around the globe. All working together to confirm and share the Message. The SETI scientific community was completely open then, united, sharing everything they knew with each other and the world. "For that moment," the narrator continued, "we were truly one. We learned that we are not alone. And that knowledge, all on its own, has changed us forever."

Dad snorted. He hit the arm of the sofa in frustration. "Nothing's changed," he said. He's more bitter than Mom, sometimes.

I sneaked a glance at Mom. She was staring at the screen, and her eyes looked shiny—as though she were close to tears.

You'll never know how it was, my parents have both said to me. This is when they're angry again at the news, at reports of protestors shot in Texas, political scandals hushed up, new restrictions on the press. This is when even Dad's non-political tech articles are edited for "political sensitivities." When the government wouldn't let Mom go to the big science conference in Beijing. "Can you imagine—now *we're* the ones not allowed to travel!" she cried, and she and Dad just stood swearing in the kitchen together. They say I'm too young to remember what this country once was. They say I don't know, can't remember that brief period of hope and freedom, which bloomed just briefly between the dark ages. When it seemed like the world might actually come together to solve its problems. When the Message was first found, it seemed it might extend that blooming of hope forever.

Are you there, Chloe? I type in the night.
  Are you there, Sarah? she asks.

The truth is that I don't like most of the Message music I've heard. It's not because I don't like the sounds themselves. It's because I know it's mostly so fake. Musicians have to manipulate the data so much to make something pleasing to human ears. I've looked a little into the data sonification programs, so I know. People have *created* the musical patterns popular on the web and among the *Sweep of Stars* fandom. They've latched onto certain signals in the Message, stretched them out, repeated them, tricked them out with extras. Real data sonification just sounds like noise.

Last year, for my birthday, Chloe wrote me a *From the Deeps* story and sent me songs recoded from humpback whales. The songs are the real deal, captured directly from hydrophone recordings made over fifty years ago. Nothing altered, no human compositions added—just the eerie wails and shrieks and moans of the sea, gliding up and up; the pauses between cries, the purrs. Cold rippled up my spine the first time I heard it. It wasn't just noise. They were the calls of another intelligence on our world. Mom told me that long ago, she had a colleague at the Institute who studied the songs of humpback whales. It may seem weird that someone at a SETI institute would study such a thing, but the idea was that whale song was a complex, non-human communication system, and that by studying its structure, we might learn techniques that could apply to the study of extraterrestrial communication, too.

I looked up some of that guy's papers. It's all information theory, mathematical equations, plots of "information entropies." The upshot: Humpback whale songs are complex. Human language is also complex. The Message beamed to us from the stars is complex. All the decades that humans have known of whale songs, the recordings we have, the analyses done. All the terabytes of data we have of a Message sent from deep space. But we still can't understand either one.

This doesn't mean that Mom and her colleagues haven't learned anything at all, of course. They've devised whole new tools to describe and analyze the data. New technologies that are applicable to other fields. They're scanning the skies for new Messages, still learning about distant stars and planets and moons. They just haven't cracked the code to what they really want to know. The other day, I heard Mom say she's afraid they never will.

Today, Dad and I had breakfast on the deck. Mom was gone on a walk. She's been taking walks by herself every morning, along the lake or through the woods.

Dad hummed to himself as he cooked. He made his usual scrambled eggs and toast. We took our plates outside and watched the light on the lake. A wind softly ruffled the trees. I wanted to ask Dad if everything would be okay. I wanted to ask what would happen if Mom's private Institute really does shut down. Would we have enough money? Could she somehow still keep her research going? She wouldn't really join up with the government, would she? For the past few years, it's been policy that any government-funded Message research has to be classified. That goes against everything Mom's always said she believes.

I wanted to ask, but Dad looked so relaxed for the moment—staring out at the horizon, coffee in hand. He and Mom were arguing last night, after I'd gone up to my room. I heard their tense voices but not their words. And then I heard soft laughter from their room this morning. I wanted to ask Dad if he and Mom were okay. Instead, I ate my eggs and said nothing.

My parents don't know it, but I do remember what they call the "good days." I remember my parents laughing together every night, every day. All the time. Even when they were both so busy with work, even though one or the other was often out of town. Laughter over the phone, through the screen. In-jokes I didn't get, references that went over my head. It didn't matter. I felt like the laughter included me, too.

And I remember Mom showing me the stars. No one can see the stars back home, of course. Even when the wildfires aren't burning, even when you can breathe without a filter mask, even when the sky *looks* clear—there's too much light and pollution in Berkeley, California to see anything of the night sky. You have to leave to see the stars. We were on vacation somewhere green and cool, an echo of where we are now. No lake, but a meadow stretching before us. My mom holding me, although I must have been nearly too big to be held. Dad standing beside us. "There," Mom said, pointing just above the horizon. She traced for me the great Summer Triangle, its corners lit by the bright stars Vega, Altair, and Deneb. She spoke their names. And *there*—she showed me Deneb now as the tail of a swan flying across the sky, the constellation Cygnus. Somewhere in that patch of sky, in Cygnus, a star too dim and distant to see with our naked eyes. A star whose light (if we could see it) would take 289 years to reach us. Something near that star, my mother explained, had sent all of Earth a Message.

Haru and Kes have never met in the story that Chloe and I are writing. They have no idea who the other is. But they long for each other anyway. They're searching for each other without knowing.

After fighting krakens all day, Haru falls into an exhausted sleep. Just before his mind tips into darkness—on the edge of sleep and waking—he sees, for an instant, a dark-haired boy outlined against the stars.

Kes has dreams, too: of a bright-haired boy laughing atop a cyber-whale.

While Haru fights for his homeland, Kes is desperately searching for home with his classmates, unlocking Star-Gate after Star-Gate. They don't realize it, but the Gates are choosing them, not the other way around. The Gates are calling them to the worlds that need their help. And one Gate is calling Kes to a watery world he's never seen, to a home that he doesn't know exists.

"It's like the red thread of fate," Chloe said when we started this story, invoking the East Asian legend of a thread connecting soulmates. And she drew a map of the Star-Gates, red threads shimmering between them and dozens of worlds; red threads also connecting Gates to each other, a shining web. She's so talented, an artist as well as a writer. I keep her map in my head when I write sometimes; I imagine Haru, unknowing, connected by a thread to Kes so many light-years away. The Gate as a conduit for that thread, the thread spun of both desire and fate. A thread that's a song neither consciously hears.

Chloe and I talk all the time about meeting someday in real life, but I don't know how it will ever happen. How would Chloe or I afford the international flight? And what flights will even be legal in the future? I think of how Mom wasn't allowed to go to China. I wonder how far government suspicions of my mother extend—of how her open political ideals might affect me, her daughter. Tensions between the US and Australia have been growing, too. We're supposedly still allies, but everywhere, the borders are closing.

I think of my parents' stories of the good years when everything and everyone seemed so free.

Hey, I message Chloe. I can't draw like her; I'm not good at making actual pictures of starry sea-skies and maps and the characters we love. I only have words to share. I send her my stories and words.

Mom wasn't telling the whole truth when she told me the Message was intended for all of Earth. It wasn't until years later that I realized this. The truth is that it's not clear at all that the Message was meant for us. The Message encodes no detectable explanation, no clear announcement of intent. There's no transmission of prime numbers or cosmological constants, no obvious clue to crack a code. No obvious greeting to strangers. So perhaps we're not the intended recipients after all; perhaps we merely intercepted the Message on its way to somewhere else.

Maybe there are Messages constantly crisscrossing the universe, sent from one technological outpost to another, and we just happened to eavesdrop on one. Can we join the conversation? (Do we want to? Would it be safe?)

The documentary special yesterday brought this and all the usual questions up. Pundits with titles rehashing old topics. Old arguments of what to do, how to respond. Fifteen years ago, Mom saw a Message. It was repeated at irregular intervals, detected by scientists around the world, over the course of two and a half days. Do those intervals mean anything? Are they part of the Message, too? No one knows. There are radio telescopes trained permanently now at that spot in the sky. But that fragment of space is silent.

There's a story Mom hasn't told in any interview. She's told it to me. On the night of the Message, she came home very late, in the blackness before dawn. Dad was asleep. She went to my bedroom and stood by my crib. Overwhelmed by all that had happened, at the reality of the new world that we'd all just entered, the world her daughter would grow up in—Mom looked down at me while I slept, and she cried. I was a little over a year old.

And fifteen years is nothing in cosmological time, but it can seem forever in human years. Next year, I'll be applying to college; my parents expect me to. Even though I'm not sure of the point; I don't know what jobs will be available when I graduate, I don't know what I can do, and all I really want to do is see Chloe and travel and make stories.

But this is a terrible world, and few of us get to do what we want. Back home, the fires are burning, and the air is soot; there are hurricanes and drought and famine; the ice caps are melting and the seas rising, and the humpback whales are all dead. I never got to see one, and the other whales are dead or dying, too. My best friend lives thousands of miles away. We communicate with radio signals beamed from our phones through the air, but I think we'll likely never meet.

I love you, she tells me, but I don't know if she means the words the way I do. Because she says *I love you* all the time—*Love you!* she signs off on group chats. *Love you!* she tells all her friends online. And I've said those words to only a few people in my life, and it always means something special when I say it. I want to believe that it means something special when she says it to me.

Daylight is slowly fading over the deck. I see the first stars shining from a swath of deep blue. My parents are arguing from within the house. I thought that maybe things were getting better between them. Mom and Dad fought after the documentary special last night, but this morning, I heard them laughing. We went into town for dinner and ice cream, and afterward, they were holding hands.

But now they're yelling again.

I have to go, Chloe tells me. *I love you, my dear.*

I love you, I say.

She sends me a string of hearts.

And then I'm alone on the deck. I look out over the lake, over the horizon, and after a moment I find it: the great Summer Triangle, marked by three bright stars: Vega, Altair, and Deneb. If I wait, it will darken enough that I'll see the rest of Cygnus. And somewhere in that patch of deep blue is a star I cannot see, a star 289 light-years away. Something there sent out a Message, and maybe they're still there; maybe they haven't blown themselves up like people are afraid that Earth will do. Maybe those beings are talking happily to others across the universe, all the time. Or maybe they're lonely, and they haven't heard anything, and they just send out a signal every thousand years or so to say *We're here!* and *Are you there, are you there?* Two of the planets around that star are in the habitable zone, and scientific models say they're great watery worlds covered almost entirely in liquid seas. Chloe is my soulmate, my heart, the other end of my red thread. I hear the door slide open behind me. "Sarah?" my mother says. I feel her standing behind me, waiting for an answer. And suddenly, there's so much I want to say to her, but I don't know how to begin. It's been years since we've truly talked. She steps up to the deck railing beside me and looks out over the lake. After a moment, hesitantly, she puts an arm around my shoulder. Slowly, she pulls me close. I let her. And after a moment, I relax into her embrace. Mom and I stand side by side like that, silently, looking out into the night.

The Things That We Will Never Say

I've missed you.

Every Astran-orbit, I make the light-years' journey back to see you. I file the paperwork, rearrange my schedule, pack, and bring my children with me. We endure the cold of hyperspace, the lingering headache, and nausea. And now we're standing on your doorstep in the cool Earth spring.

The door opens. My stomach lurches. You look so much frailer than before.

But your face lights up when you see the children. You spread your arms. "Grandma's missed you," you say as you hug them. You and I do not hug. Touch is awkward between us.

I understand.

You'll never know how it is to travel to a distant star. To stand dizzy under a burnt orange sky, four moons giving light above. To feel the gene mods reshaping your lungs, your blood, so that you may breathe the alien air. To undergo the Kairos training and mods that allow a person to see through time.

I'll never know what it's like to be you: a single mother on Earth. Desperate and angry in the last days of Empire. You moved from country to country in search of a better life. You clung to your roots, your food, your language, even as you encouraged me to abandon them all to seek a new life among the stars.

We both know loneliness. But we never speak of it to one another.

We're in the same house again, and I feel the future blooming between us now, branching again and again into countless paths. I'm not supposed to use my Kairos training to look at them. I'm trained to look at wider swaths of time, the collective actions of millions. To seek the major branch points that determine a government's fall, a galactic war, or a genocidal plague. There's too much chance and chaos in an individual timeline—a forecaster is overwhelmed.

I'm not supposed to look; it goes against all training and ethics. Yet I feel our futures shimmering between now. What I might or might not say to you. What you might say back. The illness that might kill you within the next few months or over the next ten years.

I hand you a cup of tea. I see your hands shake, then steady.

We drink together in the pale morning light and say nothing at all.

I'm proud of you.

I'm forty-six Earth years old, yet I still long to hear those words from your lips.

You nearly say it to my children. I watch you snuggling with them on the couch. My youngest shows you a game popular on the Astran home world. My older one guides you through one of her projects, an immersive composition of song and light. "Good job!" you tell them both, and clap. You're soft with them in a way you never were with me.

I'm sorry.

I'm sorry for the silence between us. For the years I stayed away, the messages I never sent. The bitterness that I hold even now.

Are you sorry, too?

Time slips, and I see the futures fanning out before us. You walk slowly down the stairs, but with double vision, I see you fall: blood on the floor, your skirt twisted around your legs, my children crying. I see you collapsing in the kitchen while we're away, dying alone. And then I see you as you are now, frail but alive. It's several years in the future; we've returned for our regular visit, and you're smiling as you hold out your arms for the children.

I see a future in which you and I reach out to each other. In which we drop our barriers of pride. We speak without criticism or judgment. We speak from our hearts without fear.

I'm afraid.

My control is slipping. Emotions will do that: fear, uncertainty. I shouldn't see these personal timelines at all. On Astran, someone would notice; my teammates would activate the mods to stop it, to keep me focused.

You taught me not to show fear. To hide all weakness, to keep it inside. Straight back and blank face when I walked past the occupying soldiers. No tears, no matter what bullies at school did. No hint of vulnerability for others to exploit. You taught me, most of all, to hide weakness from *you*.

But that never made the weakness go away.

I know what my Kairos teachers would tell me: accept the uncertainty of all futures. Identify the root fear that muddies my vision now. Accept it. Accept and let go. Let these visions fade.

Or face that fear . . . and do what I can to resolve it.

I love you.

Futures branch and branch, an infinite array crowding out the present.

An atom randomly decays. An electron leaps energy states. A coin is flipped, a die cast.

There's always the element of chance in what happens. And for human futures, there's always the element of choice.

"No, Mom, sit down!" I say. You're trying to make lunch for me and my kids. You're wincing, and I can tell that your hip hurts again.

I know that in the days leading up to this visit, you've been pushing through pain to make things perfect. You cleaned the house. Bought gifts for the kids. Filled the kitchen with treats. When I walked in, I saw a package of my favorite chocolates on the table. Sweet custard buns beside them. Pork dumplings in the fridge, folded and ready to be cooked.

I remember all the times you pushed through pain to keep going and to push me in turn. The day our house flooded, the nights you cried after my father left. When the last plague war swept the city, and you gave me water even as you must have been burning up; I remember you brushing the sweaty hair back from my eyes, wiping my face with a wet cloth. Your voice singing softly, shakily.

I hear you singing now with my children.

All the times we hurt each other, the things we screamed. Your words that bit and made me feel so small.

Our futures spread out before us, this moment splintering again and again, chance and choice irrevocably entwined.

I clear the lunch dishes. Sunlight pours through the window. My kids are quietly playing, and you're sipping tea.

As I walk past, you touch my arm. Just one, brief pat. Your face is peaceful, the old edges softened and worn. But when our eyes meet, there's a hint of a questioning sadness in your gaze.

You drop your hand. We look away. The moment passes.

My spouse doesn't understand my relationship with you. "I love you," he tells or messages me every day. He comes from such a different family, from a culture where "I love you" is said freely, easily, as casually as speaking about the weather.

The future is infinite, but with each ticking second, possibilities are foreclosed. I watch the timelines narrow. I know now what choices we'll make. There are words we'll never say. There are distances too great, after all.

I love you.
We will never say these words aloud. But in every timeline I can see, we know it's true.

The Breaking

There was a lightning storm the night my brother and I went to the Barrier. I didn't want to go; it was such a weird request. Jamie had been acting weird and distracted for days. We trekked out to the desert's edge on my night off. The sun had just set, and the sky had that strange pewter sheen it gets before a storm.

Jamie walked up to the chain-link fence and curled his fingers through the gaps. The fence was erected so people wouldn't run into the Barrier by accident; the vast, invisible wall that keeps us all safe is a quarter of a mile ahead.

"What are we doing here again?" I said.

"Shhhh," Jamie said. "Listen."

I listened.

There was only the soft whoosh of the wind, blowing over the desert and wastelands of the east. There was nothing to see—only the flat earth stretching empty before us. The darkness closing in. It had been years since I'd been so close to the border. I shoved trembling hands into my thin coat pockets. I was about to speak again, but then the sky split open.

Lightning forking across the sky, branching again and again. Purple light streaking and cracking the dome of the world. Silence. The violet lightning in the border cities makes no sound, even when it seems to break directly above you.

"Do you hear it?" Jamie said.

I shook my head.

"It's louder on nights like this. It's coming from across the Barrier. I thought so, and now I know."

"What are you talking about?" My voice was thin and too high in my ears.

"I think," Jamie said, staring into the desert beyond the fence. "It's the Angels speaking."

No one's ever heard the Angels speak. They were silent, burning, as the roads cracked and buckled, as giant sinkholes yawned, as the air itself tore and spilled out purple flames. As people died. As reality bent. The Angels stood (or hovered) and watched.

One was watching when Mom died.

People called them Angels because of the wings. Though surely, they were no messengers from God. Not that I've ever believed in God. It was hard to see their faces. There was so much heat, so much shimmering air.

"No," I told my little brother.

I told him that he wasn't hearing anything. That he was mistaken. That the Barrier kept everything out, *everything*, and that meant any sound, any voices, too.

He couldn't be hearing what he thought. And if he did, it didn't mean anything.

"Let's go home," I said. I was shivering with cold.

"Jenny," he said. Pleading.

I turned my back on him. "I'm going home."

Strange things happen near the Barrier. Everyone knows that. That's why normal people stay away.

The eerie lightning storms. The occasional lights glimpsed from the wastelands. Electronic equipment shorts out; cell phones lose connection.

Even living in a border city can be disturbing to some. There are stories online: old traumas awoken in survivors who moved from camps in the interior to a border city. Well-adjusted, resilient people, falling prey to sudden headaches and fatigue.

I'd never heard of anyone *hearing* anything.

But I knew that I didn't hear anything.

Nothing had crossed the Barrier in over a decade. For all this time, our world had held firm. *It's different this time. It's nothing. It's not like before.* It was just Jamie, not Jamie and me. That's what I told myself over and over as I fell asleep that night.

Jamie followed me home after all. We didn't talk. There was hot water in the shower, for once. I stayed under the hot water for a long, long time. When I got out, Jamie was asleep in his bed.

It felt like a miracle when we first came to this city: a hot shower, a living space that consisted of more than one room. Privacy and space as we'd never had in the camps. Jobs and the prospect of normal lives. As normal as we could expect, anyway.

Jamie was leaving when I woke the next morning; his job at the warehouse starts early. I caught him before he left. I wanted to apologize for the way I'd behaved. I didn't know how.

"Hey," I said awkwardly, standing in the little kitchen.

He nodded, his face expressionless. "Hey."

He started to move past me. I stopped him. "Look. I'm—I'm glad you told me last night."

Something flickered across his face—a hint of wry amusement. A mix of anger and sadness. He shrugged. "It's okay, Jenny," he said. "I'll see you tonight." He pulled on his jacket and left.

This is the thing: I've been responsible for Jamie for eighteen years. Since the day he was born. That's what our parents taught me. I'm six years older, the big sister. When he was little and misbehaved, Mom and Dad—especially Dad —would punish me for it. I resented Dad so much for that.

And then Mom was gone, swallowed by a hole in the world. Dad died in a camp two years later. It's been just Jamie and me ever since.

Angels don't speak in words like you and me, my brother says. Which, well, doesn't exactly come as a big surprise.

We talked a lot about the Angels over the next few nights. I was trying to understand. I was trying to keep calm, to not interrupt. I didn't want to push him away.

So, what do they sound like?

He said that they sound like gusting wind and rain lashing against your window. But they also sound like the crashing of cymbals—very faint and shivery. And they sound like the taste of an ice cube as it slides down your throat. And like a forgotten memory as it scratches again and again at your mind.

And how do you know it's the Angels? I asked.

I just do. His voice rising on the last word. Still hurt, disbelieving that I wouldn't believe.

But I couldn't hear it. Not even when he took me back to the fence. There was no lightning storm that second time.

"It's fainter," he admitted. And he also admitted that he didn't hear the sound continuously, that it came and went.

"A glitch," I guessed. Some kind of technological glitch in the Barrier that he was uniquely sensitive to. It didn't mean anything. I urged him to ignore it.

I remember his face when I said that. It was dusk, but there was still enough light to see the doubt, the wavering, in his eyes. He bit his lip. He wanted to believe me. I could tell.

I'd gone online, of course. He had, too. Neither of us could find, among all the stories people had to tell of living near the Barrier, any mention of anyone hearing anything like Jamie.

"It's just a glitch," I told him.

He was silent.

I know what it's like to not be believed. To be asked to doubt your own senses.

But when Jamie and I saw the first signs of the Breaking a dozen years ago, we saw them *together*. The two of us, from the beginning.

He was only six, playing in the backyard at the edge of our lawn. I would have been twelve—was I reading to myself outside? Daydreaming while idly digging with sticks in our sandbox, overturning beetles? I just know that I heard Jamie yelling my name. And I saw it: the rip in the air, shimmering above his head. The first crack in our world, in the soft summer light. A horizontal line, an actual crack that spread and then flared with purple light.

Jamie was still shouting. He'd backed away, but now he moved slowly toward the light, as though to touch it. But I was there, I'd reached him. I grabbed him by the arm, yanked him away. I was dragging him toward the house, yelling for Mom and Dad. They came. They stood on the back deck and looked at the crack in the world and saw nothing at all.

My brother and I kept pointing, pleading, insisting. Our parents couldn't see. They wouldn't even step off the deck to get a closer look. "Stop it," Dad finally said. "Your games aren't fun or funny." I started to cry. Jamie was already howling.

I wait tables at a restaurant that's an homage to a city that no longer exists. Even before the Breaking, the chain had been popular for its deep-dish pizza; now, to feed the nostalgia, the owners have added Chicago dogs and Italian beef sandwiches. It's worked; customers crowd the doors, and the tips are good.

This city on the border is full of people from elsewhere, trying to replicate what was lost. Here on the edge of a desert that was once a prairie, hole-in-the-wall restaurants and shacks, as well as fancy themed restaurants sell Memphis barbecue, Philly cheesesteaks and hoagies, biscuits and grits from a deserted South. New York bagels and knishes and pizza, and gumbo from Louisiana. In tiny home kitchens, more foods from the cities and states that are gone. In those homes, all the accents and languages of lost places.

The food at my workplace is good, and it's much as I remember Chicago-style pizza to be. But what I really miss are the doughnuts from a bakery near our home in the suburbs. Barbecued duck, glossy and rich, at a crowded restaurant in Chicago's Chinatown. Dim sum with my family. My mother's food. Her Thai noodle soups and curries and stir-fries. Khai jiao—the crisp, fluffy omelets she served with jasmine rice. I make those omelets sometimes for Jamie and me, but I know it's not the same. Every time I try, I recall less of her face.

<hr>

"What do you remember?" Jamie asked me in the dark. I'd gotten home from my dinner shift, and I'd thought him asleep on his mattress in the living room. I'd been tiptoeing to my own room. It was a couple weeks since we'd first gone to the fence.

What are you talking about? I started to say and stopped. He was sitting up, a slip of shadow in the faint light from the window. His words hung in the air, quiet and urgent.

Sometimes, my brother acts like I should be able to read his mind. Sometimes, I can.

I sat next to him on the bed. "I don't know," I said. "It's all confused. I feel like I remember less all the time."

"But you saw the Angels with me."

"Yes."

"We saw everything together."

"That's right."

"And other people did, too, didn't they? How did it begin? Why didn't we run sooner?"

I stared into the darkness before us. "I don't know."

<hr>

Dad was apologizing to us at the end. And that in itself was frightening. Our dad, who had never apologized to us for anything—who had tried so hard to not show weakness in front of his kids. "I should have believed you," he kept saying. He bent over, wracked with coughing. An awful, wet cough that left a white froth on his lips. "You saw it, you saw . . ." He clutched at our hands. His grip sweaty and weak. "I should have put us all into the car that first night, driven us away. Kept going till we hit California. I should have booked plane tickets, crossed the sea, taken you back . . ."

Dad coughed again. His eyes were panicked. He said his brother's name, now dead. He said our mother's. He said something in Thai that I couldn't understand. Our family tent was surrounded by a thousand others, yet there was no one to help. Jamie was crying silently. Sputum flecked my father's mouth, fell onto his shirt; I saw the pink tinge to it, the blood from his lungs.

The world cracked open, but it took time for everyone to see. Our mother walked through the crack at the edge of the lawn. I saw her do it. The purple light danced on her arm. I wanted to call her back, to yell, but my throat closed tight. Lightning bugs were winking in and out. Crickets were calling. The summer air was so soft and warm. Mom stepped forward, her arm swinging through the broken air. Nothing happened; she never noticed. She stepped out the other side, as though nothing at all lay in between.

What do I remember? What do any of us remember?

The history as recorded on the Web is all confused. Servers throughout the affected portion of the continent failed. Data was lost forever. The original newscasts are gone. To go online now (paying with credit I can hardly afford) is to be drawn into a maze of conflicting accounts and theories.

This is what I remember: the cracks in the world growing like webs, splintering the air. The place on the playground where no kid would go—even the kids who swore they didn't see anything, that the rest of us were crazy. The bus driver swerving to avoid the torn air above the road. Roadblocks appearing at that spot and then taken down, again and again. Grownups shouting, even screaming with one another over what was real. Some of them saw, even though our parents couldn't. Dad said it was my fault that Jamie was afraid to go outside, that I'd filled his head with hysteria. *Stop, stop*, said our mother and fed us eggs and rice.

On the television: scenes of panic. Reports from the East Coast that "perceptual anomalies" were increasing there. Crowds filling the street, demanding that something be done. Other crowds disbelieving, hurling abuse at the first.

It's nothing, Mom said. That's what I remember. *A huge fuss over nothing.*

I saw the Angel in the old oak tree at the corner. Its wings beating in a blur, like a hummingbird's. The halo of blue light around it, the air warped and shimmering.

"You shouldn't listen," I said when Jamie told me he could hear Angels. "Please don't listen."

Jamie and I went to our jobs—he sorting goods at one of the new shipping warehouses, me waiting tables in the afternoon and at night. We saw each other late in the evening and on days off.

I never told him to stop speaking of what he heard. I told him to let me know if anything changed, if the Angel voices grew louder or clearer. I still thought it might not mean anything. I thought, *Wait and see.*

It's what some of the grownups said during the first Breaking. *Wait and see.*

No one at the restaurant mentioned hearing voices across the Barrier. I eavesdropped on customers as I balanced trays of food; as I poured water, set down pizzas, and then gathered up emptied plates. People spoke of jobs, of new construction and investment in the city. Politics in the Western states. Love lives. Bad bosses. Relationships and hopes for the future. No one spoke of the Breaking or of the days before.

The other wait staff said nothing. I didn't know how to bring the topic up. I thought of the few people I trusted from the last camp. We were all scattered now.

Wait and see.

This border city wasn't my first choice of a home. But there's the military base here, and the businesses supporting it—and new industry fueled by investment from abroad. The major cities to the west of us are all bursting at the seams, overwhelmed with the millions who flooded in during the Breaking; there's no room there to breathe. California has sealed its borders almost entirely. When the residence lottery matched my brother and I here, to this once small city on what remained of the Great Plains, we jumped. I figured it was a start.

This is where they dump the refugees from the lost states: along the border, in the new cities trying to grow.

I remember California. Our uncle Aa Dang, our father's youngest brother, went to school in L.A. He'd come to America following my father's path, studying engineering just like Dad. We went to visit him, and Aa Dang took us to the beach. It's my first memory of the ocean. Those gray waves were so huge, and I was so scared; it was so much bigger, wilder, than the beach we went to on Lake Michigan. But Dad was there, and he could swim better than anyone in the world; he'd grown up by the sea, and he was with me, holding me, lifting me up through the crests of the waves as they rolled in, and it felt just like flying. I was safe. Mom was back on shore, watching Jamie.

Aa Dang seemed so much younger than Dad. He teased me, but in a kind way; he laughed all the time. He had a new wife, a white American woman he'd met in grad school, and they were expecting a child. I called her Aunt Lisa, and she laughed a lot, too. Dad and Aa Dang talked about people I didn't know, family they'd left behind in Thailand. Later, they went swimming together on their own, carving smoothly through the waves, strong and confident like creatures of the sea itself, until they were nearly out of sight.

I told Jamie that we could move if he wanted. To a neighborhood farther from the Barrier, where maybe he wouldn't hear what he thought of as Angels. He shot me his classic, exasperated, you-are-so-full-of-it look. A look that said at that moment: *And how on earth are we going to afford that?*

"We can do it," I said. Rents got more expensive the farther you got from the Barrier, but still . . .

"Aren't we locked into this lease?"

"Yes, well . . ."

He shrugged. "It's fine. It's okay."

"Would it help you if we moved?"

"We don't need to."

"Do you still hear them?"

He didn't say anything.

"Do you still hear them?" I said again. Demanding.

His hand lifted halfway toward his ear, then stopped. He seemed to wince. Was he hearing them now? "It wouldn't help, Jenny," he said. "I hear them at work sometimes. When they speak, I'd hear them anywhere in the city."

Jamie started taking extra shifts at the warehouse. He began staying out late so that I didn't see him when I got home. He said he was spending time with friends from work, sometimes crashing with them overnight. I was surprised; I knew that he didn't make friends easily. He was so quiet with people he didn't know.

Don't worry about me, he said. He said I should go out more, too. I reminded him that we needed to save money. "Get that old bald guy to take you out," he said, smirking. I threw a pillow, and Jamie dodged. I'd dated that guy for only a few weeks, and he wasn't old. He just had a prematurely receding hairline.

"I'm fine," Jamie told me, serious again. "Don't *worry*."

He no longer seemed as jumpy as he'd been before. He didn't seem like someone suffering delusions. He was calmer. We didn't talk of strange voices, or the Barrier, or the past. We so rarely saw each other to talk at all. When I saw him in passing, too early in the morning or too late at night, he seemed tired, but that was only to be expected.

I thought that maybe he'd stopped hearing whatever he'd thought he heard. Or that he'd adjusted to it. That it didn't matter. That he, and everything, was okay.

That's what I wanted to believe. I wanted to believe it so hard.

To this day, no one understands what the Angels are.

Scientists say they must be extraterrestrials from a distant world, incomprehensible but still part of our material universe. Others say they're demons come to punish us for unknown sins. Spirits, monsters, eruptions of the supernatural, or true angels of vengeance, after all.

We've held them back with the Barrier, a vast electromagnetic field. By trial and error, we figured out how to repel them. But we can't destroy them. We can't make them give back what they took. We can't bring our lost homes and loved ones back.

Why did only some of us see the start of the Breaking? Why did only some of us see when the Angels first came?

Nobody talks about it in person. Everyone wants to say that they saw from the start. And online, the answers are all confused. Experts speculate about "differing thresholds of perception" and "innate sensitivity to unearthly phenomenon." Others talk about mass hypnosis and say the Angels sowed confusion on purpose. Still others find a way—as always—to somehow blame it on the old US federal government, now gone.

No one knows.

Dad was a Man of Science. Someone who loved numbers, measurement, and logic. A trained engineer. Someone who thought he saw things clearly. And he couldn't.

And Mom . . . She was an artist of a kind, wasn't she? She loved beautiful things. The sheer white curtains she trimmed with lace. The potted orchids on the windowsill, neatly arranged in a row. She liked to garnish our meals with cucumber slices carved into flowers and delicate ribbons of carrot curls. In the year before the Breaking, she was taking a class in watercolors at the local art center. An unusual indulgence for her. She brought home paintings of luminous landscapes: meadows and mountains and lakes. Soft, dreamy landscapes shot through with light. An artist is supposed to have heightened perceptions, right? Aren't they supposed to see truth?

No, she said when I tried to tell her of the Angels flocking in the trees. *No*, when I spoke of how I felt their eyes upon me, even if I couldn't see their faces through their beating wings, the shivering blue air. Her normally gentle, even voice rose in anger. *Stop listening to the other kids,* she said. *Stop listening to all that craziness.* And she actually covered her ears.

I think we were afraid, someone wrote online. *We didn't see because we didn't want to see. Somehow, we blinded ourselves to what was in front of our own eyes.*

Jamie withdrew from me, and I thought it was okay. I thought maybe he really was going out with friends at night. That he was tasting freedom in this new city, as an eighteen-year-old should.

I started going out with a few of my colleagues after work, too. I slept with one of the prep cooks, a guy with rough hands and beautiful blue eyes. He lived in a tiny space downtown with four other guys, so I took him to my place instead. We were a thing, I guess, until he decided he preferred screwing another girl.

I missed my brother.

A rare moment: I came home and found the lights on, Jamie there and awake. I was in a bad mood: rude tables, the kitchen falling behind, and customers upset; a toddler flung food and spilled her drink on me.

Jamie saw it all in my face. "I'm making a snack, want some?" he said. I watched him crack eggs in a bowl and beat them with fish sauce. Then I sat in the living room until he came out with the fluffy khai jiao and rice. We ate in silence until I felt my angry edge fading.

"Thanks," I said. We talked a little about nothing: work, friends, a video series we were both watching. And then I said, "Hey, I feel like we hardly see each other anymore." I meant my tone to be light. I was surprised by the wistfulness on his face. More than wistfulness. Sadness and even a kind of tenderness. I didn't understand at the time. After all, he was the one who'd been withdrawing from me.

It was my day off, and I'd been looking forward to sleeping in. The knock at the door was a steady beat, invading my dreams. I was confused. No one ever knocked. We hardly knew our neighbors.

I stumbled to the door in the T-shirt and sweats I'd worn to bed. It was the woman across the hall: Her face and everything about her was frazzled. She was so, so sorry, but would I mind watching her kid for an hour? Teresa—her name came fuzzily to my half-awake mind. I'd watched her kid once before when we first moved in. Teresa explained that her husband should have been back by now; his work shift was done, but his ride had broken down, and she couldn't afford to be late for her own job. It would only be for a short time, and she'd make it up to me, of course.

"Sure," I said. The poor woman seemed on the edge of a breakdown.

I followed her to a one-bedroom apartment with a layout that mirrored the one Jamie and I had. Unlike ours, the living room had no mattress; I knew that their daughter shared the bedroom with her parents. Toys and sheets of paper were scattered on the floor and over a table. "Rosa!" Teresa called, and a child of four appeared. Rosa looked at me solemnly with big brown eyes.

"You remember me, right?" I said when her mother left. Rosa nodded. She sat at the table and pressed a blue crayon to paper. She drew a swooping curve.

"Pretty," I said. "What are you drawing?"

She gave me a long, wary look.

"Oh, come on, it's not a secret, is it?" I didn't remember her as so suspicious before.

She looked at me levelly a moment more. Then she bent her head and drew another curve. "They make the air blue," she said.

I felt a chill.

I looked more closely at the other pieces of paper on the table and on the floor. All covered in crayon scrawls. All blue, with zig-zagging lines of purple. If you knew, you could imagine that they traced wings and rips and shimmering air.

I tried to speak lightly. "Did your parents tell you about the Angels?"

She shook her head.

"Oh. Um, did someone else, then?"

She didn't answer.

I felt both foolish and uneasy. I took a seat across from her and joined her in drawing. I doodled aimlessly with a red-orange crayon. Red. I'd been dreaming of something red that morning. Fire. Explosions, plumes of thick smoke. And for a moment, I saw again a line of trees catching light, blazing up into torches. A wall of roaring flame along the highway. I was in the car with my family; we were trying to escape, Dad driving as fast as the traffic allowed; and I whimpered and squeezed my eyes shut, but even so, I could feel the Angels watching through flame.

"They're coming," Rosa said softly.

"Who?" I whispered.

She tapped her paper. "These. The bright ones."

"When? Who told you so?"

She pressed her lips together.

"Rosa, has my brother been talking to you? You know Jamie, the skinny guy who lives with me?"

She shook her head.

"Who then? Who's been talking to you about Angels?"

She refused to meet my gaze.

I lowered my voice, tried for a conspiratorial tone. "Rosa. It's okay. I won't tell your parents. I won't tell anyone else."

"Promise?"

"Double promise. Triple."

"You'll believe me?"

"I will."

She looked up at me from under long lashes. And then she cupped a hand around her mouth and stage-whispered what I already knew she would say. "The Angels told me."

It was like my stomach dropping, gone. Like falling and not hitting ground.

I heard my voice, flat and mechanical. "What do they sound like?"

"Like wind." She rounded her mouth and went *Oooooooo.* "Like rain. Like people, but louder and softer and shivery." She frowned, thinking. Then she smiled, proud to come up with the right comparison. "They sound like ice."

I texted Jamie when Rosa's dad got home. *We have to talk,* I wrote him. *Please come straight home tonight.* And then I hit send and I waited.

When the world finally shattered, it happened so quickly.

A web of cracks pulled tight, tighter, until everything burst: pure chaos flooding through.

Planes vanishing from the sky. The earth opening underfoot. Bridges cracked in half, skyscrapers tilting.

My father numb before the news reports. His youngest brother lost on a flight to Orlando, the jet vanishing from radar just as it started to descend. Aunt Lisa gone along with Aa Dang, along with their daughter, my cousin, a hazel-eyed girl of five. They'd been on their way to a family vacation at Disney World.

And now there was no denying it, the Breaking, a tide of madness rolling across the continent from east to west as the bonds of reality snapped. As hair-thin cracks tore themselves wide into gaping holes visible to all—swallowing planes, roads, buildings, and people. Whole neighborhoods. The purple light bleeding over everything, the air on fire. The Angels watching, silent. We saw it on our screens—until the screens went dark. Heard the screaming voices before they cut off.

We looked up, and outside the windows, we saw them hovering in the backyard. Gathering in the skies.

My parents saw, but they were paralyzed, in shock. They didn't grasp the direction of the rolling tide, the inevitability of it reaching us, too. By the time we ran, everyone around us was running.

We eventually left the car behind, abandoning it on the clogged highway along with so many others. No gas to be found anyway. Westward, westward, to where the world hadn't cracked, no "perceptual anomalies" reported. A ragged mass of humanity, walking. It was late fall now, but so hot. Unseasonably hot. How long had we been in the sun? I handed Jamie the last water bottle. Why did our mother stop? What was she staring at? I saw the blue air, a blurring of white wings. A seam opened where none had been. A flare of violet light. I screamed, dragged Jamie back. Our mother said nothing. She was no longer there.

By the time we reached safety—by the time the first version of the Barrier was up, the protective field developed by scientists and engineers who would be hailed as heroes—Jamie was no longer talking. Two years later, when our father died, Jamie stopped talking again for a month.

I'm waiting for my brother to talk to me now. I waited all day for him to text me. I called and messaged, again and again. Finally, I called his workplace and found that he'd never come in.

I was already running out to the Barrier when I heard my phone chime.

And now I'm here at the chain-link fence where Jamie and I stood months ago. It was spring then; it's fall now. A storm is gathering. In the dark clouds high above, I catch glimpses of lightning. A wind is blowing from across the Barrier, across the empty wastelands.

My brother is out there somewhere. Where I can't see, where only the Angels roam.

I have my phone out, and I keep reading Jamie's last message. I still don't understand.

Voices. Footsteps. Not before me, but behind. There are others gathering at this section of fence. People seemingly of all ages and types, dressed against the chill and shadowy in the failing light. They've come seeking their own loved ones. Waiting for them, like me. Their voices fall silent, and we look out together through the gaps in the fence.

The Breaking never stopped, Jamie wrote in his message. *It was only on pause.*

And I understand that. I understand that there are no safe places. I think that I've known it, deep down, for years. Years in which I dreamed of getting as far from the broken lands as I can—saving money for the passage and entrance fee and taking Jamie with me to California, to the westmost edge of the continent, to the place where my father held me in his arms in the sea. And beyond that sea are countries as yet unshattered, marred only by slight cracking before the Barrier technology spread and took hold. In a distant country, there are relatives I barely know, but they never came for Jamie and me. There are too many restrictions to the world now.

When he was sick, Dad said that Jamie and I would only have each other. He always said that family is everything and that I was in charge of my brother. Mom was gentler, but she'd always said much the same. So it makes no sense that Jamie should leave, that he says he has to go talk to the Angels. I can't understand how he heard when I didn't. I can't understand how he claims to be among some select group of people, called before everyone else to cross into the wastelands, chosen to hear and respond and initiate the next steps of change. Because he's not that special. He's no one special. It's bullshit that he claims to want to protect me, that he says he's going forth to smooth the way. He's not a hero or a sacrifice. He's just my brother. My baby brother.

The wind picks up, howling across the Barrier. It stings my face and pulls cold fingers through my hair.

And as the purple lightning flashes soundlessly above, I hear rain where there's no rain at all. I feel ice in my throat. A shivery echo in my bones. Voices, singing.

I press against the fence, and the people around me are doing the same. Far off, purple lightning strikes the ground, splitting the empty, wasted lands. There's a shimmer of blue. I imagine white wings. I imagine my brother walking back to me. But I don't know what he'll look like now. What form he'll take, how he'll be transformed.

I see Rosa among the crowd with her parents, her face perfectly calm. She's not big enough to climb the fence, as Jamie and his companions must have done, but she's talked her parents into bringing her here. They listened to her. We're all listening, and we stare out toward a Barrier that is even now crumbling, humanity's best technology all useless. Ice sings through my bones. The earth cracks before me.

I should have listened sooner. Jamie, I should have believed you. I'm sorry. We had so little time together—you and me, our parents, everyone here. The world when it was still whole. We didn't see, and then we didn't listen. I'm sorry, I'm sorry. The Angels' song rises and the air shivers blue. I strain my eyes toward the horizon, even as cymbals clash and a thousand voices cry. It's the next change in the world, the next phase, the next steps of the Breaking.

PART TWO
Farther Worlds

All the Souls like Candle Flames

You know of the Sea Witch, of course. Even in your inland towns, you've heard her name; you know that she collects drowned souls and keeps them in her cold halls under the sea. All whose bones lie under salt waves belong to her —merchants and kings, queens and servants, pirates and raiders and innocent babes. Ordinary sailors and fishermen, too, of course. Far too many of those from our shores.

You've seen the charms we weave to keep the storms at bay. You've heard the prayers for fair winds and a safe journey home. But what if you're already dead, fishes nibbling through your hair and seaweed twisted 'round your limbs, your flesh dissolving in the cold ocean tides? Who is there then to save your soul from the Witch's black halls?

That's what *these* charms are for, you see. Go ahead and hold one. Feel how smooth it lies in your hand. It's strong wood from deeply rooted trees. See how fine the paint job, the black eyes and stripes along the side. No, don't speak to me of those gaudy charms for sale up the street. Mine are truly crafted. See the fine details, the care with which the feathers were made.

Why does a fish have feathers? You really don't know the story of Mikki, do you? I can tell you haven't been here long. No, you can keep ahold of that one. Hold it while I tell you the tale.

Years ago, this town was scarcely more than a village. Few merchant ships docked at these shores, and fine visitors such as yourselves were a rare sight indeed. But the greatfish still ran in shoals along the coast each spring, and the glittering silveroils ran to the south in the fall. The fishing fleet still set sail each fair day of the season, just as it does today.

There was a family in the village. A little girl who lived with her mother and father and older brother. The mother's true name is now lost, but all in the village called her "Gull." Her clear skin was the white of a gull's breast, and she gathered gull feathers shed on the shore. She washed them in fresh water and wove them into charms for her husband to wear. The gull soars over salt water but returns to land to nest, so we say that a gull's feathers will guide a seaman home.

It was the first bad luck for the family when Gull took ill. Until then, it had been a blessed life: the seas fair and the fisherman's nets and lines filled with fish. His wife singing as she fed and clothed and cared for the family. The children growing up healthy and strong.

Who can say what plague struck the village that year? So many illnesses in this world, fevers and chills of all kinds on this coast. The whole family took ill, coughing and pale, burning and shivering. In this story, the father and children recovered. The mother did not.

They buried her in the grassy field above the village, close to the sun and sky. High and safe from creeping fingers of saltwater, but within sight and smell of the sea. White gulls wheeled and cried above the grave.

So the children were motherless, the daughter still such a tiny thing, barely able to lift the iron kettle above the fire. The boy, just a few years older, running wild through the tall dune grass. Neighbors and relatives tried to help. There was an aunt, the widower's sister. She did her best, but she was busy with her own young children.

The orphaned girl didn't know how to make her mother's feather charms. She had watched, and her small hands were clever, but there was a knot she couldn't manage, a knack she didn't have. No one else in the village knew how to make them. The girl, who was named Mikki, sat outside her house, trying again and again to tie the feathers just so. She cried in frustration, but no one noticed; no one helped.

There was much overlooked the year that Gull died, much that was forgotten.

It wasn't just the charms or the fish dumplings and soup she had once made. Soon, Mikki forgot her mother's face. She could remember other things —a snatch of song, the touch of her mother's hand against her cheek. A fall of dark, silken hair. She remembered sunlight flashing and the sharpness of a rock hurting her foot on the beach and then crying out to her mother for help. But her mother's face, the shape of her eyes, a distinct image of her—all these were gone.

The girl and her brother grew. They learned to take care of themselves. The relatives and neighbors helped out less and less. Mikki and her brother scrambled together over the rocky shore, collecting mussels and seaweed for supper and prying limpets off rocks to bait their father's lines. The brother held his sister's hand, helping her climb over the rough outcroppings. On the way home, he took the baskets and gave her a head start, letting her race before him down a smooth stretch of sand. Then he was running, too, and when he ran too far ahead, he heard his little sister's voice calling his name, "Kerel, Kerel!" like the high, clear call of a bird.

Soon, Kerel began fishing each day with their father, and Mikki was left alone to gather shellfish and bait their father's lines. Each afternoon, she met the village boats as they pulled into the harbor, and helped her father and brother bring in their catch.

She was happy despite early loss. She had friends; she had her brother. She still had her father, a lean, hard-working man of few words. He was somber and distant, but there were times that his eyes softened when he looked at his children. There were times when the sadness in his face cleared. Occasionally, he dropped words of praise—for Kerel's handling of the boat, for Mikki's fish stew—and then his children glowed with pride.

Gull's last feather charm had long since frayed to pieces. It was Mikki's charms that Kerel and Father now wore.

Perhaps Mikki was careless. She didn't wash the gull feathers thoroughly enough. She didn't take care to promptly replace worn feathers. Perhaps it was that she simply didn't have her mother's touch. She made the types of charms that other women in the village made: simple necklaces of feathers and beads tied on bands of leather. But they weren't Gull's designs and never would be.

One day, Mikki was spreading out seaweed to dry in the sun when she became aware of a sudden stillness. The air felt tight; no birds sang, nothing called or moved. The drying rack fell from her fingers, and she looked out to sea, her heart pounding. She saw dark clouds on the horizon and a brilliant, eerie light flooding beneath.

She ran to the harbor. Other women and girls were already gathered there. The world held its breath. She saw the first fishing boats racing home, flying before a wall of light and the black storm clouds massed above.

Wind rose off the sea. A spray of salt hit her eyes. She stood on the pier, waiting. And then the world went dark, sudden as the clap of a hand. Rain poured down in sheets, and waves swelled and whipped the bay into foam.

The first boats struggled in. Voices shouted, barely audible above the surging wind and surf. Women held shielded lanterns aloft in the gloom. Lines of rope were tossed, and eager arms pulled the fishermen ashore. None of them were Mikki's father or crew; her father's boat wasn't there.

Straining, Mikki glimpsed a boat out past the harbor. She saw it sail by the rocks near the harbor entrance; she saw it making its way to safety and home. And then a sudden wave overtook it from behind; she saw the boat capsize.

Her scream joined the screams of the crowd, thin above the wind and sea.

She saw a second boat try for the harbor and saw it dashed upon rocks.

She waited and waited, frozen and numb, but she never saw her father's boat at all.

It was the gods' blessing or whim that Kerel was not on his father's boat that day. Father's crew had taken another man on board in Kerel's stead, a crew member's cousin whose own boat was undergoing repairs and who needed to feed his family. The crew agreed to let the man fish with them that day and to divide their catch with him.

And so Mikki still had her brother, though all else was lost.

At some point during that dreadful day, she became aware of Kerel standing beside her. He had returned from the river town several miles inland, where he had gone to buy goods and run errands.

It was still raining, the sky dark as night. In the lantern-light, Mikki saw the pale faces around her; she saw the wife and young sons of the fisherman who had taken Kerel's place. She could feel her brother crying next to her. She reached out, and they took and held each other's hands.

This is what we say in these coastal towns haunted by dreams of the Sea Witch: A finger bone is enough. A joint of a pinkie, a single knucklebone, the smallest scrap of flesh—these are enough to save a soul from the Sea Witch's halls, to call a soul home to rest. Take what you can, whatever you can save from the sea. Wash the remains in fresh water. Bind it in white cloth. Sing to it. You'll have to stay up a full night, singing the soul home. In the morning, rise and carry your loved one on a bier of fresh-cut wood. Carry him or her to high ground untouched by the sea. Bury your loved one, and scatter the grave with flowers.

For days after the storm, Mikki and Kerel wandered the shore, searching for their father's remains. They were joined by others looking for their own fathers or sons, husbands or brothers. Up and down the coast, fishing boats had been lost. Wreckage and bodies washed in over days. A few men from their village were retrieved—two men from the *Gannet,* one from the *Wild Rose.* But no one from the *White Gull*—-not a trace of Father or any of his crew.

Mikki lit candles for the soul of her father and the souls of the village's lost men and boys. She prayed to the Goddess of Mercy for them. On the family altar, she set out a bowl of her father's favorite stew and the barley cakes he had loved.

She went to her mother's grave and asked for Gull's intercession. She prayed that her mother's spirit might petition and win release of Father's soul from the ocean deeps. Around her, other women and girls were kneeling in their own family burial plots, making similar prayers. White flags fluttered in the field, marking the souls of those unburied and signaling them home from the sea.

Kerel went to his mother's grave with Mikki. He knelt with her, his eyes red, but his prayers were silent.

It was a hard autumn. Three boats and a dozen men lost from the village. Nine men whose bodies were never retrieved. Survivors shared what they could with the widowed and orphaned. Kerel went fishing when he could with other boats in the village, and on boats from other ports. He found odd jobs, and Mikki took in extra work mending nets and baiting lines.

Winter came, cold and stormy. The fishing fleet was grounded. Mikki stretched the salt fish and porridge with water until the grains could scarcely be seen. Her head spun from hunger.

In the spring, Kerel found steady work on a boat that launched from a port town to the south. He rose each morning an hour before dawn and returned after the sun had set. Mikki combed the beach each day for the finest, whitest feathers she could find. She spent precious money on beads and fine leather ties. She wove her charms, praying to Gull that this time she would get them right.

The air softened with warmth. The trees were in full leaf, the fields abloom with tiny, bright flowers. Birds were nesting on the cliffs. Now the sun shone even after Kerel walked in the door after a full day's fishing. He whistled and began speaking of plans to invest in a new boat with friends. Mikki's hand went to her heart as she thought of the crew he had lost. Kerel carefully pretended not to see.

Each evening, she put a few bites of supper aside for the family altar, for her father's soul. She wondered if he could taste it beneath the waves.

Spring slipped into summer and then into fall. Kerel told Mikki that he meant to set sail on a merchant ship to southern seas.

"Six weeks down the coast to Ibrin," he said. "We'll unload and take on new cargo, continue down to the point, and then sail east to the Thressian Islands. We'll avoid the winter storms here and ride the westward winds back. Three months in all, but Mikki, it's better than kicking my feet at the fire through another winter if the season here is poor. I'll make enough money for the payments on my share of a new boat this spring."

Mikki stood still, her dark eyes wide.

Kerel's own dark eyes pled with hers. "We've saved and I borrowed an advance on the pay," he said. "Enough for you to be comfortable. Our aunt and uncle will keep an eye out for you."

Mikki's cheeks burned as she realized that her brother had already made up his mind, had already laid out his plans.

"I . . . I told Jacil," Kerel hesitated. "I know that you don't like it that I told him first, but he's promised to watch out for you." Jacil was one of Kerel's friends. A nice boy.

"You like Jacil, don't you?" Kerel's tone was light. She knew what he was asking.

She thought of a boy who had sailed on Father's crew. Kerel's dearest friend. He had had freckles and beautiful hands and a quick smile that flashed like lightning. She had never spoken of her feelings for him. She knew that Kerel mourned him at least as much as he mourned their father.

"Yes," Mikki said aloud. "I like Jacil well enough."

It's not only the souls of the drowned whom the Sea Witch calls. Sometimes, she calls to those still on land. A child on the beach goes missing. A young woman goes for a walk on the cliffs and never returns. An old fisherman disappears from his bed in the night.

Usually, there are signs. Usually, it's someone bereaved. Every village has its tale. A widow or heart-broken lover, a bereft parent. A seaman who escaped a wreck but saw his captain washed overboard and his friends drowned before his eyes. Such a person's own eyes may turn empty, unseeing. He doesn't respond to his name; he doesn't see the sunlit world. His soul is trapped underwater, wandering the ocean floor.

If you can see the signs, you can perhaps keep the body safe until the soul returns. You can keep watch, keep vigil. A family will string feathers over the doorway along with branches and sprays from a rowan tree. Family members will feed the afflicted tea with bitter herbs. Sweet-leaf will be burned on the fire.

If there are no warning signs, there is nothing to be done. A girl vanishes, called down to the ocean depths. A boy jumps suddenly from cliff or boat or pier. Afterward, the village will whisper of missed signs, of the Sea Witch's irresistible song. Mothers will continue to comb the shore, searching for a scrap of bone to bury.

Mikki went to the docks of the southern port-town to see her brother off. Other family and friends accompanied them. As he went to hug her, she handed him a pouch. "Ten feather charms inside," she said. "Each time a feather frays, take it off and put a new charm on. Promise me."

He smiled. "They don't wear out that quickly, Mikki. I won't be gone that long."

"You don't know how long you'll be gone." She tried to keep the tremor from her voice. "When you discard a charm, throw it into the sea. Maybe—maybe it will find its way to someone. Someone who could use it. They're weighted with beads of stone."

He held the pouch to his heart. He made as though to speak and then stopped. His expression was unreadable. He hugged her tight, and said only, "I will."

Another hard winter. Wind and rain and the seas churned white with foam. Thunder and crashing waves a nightly lullaby. Mikki's cottage roof leaked, and the walls shook in the wind. The cold seeped in like a relentless tide.

The fishermen were stranded on shore by the weather, adrift and grumbling. Mikki saw children hollow-eyed with hunger. Kerel had spoken truly: There was money enough for her to eat, and so she went from house to house sharing her barley-cakes and bread.

Mixed in with the scream and whine of the wind, mixed in with the crash and murmur of waves, Mikki sometimes thought she heard other notes. A chime of bells. A female voice. Something that was almost a song. She shivered and prayed and built up her fire.

She heard word of a fishing boat lost from a village to the north. A crew of brothers and cousins. They had set forth during a break in the weather, betting on fair skies for a chance at whitefish and silveroils. She didn't know their names.

"He's safer on that merchant ship than we are on our own boats here, Mikki," Jacil said. True to his word, Kerel's friend stopped by nearly every day. He was a comforting presence, cheerful and solidly built. He had fixed the leak in her roof, although it seemed scarcely warmer than before. He held his hands to her fire now. "Calm southern seas and one of the finest boats to launch from the shipyards of Ibrin . . ."

Mikki looked at her brother's friend, at his kind, broad face. She tried to smile.

Encouraged, Jacil kept on. "You were there; you saw the *Kittiwake* set sail. Biggest ship I've ever seen. Those merchant vessels are made to carry on through storms; they can ride waves half the height of our cliffs. And the captain—nothing but good words about him from everyone I've heard. A good captain. A good crew."

"A good crew," Mikki echoed. She imagined her brother on the open sea, riding waves half the height of the cliffs that flanked their village.

"He might even be on his way back now," Jacil said. "Another month, a month and a half. Kerel will be home soon."

A month. A month and a half. Mikki counted off the weeks in her head.

A ship from the Thressian Islands sailed into the port town to the south. But it was not Kerel's ship, not *The Kittiwake*, and the crew had no knowledge of *The Kittiwake's* fortunes.

Another month. And then one more. Finally word from the merchants' guild: *The Kittiwake* had landed in the Thressian Islands on schedule at the beginning of winter, taking on cargo there as planned. It had been seen departing for the westward journey back. But where was it now?

Anchored in a warm southern isle, Jacil said. Blown off course or damaged in a storm, but under repairs and soon to make its way back.

Somewhere on the coast south of Ibrin, Mikki's aunt said. Delayed, but already on course again.

Lost in wild seas, others whispered darkly. Blown far off course and drifting under strange stars. Caught in a whirlpool that circulates endlessly, forever, near the bottom of the world. Caught in the tentacles of a beast whose face is sand and rock at the bottom of the sea.

Gone, Mikki's heart told her. Torn apart by storms. Swamped and capsized like the fishing boat she had seen last year. Broken on rocks like the second boat she had seen destroyed. Vanished, like her father's boat and like so many other boats from the coast.

"Don't," Jacil said, watching as Mikki lit a second candle on her family altar. "It's too soon, Mikki; you haven't waited long enough. Ships are delayed all the time. Did you hear of the *Plover*? It sailed into Ibrin Bay half a year late."

Mikki stared at the flame she had lit. Her dark eyes were haunted, but her voice was calm.

"How cold do you think it is," she said, "at the bottom of the sea?"

Jacil hesitated. "Mikki," he said finally. "It might be different in the southern seas. The stories they tell . . . I know I've laughed at some of them. But they believe different things there. Different gods and spirits. Maybe . . . maybe it's not the same when a man drowns in southern seas."

Mikki thought of the Sea Witch. She thought of the songs she heard in the night, the voice calling and the chime of drowned bells.

"It's all one sea," she said.

This is the story we tell on our coast: The souls of the drowned are trapped in the Sea Witch's halls. As long as their bodies lie in her realm, there can be no release.

But it's a story that some—that most—have always resisted. Children light candles on altars and pray. White flags are planted to call spirits home. Ancestral ghosts are petitioned. There is hope against hope that fate can be changed.

Mikki ran to the top of the cliffs and threw her feather charms into the sea. She watched them spin through the air—half-made things, unfinished, some of them completed but torn apart by her own hands that day. Why had she spent the winter tying them? Why had she combed the shore for the perfect white plume? Her frail charms had never done anything. They could never hold back the might of the sea.

She watched her charms tumble and fall. She saw them caught by the slate-gray waves.

She had prayed to her mother's spirit, the mother she could not remember. The only family member buried in the safe black earth. Gull had never protected anyone. She had not even protected herself.

Mikki watched the last of her charms sink out of sight. Seagulls flew beneath her, banking and soaring into the wind.

That night, she went to her aunt and uncle's home for dinner. Her young cousins chattered and laughed and passed the bread, and afterward, the family asked her to stay the night. There was no room, and yet, on another night, she might have accepted. There had been times during the lonely winter when she had curled on the floor before her aunt's fire alongside her youngest cousins, grateful to feel their sleeping bodies beside her, to hear the breath of another person. She knew that her kin worried about her. But this night, she thanked them and turned away.

She went home to her own cold house. She sat before her own empty hearth, her eyes unseeing.

"Will you marry him?" her aunt had asked. Jacil had proposed to her that morning. Mikki had not given anyone a reply.

Of course you will, a voice inside her said now. Jacil would care for her. He was a good man. And she was a girl alone in the world, brotherless and fatherless. She could grow to love him. She thought of what Kerel would have wanted.

She thought of Kerel at the bottom of the sea.

She heard the Sea Witch's song again, chiming faintly beneath the wind. A song like a flute, and then like the piercing cry of a gull. A woman's voice, singing a song she knew, a lullaby she had once heard . . . Light flashed in her memory, she felt cool hands; a curtain of dark, silken hair brushed her cheek. She was a child, lying feverish in bed, and her mother was singing to her. She struggled to get up, telling herself *This isn't real,* and she heard another voice, her brother's voice, calling to her, frightened and far away, *Mikki, Mikki . . .* She heard other voices, fainter still. The voices of all lost beneath the waves.

She felt a feather in her hand and knew it was the beautiful, perfect feather she had always sought.

She opened her eyes. The feather was real.

She traced the long feather shaft with a trembling hand. She felt the edges: smooth and strong. It was whiter than foam, white as the rare snow that sometimes fell on the coast; it glowed, and there was not a speck of dirt or color to be seen.

She heard her mother's voice and knew that this time it was true.

She closed her eyes, held tight to her feather, and let the Sea Witch's song take her away.

***

She was a little brown fish in the great ocean. A fish so small, so inconsequential, that she had no name; fishermen would not waste their breath on her. She swam through the holes of fishermen's nets; she swam past their lines, beneath their boats; she swam downward, down, and all sunlight slipped away.

She was one of hundreds of tiny, nameless brown fish. They swam in the cold depths, moving past one another without notice. The only light came from the tiny flames, like candle lights, that the other fish held in their mouths.

There were walls of stone, black and shimmering. There were forests of kelp. There was a woman on a throne, and her green hair drifted and swirled in the tides. Her face shone like a pale moon. Her lovely eyes shifted from green to gray to blue to green again. She lifted one hand languidly, gracefully, and at her signal, a small school of fish came and circled above her head, the candle lights in their mouths making a living, glowing crown.

The newest little fish, just come from the sea surface, swam forward to join them. She, too, was a servant of the Sea Witch.

***

She had served the Sea Witch for untold eons. She had served the Sea Witch all her life and all past lives she might have had. She knew nothing else. There was nothing else to know.

She swam the great ocean looking for drowned souls to bring back to the Sea Witch's halls. She swam through great wrecks, ships near the size of palaces; she swam through rusting black cannons and broken chains. She found some souls still drifting near their bodies, confused. Other souls had already been washed far from their remains, whole crews scattered across the sea.

The souls were little lights floating in the deeps. Tiny golden lights—the sight stirred some memory within her. Whenever she came across a soul, she took it into her mouth and swam back with it to the Sea Witch's halls. In those silent halls, shelves stretched endlessly along the black stone walls. The little fish would deposit the soul carefully upon a shelf, there to join an endless line of souls shining steadily at the bottom of the sea.

The Sea Witch sat amidst this all, watching the lights increase around her. Her eyes flickered with the colors of the ocean surface. Sometimes, her eyes looked sad.

Sometimes, a soul would try to speak.

They would whisper as the little fish took them into her mouth. They would murmur snatches of their memories; they would plead with her for a glimpse of the sun, a breath of air. She did not understand their words. She carried them with her, deep and deeper still, until, at last, their voices faltered. They were silent as she placed them on the waiting shelves.

She knew the valleys and hills of the ocean floor; she knew the wide plateaus, the vents of fire, the canyons and trenches and undersea mountains. She knew all manner of human ships and boats. She saw remnants of human life spilled from the wrecks: cracked plates and cups, a shaving blade, a woman's comb. A child's doll, the porcelain head broken open, the silken hair rotted away. She saw all manner of corpses and bones, and the talismans that many wore or left behind. Figures of gods and spirits, carved in wood and gold and ivory and jade, hung from chains of silver or gold. Amulets stuffed with dried flower petals; vials of blessed, black dirt. Lockets with loved ones' pictures. Lockets that held pieces of parchment inscribed with prayers and spells.

She saw a charm of feathers twisted around the neck of a freshly drowned corpse. The soul still floated nearby, bobbing in gentle currents. She stared at the decaying feathers, and something stirred within.

Ten feather charms. She had given ten charms to someone, a long time ago. Charms weighted with beads of stone. Each charm woven for a face she could no longer picture.

She found the first one tangled on a coral branch in tropical seas. The beads glinted; the leather bands were still supple and strong. The feathers looked as fresh as the day she'd tied them but shone white-hot like pieces of the sun. Caught in the charm's loops was a single glowing soul.

The little fish bit and pulled at the charm, at the tangle of feathers and soul. The soul whispered, and she felt it break free and slide inside her. She knew her name. She remembered everything.

"Kerel," she said.

"Mikki," he replied.

The feathers slid off the leather ties, one by one. She felt them cling to her, melt into her scales. They flared, and she was an explosion of light. Then they dimmed, and they were merely ordinary brown scales, a part of her like the rest of her skin.

She began laughing shakily, giddily. "You're so far from home," she told her brother, and he wept because so was she.

It was easier to find the others, then. She heard them calling to her across the sea. They had all drowned off the same coast, within a few miles of one another, yet their bones had been tumbled far and their souls even farther. She could hear their voices clearly now; she understood their words. Kerel knew them, too, and he helped her find the souls of the men from their village, all who had drowned in the storm that wrecked their father's ship.

Hathir, solid as an oak tree, and gentle and kind. He had been like a second uncle to her.

Feren, thin as a grass-blade, who quipped and laughed at his own jokes.

Karsen, who whittled spinning tops and toys for the village children every New Year's celebration. Athel, barely more than a boy, who used to flick her pigtails when they were children. Farsil and Kiernan and Relis . . .

She found them held in glowing feather-charms, entangled in seaweed and coral, caught on the rotting mast of a ship or the edge of a rock. Anchored and waiting for her. She took them into her mouth, and she took the feathers for new scales.

"You can't hold us all," Kerel warned, and it was true. They were too many, too heavy and bright. They burned her cheeks, her teeth.

"Hide us," they whispered, and she unwound a feather charm and used it to tie them all together to the corner of a jagged rock. She tucked them into a rock fissure.

Kerel she did not release. She had swallowed him, and he stayed within her, lodged beneath her heart.

Five left. Four. Three. Two.

She found him, the freckled boy with the brilliant smile. The one she might have loved had they had more time.

"I saw him," said the soul who had once had beautiful eyes. "He was with me; he tried to save me. And then we drowned, and a brown fish took him away."

And Mikki and Kerel knew where the last soul, their father, had gone.

She swam back over the great ocean plains; she swam over the undersea mountain ranges, the valleys and trenches and vents of flame. She returned to the Sea Witch's shimmering black halls.

She looked at the shelves and shelves of souls and despaired.

None of these souls spoke. None called out to her. There were no shining white feathers coiled around her father—nothing to mark him from the rest. He had been taken before a charm could find him and hold him fast.

"Where do I begin?" she whispered. And Kerel within whispered, "At the beginning."

They moved down the endless rows, the golden lights burning steadily around them. Servants of the Sea Witch came and went, adding new souls to the shelves. All ignored Mikki.

She called out, and the vast silence drowned her voice. No one replied.

"He never did talk much," Kerel said.

She laughed weakly. But a pang hit her fish-heart as she thought of how little she'd known him, her quiet, grieving father. She'd thought that maybe he talked more with Kerel, that Kerel surely knew him better, for they had gone out to sea together each day . . .

Mikki and Kerel went on. On and on. Ever closer to the heart of the Sea Witch's labyrinth of halls. They saw her at times, walking in the distance, her hair drifting luminously behind her.

How much time had passed? How long would the Sea Witch let Mikki roam these halls?

Days later, years later, an unknown immensity of time . . . Kerel froze within her and said, "Mikki. *Here.*"

She stopped. The little lights burned before her, each one exactly the same.

"Here," Kerel said again, although his voice was uncertain. "Somewhere here, one of them, I can feel it . . ." She swam in a slow circle. Kerel, inside, tensed with frustration. "No, not that one, not that one, but close by, I know it . . ." Loss echoed in his voice. Loss that did not begin on a single storm-wracked day but that stretched out from the years before.

"If we had a feather charm," Mikki said. "Something to call him, something to catch him . . ."

Kerel was still. When he finally spoke again, his voice was strange. "Mikki, I can feel a feather inside you. A feather in your heart."

It was as though the cold ocean had vanished. She remembered sitting alone in a dry room. She remembered holding a beautiful, perfect white feather in her hand. The feather her mother had given her.

"Take the feather out," Mikki told her brother.

He pulled it from her heart, pushed it up her gullet, and helped her hold it in her teeth so that it could shine to the outer world. She swam slowly before the shelves of souls, the feather incandescent in her mouth.

She saw the Sea Witch enter the far end of the hall.

Now souls were waking and stirring all around. Their voices were like the rustling of leaves in the sunlit world. They were calling out to her, to the shining feather she held.

Mikki saw the Sea Witch draw near. At the other end of the hall, a school of fish turned and began to swim toward the feather's white light.

Kerel gasped as the Sea Witch's face came clearly into view. Mikki knew that he saw it, too—the fine bones of her pale face, the graceful curve of her eyes. The Sea Witch resembled their mother.

The feather blazed in her mouth; she was blinded by it. But she heard a voice, familiar, quietly speaking her name. She swam to it, unseeing. She felt a soul push up against her feather and make its way through the barbs into the quill. The light increased still more; it was intolerable. The soul moved up the quill, and the light flared through her; her bones hummed. And then the light dimmed, and she knew the feather was a part of her again, a feather-scale like the rest. Her father was within her. "Mikki," he said softly. And then, "Kerel."

Fish eyes cannot cry. But she felt something in her contract, and then loosen and ease. She felt her father settle in next to Kerel. She held the two of them now, her family. Two golden lights nestled beneath her heart.

The feather from her mother had dimmed, but it did not go out. It shone still in the darkness. All her feather scales shone. She was a white light, a beacon. Souls around her cried out.

A feather charm flashed above. A string of feathers holding eight souls, men and boys from her village. Lost crew of the *Gannet*, *Sweet Rose*, and her father's boat, *White Gull*.

She swallowed them all, taking them within her. The last feathers became her last white scales. And the souls were not heavy, as they had been before. They were light itself. They were sails full of wind; they were lanterns of hot air, pulling her upward.

She began to rise.

She heard the souls on their shelves calling for her. *Take us! Take us with you!* they cried. She gulped souls down as she floated past. They slid in and told her of their pasts. A slave thrown from a ship for disobedience. A sailor whose foot slipped on a wet deck. A girl who drowned herself from grief.

She was rising toward the ocean surface. She was buoyant with souls.

"You can't take them all," Kerel whispered as she rose faster and faster.

And another voice, a new one, said, *No. You can't take them all. But you can take all you can.* It might have been her mother's voice. It might have been her own.

Far below, the Sea Witch stood and watched. Her green-grey eyes were expressionless. Her hair and dress billowed in invisible currents, and her servants watched silently with her.

But Mikki was looking upward. The surface was rushing toward her. She saw the light growing stronger and clearer. She remembered the sunlit world, the life she had lived there. She had time to mourn it, to mourn what might have been. To grieve the life she might have chosen: marriage to Jacil, children with him, an ordinary life in the village with living family and friends.

The surface rushed ever nearer. Her scales had turned to feathers. She thought she saw the sky. And then her last thoughts disappeared. She was flying upward, and there was no separation between water and air. She was melting into the light, she and her father and brother and all the souls she could carry with her wings.

But our story does not end here. Not quite.

You might understand it now, that wooden fish charm you hold. The little shrines you may have seen along the shore, at the foot of a pier. Shrines to the fish-bird, the bird-fish. Prayers to both the White Gull and Brown Fish.

No? Then let me explain. It is said that Mikki did not stay in the Realms of Light. It is said that she went back for the souls she could not save. She scours the oceans even now; she enters the Sea Witch's halls and takes souls from the very shelves. The Sea Witch merely goes about her ancient business, collecting drowned souls; and Mikki goes about her business in turn—Mikki the Light-Bringer, Soul-Savior, the Winged Fish.

Did you keep count during the tale? Ten charms she gave Kerel: one so that he would always have a charm to wear and nine to be tossed to the sea. But the tenth charm never found their father. Perhaps it found a different soul to save; perhaps Mikki has already used it, rescued that soul, and taken the feathers. Or perhaps this is what she uses over and over, this single charm, saving lost souls one at a time.

And the Sea Witch in her black halls: Perhaps she is merely holding the souls in place for Mikki, keeping them safe on her shelves. Perhaps that has always been her ancient task. Is that why she sings from the sea?

This is a story we tell each other, here on our lovely, perilous coast. Here, where storms blow and bells chime in the deep, and we pray and light candles in the dark.

Of Milk and Blood

The rifle feels heavy and unbalanced in her hands. Her knees are shaking, her arms weak as water. Her world has narrowed to a spot fifteen paces ahead. In the barn's dim light, what looks like a young man lies stretched on the floor, dark hair spread out like a pool of ink. As her heart clangs within her, the figure groans and lifts its head. Dark eyes meet hers, fever bright. Delicate features in a face pale as snow. A human face, but what rises from its head betrays the disguise. Winter light washes in through the door behind her and catches on onyx-black horns. Beautiful horns, glossy and bright, rising straight from the head and then curving back and slightly outward like the horns of a goat. The horns of a demon. The unmistakable sign of devil-blood.

This is not the first time that Alis has encountered a demon.

She was born in these hills, and every child here grows up among spirits and devilry. Demons sour the ale and spoil the meat, rot grain in the storehouses, and blight corn in the fields. When the bread fails to rise, the baker crosses herself and throws salt on the fire to ward off evil. Demons spread fevers, coughs, oozing pustules, death. They hoot from the bodies of owls and invisibly pinch new-born babes so that the infants scream from midnight onwards and households grow haggard from lack of sleep. Demons torment innocent maidens and youths with terrible dreams so that young people wake flushed and shamed before dawn, their bodies still tingling from a devil's sinful caress.

All this Alis knows. But she knows the monster before her in a different way.

It stares straight at her, recognition in its own eyes. Those eyes are pleading, huge and black. It's as beautiful as she remembers. The shape of a boy in his teens. Thin and dirty and dressed in rags, clearly ill or injured—yet beautiful still. So pale that its skin seems to glow with its own faint light. It has not aged in the intervening years, but Alis has, and her mind reels at the gap and collapse of time: she was a child, but now it's the one who seems so vulnerable and young. Yet in the same instant (such are time's trickeries, it loops and doubles upon itself), she is again eight years old, terrified and entranced, alone with it on her parents' farm.

Ahkara. Horned demon. Drinker of milk and blood.

Its head droops back down. It lies still, eyes fixed upon her. Weariness and wariness and desperate hope on its face.

She had not thought of it in years.

Years during which the memory of a moonlit night was buried so deep that her heartbeat neither skipped nor sped at the mention of ahkaran. Years during which she milked cows and skimmed cream and walked daily to the springhouse without fear. Years during which she listened to sermons on devilry and sin without guilt.

Only in the first few years, the nightmares. After she had buried deep that night of fire, she would occasionally dream of cool moonlight and water. A presence walking with her, its low voice calming her. Softly, it spoke a story that melted fear. But even as she dreamed, she could never quite grasp the words.

She would wake, and even that hint of memory would evaporate like dew in the sun.

Now it's here again, the monster, bursting through the long miles and years that have passed. A veil in her mind is torn and memory sings. Through the shock, she fights to stay on her feet, keep steady. Toward the back of the barn, she hears her cow shuffle and kick at the floor.

Mother! her son had called to her just minutes ago. *There's someone in the barn!*

She hadn't known when she ran to the springhouse all those years ago. She hadn't known of how ahkaran come down from the highest peaks of Stone Mountain during times of human suffering, times of famine and war and disease.

They do not cause these disasters, but they ride in such disasters' wake, feasting upon misery and adding more of their own. They steal milk and cream from dairies and suck milk straight from cows, leaving them forever dry. They draw blood from the ill and injured, hastening death. It's said that a hungry ahkara may even attack an uninjured human, drinking with hollow fangs the blood of children or women found in the wilderness alone.

Alis hadn't known any of this. She was young; there are so many different demons in the world, and her parents and elders had not yet told her of this one.

But she'd still been afraid that night. She stood mutely when her mother made her request. Her mother had to ask again. *Be a good girl, Alis*, Mother said, an unfamiliar pleading in her voice. *Go get us some fresh water.*

A low fire on the hearth and lit lamps in the room. Mother looked so pale and exhausted, holding the baby. Sweat dampened her hair into dark streaks across her forehead. Alis' little brother had been crying and fussing all day, but he was now silent in Mother's arms, hardly moving. His eyes were open but dull.

Alis was scared to go out into the night alone, to cross that great sweep of darkness by herself to the springhouse. But her family was sick, all of them: a fever raging up and down the valley. The evening's water had been spilled, and when she'd touched her baby brother earlier, it had been like touching a pan from the fire. *Alis.* The pleading in her mother's voice scared Alis more than anything yet. Father was lying abed as he'd been for the last three days. Only Alis was well, still steady on her feet.

Moonlight shone overhead as she ran to the springhouse, to the furthest of the farm's outlying structures, the little room of stone enclosing the family spring. The sky above was a luminous blue-silver, blotting out the stars. The silhouette of Stone Mountain on her right, a world of shadows at her feet.

It was owl-demons that she feared as she ran. The call of a death-bird or flight of a witch. Bears and wolves and slinking night-cats.

When she reached the springhouse, she found the door open.

She saw moonlight on the figure within. The face of a beautiful youth. Horns like black blades, curving above.

Back then, the creature had been older than her, but now it looks so much younger. Not many years past her own son. It's cold in the barn, so much colder than that spring night long ago. Her fingers are numb. She sees her breath, though not the ahkara's.

She steadies her rifle.

Wait, it had cried. *Don't run!*

That was her mistake: listening. No one had warned her against that.

Desperation in its voice to match her mother's, to match her own. *Please,* it said. *Wait.*

She had. Fear and fascination bound her still.

It stood before the trough of flowing spring water where Alis' mother kept pails and crocks of milk and cream to cool. It held one of those crocks in its hands.

For my sister, it told her. *She's ill. She needs to eat.*

Its voice was a human boy's. Husky and raw, strained with fear.

She only needs this little bit of cream, the demon pleaded. *Don't tell anyone, not yet. Give us time. I won't come here again.*

Moonlight flashed off its horns and seemed to emanate from within its face. Its eyes held hers. Desperate, yet somehow gentle, too.

It was the gentleness that seduced her.

She was still afraid to walk back to the house alone, and somehow, it knew that. It walked with her partway as she carried her pail of water in both hands. It talked softly, soothingly.

Do not listen to demons, the priests and elders of the hills said. On the night of the fire, they warned emphatically, *And never ever listen to an ahkara.*

Alis hadn't told. She'd never told.

She'd given her mother the spring water, dipped a cup for her to drink. Mother had thanked her tiredly and kissed her on the head.

Distracted, Mother didn't notice the missing crock. Then Alis herself took ill; her insides turned hot while her skin pricked with cold. She was put to bed, and she dreamed of cold milk, cold cream, and cold butter on her skin. She heard low, worried voices. She understood that her mother had noticed the missing crock after all and that a cow in the upper valley had gone completely dry.

More cream missing from a neighbor's springhouse, and a side of meat as well. Cows dry in the morning when they should have been full. Word spread: an ahkara in the valley. Come down from the heights of Stone Mountain to feast on the human suffering below.

And the fever, still sweeping up and down the hills.

No, Alis said when she heard of preparations for the hunt. No one heard. Her hands clutched at the necklace of woven gold-grass which her mother had given her to keep the milk-stealing blood-sucker away.

She was still recovering, still taken by chills, when the hunt returned. Her father held her by the hand as the family walked into town to see the monster burned. Households scattered up and down the hills had come to bear witness. The story had been told and was told again: The demon had been tracked to a shallow cave and was found lying motionless beneath rags and leaves amidst stolen crocks and pails. But it was only playing at death. As the hunters approached, it opened its eyes, then it opened its mouth—and brave Ger Woodsburr of the upper valley shot it dead through the chest.

Alis watched the body tossed on the heap of branches. It tumbled like loose sticks, a mess of blood and cloth and long white hair. White horns, gleaming. A female demon, the priest and hunters had reported.

The priest poured the oil and prayed. White hair and cloth caught flame. Alis' little brother cried in his mother's arms. Alis hid her face. Her body went cold and hot. *It's the sister*, she whispered. But amid the cheers and revelry, no one heard her speak.

She buried it all—the meeting in the springhouse, the night of flames. The sick crackling and the smell of burning meat. The horror and guilt that could never be expressed.

And nothing happened; nothing has happened in the long years since. She let a demon escape, she never told, but she has not been punished for her sin, not yet. There have been deaths in her family: childbirth fever took a cousin, an uncle was killed by a falling tree. But nothing has touched those closest to her. There have been no signs of another ahkara, despite hardship and hunger and war.

Until now.

Mother! her son had called. His eyes more excited than scared. *There's someone in the barn!*

The barn door left carelessly open. Drops of blood in the snow.

No one to take care of it but her.

Alis breathes. She has her rifle. Her husband has shown her the handling of it. Necessary, in this year of absent men. Grown sons and young fathers all conscripted into a meaningless war in the west. She's brought in the crops alone, slaughtered her pig alone, harvested and smoked and prepared almost all the winter stores alone, with the help of her young children and, every now and then, a kindly neighbor.

She's alone now. The nearest neighbor a half hour's walk over the ridge. Her kin in a low valley further still. Her children locked in the house where she'd told them to stay.

The ahkara stares up at her. A demon who looks like a boy, lying seemingly helpless before her. In pain.

Demons often assume a pleasing shape, the priests and elders warn. They sway human hearts through pity. They feign at being hurt and helpless; they take the appearance of children in need. They blind human eyes with false beauty.

One must be strong to survive an encounter. One must trust in truth beyond mortal eyes. A moment of hesitation, and you may feel the hollow fangs at your neck. Your soul will be lost.

The village priest spoke for a long time on the night that the white-haired ahkara burned.

Be on guard, he had said. *Protect your soul. Don't listen to anything a devil says.*

She was a child and she hadn't known anything. She listened. She believed.

My sister is like you, the ahkara had smiled. *She also doesn't like walking in the dark alone.*

It kept to the edge of uncleared forest as they walked. The owl-demons were harmless, the horned one insisted.

It told her a little about the world from which it came. The heights of the cold, stony mountain. The purity of the air there. The storms that sometimes forced the ahkaran down so that they had to scrabble for a season in the human world.

We're not that much different from you, it had said.

The veil on her mind is gone. It's taken mere seconds for the memories to loosen, to rush through her body. She remembers all.

Her breath clouds the air. She hears the cow kick again at the back of the barn. Her only cow, which she and her children need to survive.

Her children, only steps away, alone in the house.

The ahkara lies before her, its eyes wide and pleading. The gentle-seeming spirit which has haunted her dreams.

She knows what she must do.

The demon sees the decision in her eyes. Its own eyes change. The desperation that drove it here—to seek shelter in a barn in broad daylight, to seek out a human it once knew—this desperation fades. Resignation takes its place, and something else.

Alis doesn't see the betrayal in its eyes. She doesn't look. As it attempts to speak, she doesn't listen. She pulls the trigger as she's been taught. The shot is deafening, and the recoil numbs her shoulder. The blood that flows is a brilliant red. As red as human blood.

Between Sea and Shore

The world is filled with spirits who would take a child. The *gundarram*, who hide in banana trees and send out their foul breath to sicken sleeping infants. The *gargar* demons with red fur and black wings, who fly through the rainforest looking for naughty children to snatch. *Momimo*, who appears as a little lost boy crying in the mangrove swamps, begging children and adults alike for help. There are even spirits who steal the lives of babies still in their mothers' wombs.

My aunties warned, scolded, and threatened me with such tales. My cousins and I retold the stories we heard, alternately terrified and delighted. But my mother never warned me of the spirits of the jungle. The only ones she ever warned me against were the Nai-O, the beautiful swimmers, the shapeshifters of the sea.

Sometimes, I can see dolphins out in the bay. A flash so quick I can hardly be sure: a silver arc, a moment of flight, the curve of a leap that drags my heart along with it. Sometimes, I see a pod: two and three and more leaping and spinning together, breaking again and again out of the water into the empty air. I stare at them from the shallow water near the shore, a scoop-net in my hands. I can swim, but I will never get close to them; I can't swim that far, and I will never be allowed in the painted boats that venture out to the deeper waters beyond the reef.

All I can do is stare.

"Dolphin blood," some families are said to possess. It is known that the Nai-O, who delight in taking dolphin form during the day, sometimes take human form on land at dusk. There are tales of young women seduced and left carrying half-human offspring. Men are no less lucky—they are often driven hopelessly mad by an encounter.

"But why? Why would they even leave their home?" I asked once. I could not fathom it. Some say there is no death in their undersea kingdom, no suffering. Beautiful music plays; the water is cool and refreshing; the Nai-O, ultimately neither dolphin nor human, laugh and dance under the waves. Some say they live in castles of coral and moon-pearls. Some say they eat fruit off plates of shining gold.

"They're drawn to humans," Auntie Tippi said simply. It was the resting hour after the mid-day meal, and we lay under the thatched palm shade of Auntie's small courtyard, too drained by the heat to move. Even my little brother was too hot to run about, and he lay draped on the ground at my feet like a beached jelly. "They're drawn to human songs, human music." Auntie slapped at a gnat on her arm.

"They're drawn to the human world because it's different," an older cousin guessed. "Maybe even spirits want to see new things."

One of the littler cousins pinched another, and wails split the air. My mother spoke quietly, so quietly that perhaps only I heard. "They're drawn to sorrow," she said.

There is no shortage of sorrow in our world. Every few years a great storm batters the coast, tearing the roofs off our homes, flooding our fields, and breaking our boats. Unlucky men and boys are caught and dragged under by the sea. People are bitten by snakes and poison spiders, lost to the jungle. Rains bring the coughing sickness and sun brings the prickly fever. Shallow wounds blacken and rot. The *gundarram* steal the breath of babies, while other spirits take the breath of laboring women and babies together with a single hand.

There is sorrow in my household. I have always felt it. My mother goes silent, and her gaze slips past me, staring at what no one else can see. She was pounding herbs and salt into a paste for dinner, but her hands have grown still. I, in turn, grow nervous, for Father will yell if dinner is not made to his liking. "Mother," I say tentatively. I cannot predict her moods. There are days that she smiles and laughs, and she is with me and my brother. But other times, she snaps at us; her voice goes shrill, and she bursts into tears. She sings to herself songs from her old village, but she won't teach them to me and gets angry when she hears me singing them in my turn.

"Mother," I say, and she might come back, or she might not. Father can't stand to see her this way. I gently take the mortar and pestle from her hands and try to finish dinner myself. I'm not as quick or skilled as she can be, and Father will grumble when he gets home. But he would grumble anyway.

Many women have sorrows. Many women have lost children. My mother is not the only one. But she's the only one I know who loses herself like this, who grows clumsy and forgetful even as she's cracking open a coconut or spreading fish out on racks to dry in the sun. She is weak, I think to myself. Accursed. Why else would she lose two children still in the womb even though she wore a garland of shells and fresh *sippi* flowers every night? Why else would she be unlucky enough to lose my other brother to the rain-sickness when he was barely a year old? Why can't she be like my aunties and the other women—often short-tempered and scolding, yes, but also strong and stoic and always capable?

To escape her sorrow, I run to the sea. I laugh and dive and splash with the other children. We wade in the shallows with our scoop-nets, catching crabs and small fish; at low tide, we dig up clams. I'm only a girl, but I can swim faster and farther and hold my breath longer than anyone, even Rakao, the son of the chief fisherman. He and I dare each other to swim out farther and farther until we're nearly at the reef, and it's just the two of us, floating on our backs in the warm still water. The blue sky tilts above like a second ocean, and we're weightless, suspended between expanses. I think that my body might go transparent with water and light. I think that I might stay like this forever. I think that I might never leave.

Then I hear Rakao's voice crying out that there are dolphins.

I turn upright to look. We see them flashing beyond the reef, past the fleet of fishing boats. A man in one of the boats is angrily waving his arm at us—Rakao's father—gesturing at us to head back.

So we do.

"My father is taking me out tomorrow," Rakao boasts when we are back on shore. "He says I am old enough now to be of some real help."

I am silent. It's true; he is old enough. Rakao's father first took him out to the reef when he was six, but such trips have not been regular occurrences. I see now that they will soon be; he will learn to use the lines and elaborate nets and traps that only the men can use, and he will spend every day on the reef or open ocean while I stay confined to the inner lagoon with the women and children.

He doesn't notice my silence. He's chattering as we walk back to our homes. He heads to the chief fisherman's house of multiple rooms, while I walk to a small house that needs new thatching for its roof. I find my little brother crying inside, hungry, and my mother just sitting on the floor, staring blankly out through the open doorway at the sea.

They say that festival times are the riskiest for a Nai-O encounter. All the voices of a village lifted in song—the swirl of melodies, the sounds of flutes and drums—it's like a great fire in the dark. The Nai-O hear and come. The priest always draws a protective circle around the main celebration space. The elders jealously chaperone the young maidens and youths.

Still, there are tales. There is the story of the girl who foolishly ran home in the dark by herself to fetch a belt of shells to wear. She met a Nai-O and nine months later gave birth to a child with silver hair and fingerless hands like fins. The baby gave a single high, nearly soundless cry, and then died, unable to breathe this world's air.

And there is a story that took place in our own village, within living memory. Old Uncle Turo was once the handsomest youth of his time. The great-aunties sigh and shake their heads, remembering. He was brave and gifted, and reckless as only a young man can be. No one remembers how or why he slipped from the New Year's festival. But when they found him the next morning, it was already too late; the once-laughing boy was sitting empty eyed in the sand with seaweed in his hair. He never spoke sense again. He drifted aimlessly about the village and sang at the sea; he grew old, rocking and mumbling to himself. He lives still: a silent, bent man forgotten in corners until someone chances to remember and tell the old story.

And then there are the other tales. Stories of the ones who were not seduced and abandoned but taken away altogether.

Don't walk by yourself at dusk, they tell the youths and maidens. *Don't sing alone near the sea.*

The aunties of the village look after my brother and me. They pull him out of the mangrove swamp and then scold me for not keeping an eye on him. They watch us alongside their own children as we play. We call all the older women of the village "Aunt," but Auntie Tippi is our real aunt, our father's younger sister. She reminds Mother that our small garden needs weeding, that it's time to pull the *aro* roots. She tells Mother that Little Brother has outgrown all his clothes. We harvest shellfish and gather palm fronds with her family, and she and Mother weave baskets together in the late afternoon as my brother and I play with our cousins.

Auntie Tippi's fingers are gentle as she threads flowers through my hair for the Harvest Festival. "Your mother wore flowers like these when we first met," she says, smiling. "You're already nearly as pretty."

I feel myself go still. My mother—my tired, drab mother—was once pretty?

I've never heard Auntie Tippi say anything like this before. I've never heard anyone in the village talk about what my mother was like when she was younger, before I was born.

"Was that at the Harvest Feast?" I ask. "When she and Father first met?"

But my aunt looks as though she regrets her words. Sadness like a shadow flickers over her face, and she doesn't say anything more.

My mother is the only one who says that the Nai-O take small children. She's the only one who has ever said so.

I was playing alone on the beach. I was perhaps four years old. It was the cool time of evening when families gather to enjoy the reprieve from the heat; children splash and run in the sea as their mothers sit weaving baskets and the men mend nets or clean out traps for the next day's fishing. The fishing boats have been dragged ashore, and their painted eyes and charms glint in the day's last light.

I had wandered far from my friends and from any adult. Orange streaks from the falling sun lit the sky, but my feet seemed to be moving in a separate world of darkness. I watched my own feet splashing through the dimming water; I followed them, fascinated, as though I were following the appendages of some mysterious creature. And I was singing a lullaby as I went, something my mother would sometimes sing to me, a song from her own inland village.

Kirri, kirri sing the little birds.
They call for you in the dawn.
Mik, mik calls the mouse in the field.
He misses your shadow passing by.

I was singing, and was there an echo I heard, a second voice tracing those words? I sang louder, and it seemed that the waves were growing stronger. That second voice sang with me, a half-beat behind, and I could hear the curiosity in its uncertain refrain. The current sucked at my legs . . .

And my mother was screaming my name, running at me; she grabbed me and swung me away from the water, up into her arms. "Don't," she cried. "Don't ever sing that song, don't sing here at night, don't you know—" She shook me, she was so angry, and I saw the tears glinting on her cheeks. I burst into sobs.

The Nai-O, she explained as she carried me crying back up the beach. The Nai-O, the singing dolphins, didn't I know that they took small children?

My friends didn't believe me.

"The Nai-O don't take children," Rakao said, frowning. "Or not little ones. They take the older ones, the ones who are almost grown."

"Everyone knows that," an older boy, Kaavo, scoffed.

"My mother said so," I insisted.

Kaavo tapped the side of his head with two fingers, the same gesture people made when they spoke of Old Uncle Turo. "My mother says your mother is crazy," Kaavo said.

My mother was not crazy. Not then.

Back then, she still sang to me and stroked my hair and held me in her arms. She spoke and listened and looked at the world, even if her eyes were sometimes scared and sad.

I kicked that boy in the shins for disrespecting one of his elders.

The seasons blur—planting and harvest and sun and rains and sometimes a cool breeze off the sea, stirring the air. The Four Great Festivals slowly wheel around in their turn. There are harvest seasons for fish as well as *aro* and rice— there are times when the large spotted *specka* run and a full moon when huge schools of *berbekki* throw themselves into the fishermen's nets. Rakao tells me of all this when we meet. He tells me of the great green turtle nearly as large as a man, whom they call "Grandfather," and who greets them every day on the reef. He talks of bright fishes with colors and patterns I've never seen—too clever and quick to be caught. He speaks of undersea forests of coral. He tells me of rowing past the reef into choppy water, of feeling the boat rise and fall; the lurch in the stomach, the great rolling hills and valleys of water.

Father takes Little Brother out to sea as well, although not often. He's not a patient man, and Little Brother gets bored and restless in the confines of the boat.

Rakao meets me at the beach as the sun is setting. He tells me of the pod of dolphins he saw, closer than he's ever seen. He gives me a piece of pink coral.

How do you tell a Nai-O from an ordinary dolphin?

The differences are subtle. Some say the Nai-O are slightly larger. Others claim that they are smaller. All agree that their skin is brighter, more silvery. They leap just a little higher in the air, cut through the water just a little more swiftly. They are curious and fearless, and often swim alongside boats. At sea, the Nai-O are almost considered good luck; they often bring good weather and fish.

Still, it's best to keep your distance. It's best not to draw their attention.

Rakao says he's never seen one but promises to tell me if he does.

When the rains fall, it's time to light candles for the dead. On the family altar, Mother places coconut shells of fresh water and jasmine flowers. We peel and cut guava fruit as an offering. We kneel and recite prayers for our relatives' well-being and blessings: ancestors I've never known, my father's parents, and their parents in turn. My father's siblings who died in childhood, and his older brother who died before I was born. We and Auntie Tippi are all that's left of his family.

In my mother's village they pray for her ancestors and family but here she makes offerings for her husband's. She and Father's lost children are the last names to be spoken. Her tears start before she gets to her first son's name; she's crying as she lights the candle for Father's older brother, for an uncle I never knew.

The stories always leave something out. What happened to the girl with the belt of shells after she gave birth to her Nai-O baby? What happened to the half-Nai-O children who survived, whose descendants are said to live in certain villages on the coast? Were they happy? Did their mothers love them? Did they ever long to leave their human families and go to live in the sea?

Rakao and I meet when we can. It's hard, for we're both busy with new duties. It's been years since we swam in the lagoon together. Long ago, I was told to put on a maiden's proper clothes, to leave the sea to unshirted little girls.

But we can still meet on land, for a short space each day. We can still talk and be together.

We're almost always surrounded by others—family and friends gathered around us on the beach or working with us during chores. But there are still moments when we catch each other alone during the daily routine—moments when he still seeks me out, meeting me by my home. He spends most of his time with the other boys, of course, working with them, trading cheerful insults with them, kicking around a woven rattan ball. But I know he speaks truly only to me. We stare at the sea and wonder aloud about the islands across the water. He tells me the stories he hears from visiting sea traders. He talks of running away to join them. He tells me of a quarrel in his family, of something his father said. He speaks of the expectations of his father and of the expectations of all his uncles. It's like a dozen eyes always watching you, he complains; it's like the heat of the sun always on your back. And then suddenly, we're laughing at his imitation of a stern old uncle; we're laughing at an auntie's manner and at some silly happenstance; we're laughing at nothing at all.

I ask him to tell me of the sea.

He smiles. "You're the one who should be on the boat each day," he says.

Later, I watch as he swims freely in the lagoon with his friends. I think of a game that the two of us used to play. When we were children, we built a great boat out of palm fronds and branches: the greatest boat that has ever been, a deep-sea voyaging canoe with sails like white wings. We stocked that boat with coconuts, and Rakao caught a shark to tow us, and we sailed across the ocean to the lands beyond the sunset.

———

I heard two new Nai-O stories last year. It was at the Clear Moon Festival, and I heard them from a girl from M'kai village. She was visiting with her family, honored guests of one of our chief families. She told us the stories as she and her mother helped with the feast preparations: pounding roots, shelling nuts, and folding countless banana leaves around fillings of sweet rice and fruit. *A story*! we demanded while we worked, for it was the fee asked of all visitors. The girl smiled demurely and glanced at her mother. The woman nodded, and the girl, clearly proud to tell a story she had learned well, told her tale.

Long ago in M'kai village, there lived a gentle young man. He was kind and well-liked, a good fisherman and hard worker. But he was also an odd, dreamy youth, prone to spells of silence and unexplained sadness.

One day, this youth was out at sea with his brother when a large dolphin, bright silver in the sunlight, surfaced next to them. The dolphin followed as they rowed out to their fishing grounds, and fish flooded into their nets. They could scarcely drag them all into the boat.

From that day on, the dolphin visited with them. Nearly every day she appeared, leaping and swimming beside them. She swam so close that the men in the boat could reach out to touch her. But it was only the younger brother, the sad-eyed dreamer, who did so.

The dolphin brought fish, and the brothers brought home nets nearly bursting with their catch. Their mother and sisters were nearly worn to exhaustion drying, salting, and preparing for trade all that could not be eaten in the village. Their father strutted and grew fat with pride.

But even as they grew rich, the family and others worried. For the younger brother cared nothing for dried fish and money, nor for fresh fish, either. If he had been somewhat dreamy before, he was now three times worse. His eyes turned ever seaward, and they looked only to the silver dolphin that greeted him each day.

The unease grew. The boy's older brother had married, and now the father tried to marry off the younger son as well. But the boy would not look at any of the girls that the matchmakers found for him. He cared only for going to sea and singing to the dolphin from his boat, regardless of the warnings of others.

And then, one day, it happened. One day, the boy simply swung his legs over the edge of his boat and slipped into the sea after the dolphin who waited for him. The elder brother saw the sleek silver shape in the water; he saw the younger boy reaching for a fin; he watched the boy slide smoothly onto the dolphin's back. The elder brother shouted and jumped into the sea after them. But the dolphin and boy skimmed through the water quicker than bird-flight. Men on other boats saw as they flashed past, and they watched as the dolphin dived deep, the boy holding onto her fin. No one ever saw them again.

There was a silence as the girl finished her story.

"No one?" said a young girl-cousin, a child of four. And she began to cry.

There was a rush of soothing words and comfort for the child, and then praise and questions for the tale-teller. The girl from M'kai flushed under the attention. "No," she said in response to one question. "It's the only tale like it that I know." She paused. "Or maybe not. There's also a story of a girl who went into the sea after the Nai-O. Some say that she had met one on the beach the night before and afterward refused to be left behind. Some say that she was part Nai-O herself. For one dusk, she took off her clothes on the beach—in front of everyone—and walked naked into the sea. There were shouts, and someone tried to go in after her. But something of the Nai-O's speed touched her then, for she swam faster than was human, and she disappeared into the waves."

<hr>

"Do you think she's pretty?" I later asked Rakao about that girl from M'kai. Everyone knew that she and her family were visiting because our head chief was looking for a match for his son. All through the festival, people had gossiped of it. The girl was generally held to be beautiful, with her large round eyes and shining black hair.

Rakao shrugged. "She's pretty enough." He grinned and flicked away a wisp of my hair that had fallen into my eyes. "I hear her younger sister is even prettier."

I'm nearly of age, and my parents should be looking for a husband for me. But my mother looks through me, lost in her own world. My father has never looked at me at all.

<hr>

Sometimes I can't sleep at night. I slip outside, then, and I sit just outside our doorway, watching the sea. The black waves glitter and heave. Beneath the roar of the surf, beneath the rhythmic pounding as familiar as the beat of my heart, I think I hear another sound. Another song. Voices. It's not the voice that once sang my words back to me when I was a child. It's not anything repeating human words or trying to understand and imitate human song.

It's something pure. Something of water and starlight and sunshine and cold. Something of deepness and vastness and height. Something I can't grasp. I try, I concentrate, I reach out—and it fades and melts like foam on the sea.

The Harvest Festival nears, and Auntie Tippi says she'll help me with my festival clothes. It's been a good season for rice; each family's granary is full. It's been a good season for fish; the migrating *berbekki* passed by the coast in schools so thick they were said to resemble black clouds beneath the water. I'm fifteen, and I will be joining the women's chorus in the singing this year.

Rakao is nearly sixteen. I hear that his family has been consulting the matchmakers for his bride. I hear that a girl from an inland village has been invited to the festival to meet him.

"Why would I wish to marry an inland girl?" Rakao says to me in disgust. For once, we're alone together on the beach. "She won't even know how to properly clean a fish!" he says. Has he forgotten that my mother is from an inland village? Or is he remembering it all too well? I hate this other, unknown inland girl, yet I also feel a brief, intense desire to kick Rakao in the shins.

"Her father is wealthy, and they say the *kanat* should be renewed . . ." Rakao's voice falters. The *kanat* is a bond between families and clans; it's a bond between villages, too. Each family and village is bound to others in a complicated web that only the priests and matchmakers, those wise women with their marked tablets of bamboo wood, fully understand. I think of my own family's ties, of the *kanat* that brought my mother and father together.

"I'm too young to marry," Rakao says. I look into his eyes, and the panic in them is like something I would see in my little brother just a year ago— before he grew too old to run to me for comfort and a hug.

Rakao is right. He's younger than most boys when their families start looking for a bride. What have the matchmakers said to them? Are they only trying to seal an engagement? The girl from M'kai never came to our village; they say our head chief waited too long, and her family accepted a different marriage.

"Nari," Rakao says quietly, calling me by my name. His back is turned to me; he's looking out at the sea. "Do you remember that game we used to play when we were kids? The one about building a great boat and sailing across the sea to the other side of the world?"

Could I ever forget? I think. I feel my heart clench.

"I still wish sometimes that I could run away like that," he says now. We're both quiet, and when he finally turns back to me, his eyes are calm. "I wish I could sail away in that great deep-sea boat." He smiles a little sadly, fondly. "Or that I could meet another girl like you."

I can't tell him what's in my heart. What my heart wants is impossible. I blink quickly and look away.

I can't marry him; I know that. There's the *kanat*, there are blood ties, there's tradition. Marriage within a village is discouraged. There are exceptions— Auntie Tippi was allowed to stay and marry her village sweetheart. But the matchmakers pored through their charts of bloodlines and ties; the priest cast shells and prayed. A dispensation of the type given to her and her sweetheart — kind Uncle Kanoa—a dispensation granted by gods and ancestors and elders and family alike—is granted once a generation, if that.

And why would Rakao's family seek such a dispensation for us? He is the eldest son of the chief fisherman of our village and nephew to the head chief. What am I but the daughter of a dwindled, accursed family? We may as well ask the gods for a dispensation allowing me to go to sea, to sail beyond the reef in the deep-sea boat of mine and Rakao's imagination.

Rakao and I have never spoken of any of this. He flicks my hair and teases me. And he calls me "Cousin," the greeting that we all give one another in our village. The proper greeting.

My mother is always worse near the time of the Harvest Festival. This year, she couldn't even be relied on to participate in the village's shared rice harvest; I took her place in the village fields, trying to work doubly hard under the accusing eyes. She stayed in bed, sleeping or staring blank-eyed at the wall.

But something seems to rouse her this year as the festival preparations get underway. She watches me as I sew bright beads on the shirt I mean to wear. She comes to listen when I and the other women and girls gather to practice our songs.

"Don't go," she tells me one day. We're alone in the house, just her and me. With both the rice and fish harvests in, the men have been indulging in impromptu pre-festival activities; Father is drinking rice wine with the other men, and Little Brother is off with his friends. He takes every chance he can to flee our home.

I look at her in surprise, for I had thought her asleep. In the lantern light, her face is a patchwork of shadow and golden-lit skin. She's sitting up straight, and her hair is a flow of shadow, catching the light dully here and there.

"Don't go, Nari," she says urgently, and something in her voice reminds me of that day when I was four, when she rescued me from a suddenly threatening sea.

"Don't listen to him," she says, and I realize she's weeping. "He can't take you, he can't keep you; it's all a lie. You don't belong there. I didn't belong there. But I don't belong here, either. Nari, you won't leave me, don't leave me." Her thin arms stretch out to me. I am terrified. I promise her that I won't leave her; I promise not to sing by the sea; I promise her anything she asks. But I don't leave my seat to cross the room to her and comfort her. I don't touch her at all.

I have always loved the music of our festivals. The drum-beats that pound in your blood and move your feet; the high, clear notes of the flutes sweeter than birdsong. But the human voices are sweetest of all: the choruses interweaving their separate lines of melody, the voices rising and falling and rising again in a sound that melts away time. We rehearse in groups: the youngest children in their own choir, girls and boys separate from the women and men. But on the nights of festival we all come together, and together, we sing songs of thanks and praise; together, we sing old stories and legends into being. No one sings alone.

When we sing like this, I can feel myself disappearing into the music; I can lose myself completely. And I can believe that spirits from the sea would want to hear this. I can believe that they would leave their undersea paradise to listen to us, to try to share in our songs.

People from other villages trickle in, as happens every Harvest Festival. Visiting chiefs and elders, relatives and marriage prospects. I know when the inland girl and her parents arrive. Rumor travels fast, and the day after their arrival, Rakao himself comes to my home to tell me.

"She's stiff as a dried fish, Nari," he tells me miserably. "We had to share *sippi*-leaf tea with everyone watching. Then they left us alone to talk. It was horrible."

I try to say something sympathetic, but my heart is beating fierce and glad.

I wonder if he sees it; he looks at me sharply. And then he gives me the message he was sent with. "They want to visit with you this afternoon. The mother and the girl."

I gape, and he laughs a little as he says, "They're your blood relations, you know that, don't you? The mother is your mother's true cousin. They grew up together."

I'm still gaping at him. His smile fades. He knows what I'm thinking; he knows me so well. "It will be alright, Nari," he says softly. "Your mother's been doing well; she'll be alright."

But she's not.

Silently, I serve juice and sweet rice cakes as the woman, this Auntie Ona who I've only just met, struggles in conversation with my mother.

Auntie Ona seems kind. Her face is round and pleasant; she sits and talks of how glad she is to see Mother again. She says it's a comfort to think that her daughter might marry into a village where there is at least one kinswoman, one good friend, to help guide her. She praises me, says that I am beautiful and well-mannered, and mustn't Mother be proud?

I'm not supposed to speak unless spoken to. So I sit at the low table and sneak glances at the girl across from me: Rakao's intended. She's tall and skinny where her mother is soft and round; her face is long and plain. Her expression floats between vacancy and unhappiness.

"Oh?" my mother says absently in response to the other woman's words. I can see her drifting. She seemed to behave well enough when our guests first arrived; she smiled and embraced them both. But I saw the flash of shock on Auntie Ona's face just before she reached out to hug my mother. What did she see?

I try to look at Mother through a stranger's eyes. She's dressed neatly, and her hair is combed. But she's so thin, so fragile looking. Her hair is brittle and tipped with white; she looks far older than Auntie Ona, who is the same age. And she's shown no real warmth or interest in her cousin, whom she last saw fifteen years ago. She's barely asked any questions of the daughter. She nods and drops polite syllables here and there, but she's distracted; it's as though she's listening to a different conversation in the room, one that only she hears.

I think even the skinny girl across from me is beginning to realize that something is wrong; she seems to come out of her own distracted thoughts to look with puzzlement at my mother. I feel a kind of queasy shame in the pit of my stomach.

"Nari," Auntie Ona says, turning to me with desperate enthusiasm. She praises my cooking and plies me with questions. I answer, feeling my face hot with embarrassment. I don't want either of these guests here; why do I care what they think? Mother is leaning against a wall, her eyes unfocused, some-where else entirely.

And then, suddenly, she is paying attention again. "Marriage?" she repeats, looking at Auntie Ona. Auntie had just been mentioning again her daughter's possible betrothal to Rakao. Mother looks at the girl, and tenderness fills her eyes. "Oh," she breathes. "Do you love him?"

It's a breach of etiquette so great that we're all speechless.

My mother shakes her head. "I loved him," she says. She sways a little in her seat. She says it like a song: "I loved him. I did. I did."

I go to bed early that night.

I lie on my mat and think fiercely that I don't mind how Mother behaves; I don't care what those inland relations think. Perhaps Mother has even scared them away from marrying into this village. *Look what happens when inland girls come here.* Good, I think; Rakao will thank me. That girl should thank me, too. It's obvious that she doesn't want to marry Rakao and live here; it's as plain as her face is.

But part of me wants to cry and then run to the house where Auntie Ona is staying and knock on the door and beg her to talk to me. *Tell me*, I want to say. Tell me what she was like when you knew her. Tell me about the girl you remember. Tell me who my mother used to be.

I don't ask anyone about the last words my mother said to the girl. I know that she wasn't talking about Father. I know that she's never felt that way about him.

"I won't marry her," Rakao tells me, waiting for me outside my house in the early morning light. He knows that I'll be the first one up during these slack days of holiday. "They can't make me; I refuse."

"Good," I say, my voice low but as strong as his.

Something of the fierceness in him seems to leak out. We stand staring at each other. The sky is whitening around us. But in the early blue shadows, it's still hard to make out his eyes. I don't know what I see there.

"Well," he says. He sounds confused. "I just wanted to let you know. They'll be looking for me back home . . ."

"I know," I say. And I feel as though I'm answering a question he's never asked.

We stand still a moment more. The moment stretches and echoes; I feel as though the world is tilting. "I—" he stops. "I'll see you tonight," he says finally. "At the festival." And then he turns and is sprinting away from me, past the row of stilt houses slowly emerging from the dawn.

Tonight. The first night of Harvest Festival. It feels a year away.

I've never told anyone how I sometimes hear the ocean singing. I've never even told Rakao.

It's not just at night that I hear the music. Now I sometimes catch it during the day, in whispers beneath the wind and surf. I hear it calling while I hang clothes up to dry, while I sweep the floor or prepare supper. It pulls and teases at the edge of my hearing. It's something that can't be held, can't be grasped—like water itself.

But I hold still and try. I let the music into my mind, as much of it as I can. I feel it moving and spreading through me. Then human voices interrupt the song. My mother calls my name. The music's gone, and even in the hottest sun, I feel myself shivering.

I sew the last bead on my new shirt. I help carry armloads of floral offerings to the temple grounds, where the festival will be held. I help Auntie Tippi and the other women cook for the Harvest Feast, and then Auntie Tippi braids my hair.

I walk to the festival grounds with my family, holding onto Mother's hand. Little Brother runs ahead of us, looking surprisingly grownup in his new clothes.

I take my place in the women's choir for the first time. I catch Rakao's eyes in the men's choir across from me. He nods.

I'll tell him, I've decided.

I'll tell him and he'll agree with me; he'll think and feel exactly the same. Together we'll find a way to win over the elders and families and everyone. It's right, he'll know it's right; what we have goes beyond *kanat*; Rakao and I will make our own *kanat*. He feels it just like I do. Doesn't he?

But there's no time to say anything now.

Now there's singing, melodies tossed back and forth between the separate choirs; melodies entwining, voices running over and under and around one another. There's music rising in me and from me. Now there's the great bonfire and children running about giggling in the shadows. Later, there will be the patterned, formal dances of the different age groups, and later still, the dancing for all ages.

I try to find Rakao after the singing, but there are so many people. New faces from outside the village, new youths as well as new young women. I find myself caught in introductions, even as the daughter of a poor low-status fisherman. I see Rakao on the other side of the fire, still playing host to the long-faced inland girl.

Two of my other friends, Auntie Tippi's older daughters, grab my hands and pull me into a dance.

Later I see that inland girl talking to one of the visiting boys from outside our village. Rakao is standing off to the side, looking relieved.

There's no time to talk to him alone during these days of festival, but there's time for my mother to cling close to me, to worry at me. "Where are you going?" she says. "Where are you?" Her thin hands clutch at me. She hasn't gone to a Harvest Festival in years, but now she goes each night, stuck to my side. She lets go reluctantly when a boy takes my hand to dance. She pleads, "Come back soon," as I step away to fetch a drink or fill her banana leaf with rice.

"Stay close," she whispers, her nails digging into my wrist. I grit my teeth.

From the side of my eye, I see our priest walking a circle around the celebration space. He's sprinkling blessed water on the ground, keeping us safe from jealous spirits of the sea.

Rakao and I glance off each other in the bright chaos, stumbling into each other and then spinning away again. He seizes my hand during one of the dances; he spins me till I'm laughing with dizziness. I see his smile before the dance line moves and turns, and I'm handed to the next partner.

My friends are gossiping under the trees. Rakao's inland girl and her family left this morning, off to prepare for their own village's Harvest Festival. A few last visitors are expected tomorrow. That family from M'kai, the one that came to the Clear Moon Festival last year—have I heard? They're coming back, this time with their younger daughter. And a son, too.

This last is said with a sly smile by a girl-cousin. There's laughter.

But I'm not paying attention because Rakao has joined our group. He settles in with ease, joining the conversation in mid-flow. Does he look at me as I look at him? Our eyes keep catching. Even as he laughs at his cousin's joke or debates a fine point of fishing technique with a friend, his eyes keep returning to mine. It's as though we're holding a separate, secret conversation. I feel my heart blooming with each look.

Tomorrow night, I think. Or the day after. We'll find the time to talk. We will.

That night, I hear the music of the sea in my dreams. Larger and louder than I've ever heard. Even in my dreams I can't grasp it, but dimly, I sense its themes. Something about wind and waves and tempests. Something about depths and freedom and the flight of the gull. Starlight in a black night and a far distant shore.

It's the last night of the Harvest Festival. I'm standing with the women's choir, waiting for the singing to begin. My cousins are chattering behind me, still gossiping of the family from M'kai. Cousin Palani saw them today; she's nearly swooning over how handsome their young son is.

Then I see them myself. They're taking their seats among the honored guests. I recognize the tall, broad-shouldered father with his greying hair. I recognize the graceful mother. I see the son they've brought with them, and the young daughter, sister to the one who told the Nai-O stories last year.

Rakao is with them, guiding them politely to their seats. I realize that the rumors he told me last year were right. The younger daughter is even *prettier* than her sister.

It took me so long to understand.

A name spoken and a name misspoken. The things my mother said and her tears over an uncle I never met. The silence in our household. The story I finally coaxed from Auntie Tippi about my mother's first betrothal. The way my mother warned only me against the Nai-O, and never my brother.

The night that Father came home late, drunk on rice wine. I was sitting in the doorway, looking out at the sea. He almost stumbled over me. I said something, I don't remember what—perhaps it was just his name, "Father." And he was silent. I could feel him looking at me in the darkness—a rare thing, for he never looks at me. "You're not mine," he said finally, flatly, and he pushed past me to his bed.

These are the memories that finally fell together in my mind. These, and the music of the sea.

It's surprisingly easy to run away from a Harvest Festival.

The aunties and uncles think they're keeping watch, but they're distracted with food and drink and dancing and talk. The circle the priest has drawn has no power over humans; it's easy enough to step over.

It's easy enough to run into the darkness, to flee.

I watched for as long as I could bear it. I watched Rakao talking with that M'kai girl after the singing; I saw the way the two of them made a private circle in the golden lantern lights. I saw the way he looked at her. And the way she looked at him.

Did he ever look at me that way? Did I imagine it all?

Even if I didn't imagine it, it's not me that he'll marry. I heard the gossip swirling before and after the singing. A marriage was not made last year between the older M'kai girl and the head chief's son, but the priests are insistent that a *kanat* be arranged between the two villages. It's overdue, they say.

And Rakao is the head chief's nephew. If he marries the younger M'kai girl, the clans will still align.

From what I saw, I don't think he'll object.

It was easy enough for me to slip away from my mother, to wait for a moment of distraction. I fled the Harvest Festival; I ran to the sea.

My throat is burning, and pain cramps my side. I've run so fast, so far. I'm at the very end of our village's strip of beach. When I turn to look back, I see the lights of the festival tiny and golden against the great night.

I pant, catching my breath.

It's not the Nai-O's fault, I know. It's not their fault that some people can't choose. It's not their fault if some are left stranded behind, unable to make the leap, to let go fully of their human ties. The Nai-O don't mean us harm. They're only curious. They only want to hear our music. And to offer us their own.

I know the Nai-O never meant my mother harm.

The sun went down long ago, but it doesn't matter. It doesn't have to be dusk. A nearly full moon lights the sky and burns a cold path across the waves. I face the sea and begin to sing.

I don't sing the songs of the Harvest Festival or any of the songs of my village. I sing my mother's songs. The sad, lonely songs of her inland home.

And I know that years ago, she stood on this shore and sang these same songs at the sea. She was lonely and sad. She had fallen in love with a boy at a Harvest Festival and had been pledged as his bride. But illness took him before the marriage could take place, and to preserve the *kanat,* she was wed to his younger brother, the last of the family line. A younger brother who Auntie Tippi claims was not always so grim and rough but who was forced to grow up and old before his time. A brother who could never take the place of the one who was lost.

The inland girl was alone among strangers with a man she didn't love. No one warned her of the Nai-O. She didn't know.

But I know, and I sing her songs now, flinging my voice out over the waves. Her songs are filled with human sadness, but I realize that I myself am no longer sad. What's burning through me is exultation. My voice rings stronger and truer than it ever has.

I sing to my father who came from the sea. I sing to my home and all my undersea kin.

They sing back, and I begin to undress.

I take off the beaded shirt of which I was so proud. I take off the matching skirt that Auntie Tippi made for me. I take off the necklace I always wear, the necklace made from a piece of pink coral that Rakao gave me when we were ten.

I let these items fall onto the sand, and I step into the sea. I think briefly of my little brother, but he's almost grown—he doesn't need me anymore. I wade in, and the cool water closes over my thighs. I hear a voice calling my name. My mother's voice crying frantically for me. But I spread my arms and kick forward, gliding into the waves. The music of the Nai-O rises for me, and I understand it at last; it fills my head and my body and bones, catching and lifting me to the stars, to the deeps.

Wings

Last night, you were a great black cat, larger than me, with shining green eyes. You stretched out on the bed, and I curled against you, the back of my head against your belly. Your purr of contentment vibrated through me. I fell asleep, so happy that I nearly didn't think of your former self.

When I wake, you are gone.

I go to the window and look out. There's a white heron in a pine tree waiting for my gaze.

Sunlight strikes your white feathers. You shine against green needles.

I wish you weren't so far away.

There was a whole week when you were a fish. A beautiful goldfish, long as my arm. Patterned in gold and red and orange, with flowing tail and fins. It was a full day before I found you in the pond under the willows. I was so relieved that I cried. I brought you bread over the next several days, and you swam close to me to take it. But not close enough to touch.

There are times when we can't touch. Can't even breathe the same air.

You were a red-winged blackbird next. You perched outside my bedroom window and woke me with your song. A run of trills, repeated again and again.

When you were still human, you told me love stories.

Two birds nested in the woods, you read.

Lamplight golden on your long, slim hands as they touched the page. Your face in shadow. Your voice a clear, resonant baritone, soft in the falling dusk.

You spoke of doves that served as messengers between lovers. Of magpies who formed a sky-bridge to unite a husband and wife. Of lovers who drowned and were turned into kingfishers by a merciful god.

Of lovers lost and parted forever.

Two birds in the woods, you read. And then one woke to find itself alone.

We fled before my mother's rage. It is one thing for a princess to play with the latest court poet. It is quite another for her to marry him.

We fled to an enchanted island in a great lake, where we could always be together. But my mother twisted the enchantment, making of it a bitter joke.

She knew that I fell in love with your voice and stories, so she took them both away.

I speak, but you never answer in words. I wind my fingers in your fur or stroke your feathers or scales. I listen to your purr, your growl, your squeak, your chirp. When I can, I tilt my head to listen to your heartbeat.

There is a desert of pink sand, you told me. We lay together in my mother's gardens, under the weeping willows.

At the edge of this desert, you continued, is a city carved of cliffs striped rose and gold. The air smells of cinnamon. At dusk, a thousand bells ring.

Our hands reached each to each. Our fingers intertwined.

There is a city by the sea, I said. A city carved in pearl and mother-of-pearl, built of coral and shells. A city that shines like light on water. The people carry lamps of phosphorescent fish and tend gardens of swaying anemone.

This was how it happened: with stories. Stories from books and song and memory. Stories spun of our imagination, pure fantasy, traded back and forth between us, growing wilder with each iteration.

Stories of our hearts.

A man stood on the walls of his city, you said. His heart was a white bird which he flung into the sky. His heart spread wings and soared over the walls, over the desert, searching, searching . . .

She swears that you will never speak again. She promises that you and I will be together, but always apart.

She is waiting for me to tire of you. To leave this island and crawl back to her.

You are iguana, fox, beetle, mouse. Deer, fish, crow, and snake. Some forms are easier than others to hold in my arms.

You're a bee and then a spider which I can scarcely see.

Understanding flickers in your eyes as you change. You know more, and then less.

I hold on to what I have.

In the audience hall, you sang of great feats of love. A mountain of glass scaled, a desert crossed. Oceans swum. War fought for a lover's hand.

The evil sorcerer defeated. The war won. The curse shattered.

At night, in the secrecy of my bedchamber, we whispered the small intimacies of love. The tender names, the private jests. The hitch of breath and muffled cry.

And now you are absent. Hidden. I search the forest for you, wondering what you've become today. I scan the tops of trees.

I sing part of a song we made together.

She stands on the walls of her city.

Her heart is a white bird which she flings into the air.

Her heart soars over water and desert, searching, searching . . .

All the stories we told. Your hand in mine. Lamplight shifting over your face, your golden skin. The arch of your brow, the pout of your lips, and then your face filling with laughter the way water fills a bowl.

Are you sure? you said, when I brought you the silken cords that would bind us for life, that would tie a marriage knot witnessed by heaven.

I didn't care about your lack of titles, your common blood. I didn't care about the risks. I looked into your tender, wondering eyes. I'm sure, I said.

Through all my magic defenses, my mother finds ways to send me messages. Owls and ravens come marked with the glowing sign of peace, but with notes tied to their feet. The notes remind me that she's waiting. They speak of honor and duty and a greater world. They're filled with threats and promises of forgiveness.

I tear her messages to shreds.

The willow leaves turn yellow. A cold wind blows.

You change unpredictably. Vole, stag, possum. Wren, squirrel, wolf. But the next time you change to a goldfish, you remember me. This time, you take the bread from my hand.

Fall and winter, and you're a brown bear sleeping in a corner of my room. I read to you aloud. I watch you twitch in unknowable dreams. I speak. You're so far away.

I'm still telling our stories.

When you're not here to listen, I write them in ink pressed from berries and roots, stirred from pine resin and ash. I write on scraps of parchment that I find in the house. When that runs out, I strip bark from birch trees to use as scrolls.

My words pile up.

All the longing I feel, all the rage and grief, and the joy we once shared. The days of our lives now: the solitude of this island, the sunlight on water and drip of rain through the trees. My happiness when you have eyes that look into mine, that seem to understand—even a little—of what I say.

Spring and summer and fall again.

My mother's messages come this year as golden leaves blown into our home, her writing scarlet along the veins. I tear them up and ask the wind to blow them away.

You were beautiful. You are beautiful, still.

Whatever form you take, you are beautiful.

I find myself speaking less and less. My own voice grows strange to my ears.

There is a language deeper than words. A language of silence, touch, and simple presence.

This is the language we speak now.

You're a rabbit watching the sunset with me. A butterfly on my table as I write. A small cat the color of smoke, curled upon my lap.

Seasons turn and blur, and our past life feels like a dream.

Were you a poet and singer once? Was I a princess?

Did we meet in my mother's garden? Sneak kisses in the arbor? Did we tell each other stories?

Did words spill between us like a rushing river suddenly loosed?

There were cities in this dream. Impossible cities of sand and light. Music and dancing, a glittering court. Books of poetry bound in red silk. A man's voice singing, soft as dusk.

A princess in her gilded cage. A stranger from a far-off land. A story.

Wisteria in bloom. A curtain of green willow leaves. Your hand on mine as I turned a page.

Our hearts singing through our words, each to each.

I try singing a bit of poetry now.

Their hearts were white birds.

Their hearts were singing.

Their hearts flew over desert and sea, mountain and plain . . .

I'm crying.

You whine and push your cold, wet nose under my hand. Your large, brown dog eyes look into mine.

I throw my arms around your furry neck and hug you.

I miss you.

———

Two birds in the woods. The poem echoes in my mind. And then there was only one.

———

I've been afraid.

I've kept us on this island in a far northern lake. I've used what magic I have to keep us shielded from my mother's power. Safe.

Trapped.

You change through countless forms, and I stay the same. Each time, we find one another. We're together. But it's not enough.

I've been afraid to take the next step.

But I step from our little house now, in search of you. It's spring. The entire sky is ringing with birdsong. The robins are here, and the red-winged blackbirds. Waterfowl are migrating up from the southern lands. I've heard the calling of loons. Red-tailed hawks are nesting.

You're a white heron stepping delicately at the edge of the pond. You shine against the green willows.

I hold my mother's latest message in my hand. A green leaf this time, her words written in gold. She says that she has lost all patience. That she has found a way to breach my island defenses. That if I do not return, she will come to finally silence you in all ways. Forever.

I toss her message to the wind.

It's time. Even without her warning, I would know that it's time.

I swept our little house this morning. I stacked my birch-bark scrolls neatly on table and shelf. Three years of writing. My mother can read through them if she wishes. All those scrawls of ink, all to say only, I was here.

I am done with words.

You move toward me on your impossibly thin heron legs.

My love, I've clung to what I am. I've been afraid to change with you. But I'm ready now.

Your gold-rimmed eyes look into mine. I reach out and touch your feathers.

It's you. Through all your transformations—somewhere deep inside—it's always been you. It took me this long to be sure.

I can't undo my mother's spell. I can't make you human again. But I can extend the spell to myself. I can join you.

I let the protective barriers around the island drop. The wind picks up. I feel the surge of energy flowing.

It's time to leave, my love. To dare the wider world together. I can't guarantee our safety out there. But if you could speak, I know you would agree to the risk.

You stand still as I stroke your back. I reach for the spell wrapped tightly around you. I tap into the energy flowing, released, from the collapse of my wards and protections. I reach into myself and draw on everything I have.

I pull on my mother's spell. I stretch it out. I wrap it, shimmering, about myself like a shawl.

I feel my limbs shrinking and then stretching. My bones lightening. Hollowing.

You're with me. I cry out as feathers break through my skin like a thousand hot needles. My bones melt, flow, and are reshaped. Wings curve from my back. You're with me. I feel your beak on me, tenderly grooming my feathers.

Memories flash. Images of a different life. The strum of a lute, the smell of spring flowers. A man's voice calling for me in the dark. My heart was a white bird seeking yours. We met in a garden.

Sky. Sky above, so much sky, an endless ocean of it—

White wings. White feathers. Two birds. There was one but now there are two—

The last words I'll ever think, ever know.

Our hearts are flying over sea and desert, mountain and plain . . .

Our hearts meet in the sky.

We're in the sky. The wind is beneath us, the sun above, the island behind, and we're flying flying these are my last human thoughts my last words there is only sky and wind and you beside me changing forever we'll change together me and you—

Fanfiction for a Grimdark Universe

We didn't know the Dark Lord would raise an army of the dead. We never thought the young prince could turn traitor. We're menaced by ghost-wolves, stranded in an outpost on the cold edge of the world, and all signs say that we are, as our first-year Master of Field Operations Planning would say, "utterly fucked."

And you choose now to go through my pack and ask me about the papers you've found? To stand there with your eyes wide and confused and accusing? To ask if I wrote them, and what they mean?

Ah, fuck.

Okay. Remember when I was on assignment to that minor world in the Opal Sector? I found those stories there. I didn't write them. They're something called "fanfiction."

Yes, Jenna, the stories are about us.

I went to that world to research the "bleed-through" phenomenon. How events in one world can leak through to another in the form of dreams, images, thoughts, and myths. How the death of a sun in one universe becomes the foundation for a religion in another. How the same heroes appear in different stories again and again, under different names and faces. Narratives seep across worlds and time, reshaped and remade by artists and dreamers. On a minor world that exists at right angles to our own, the inhabitants have invented astonishing and wonderful forms of narrative—from their first pictures on cave walls to film and streaming video, from epic poems and novels to comics and digital games where players choose their own endings.

And the consumers of such media, in turn, create their own. They write and share their remixed stories on digital forums. They applaud and leave comments and "kudos." It's become quite popular as access to these platforms spreads.

You're frowning. I'll get to the point.

Look, of course I know that you're familiar with bleed-throughs. I don't mean to be condescending. I'm just . . . give me a moment. This is awkward, right?

So our own story is being told in that world. Right now. Or something very like it. The whole gang is there—Jin and Ratha and Angel and Tal and you and me. Masters Ahn and Neru. Our Academy days and the return of the Darkness and the fall of the Luminous Pearl. It's a story called *The Secret Guardians of the Ten Thousand Shining Worlds,* and it's a comic book series —you know what that is?

Hush, hush. You'll wake the others. This is why I couldn't tell you. I couldn't tell anyone outside the Commission. Yes, it's the only world, the only instance, where *we* appear as a bleed-through. No, no one knows what to make of it. The series installments always came out with the storyline lagging cycles behind our real lives. Master Neru thought about sending me to more worlds to try to find a more up-to-date version—maybe even something that would predict our timeline. Ahn freaked out and said no. Pretty much the whole Commission freaked out.

I was freaked out, too.

We wanted to find practical applications for the bleed-through phenomenon, but this hit too close to home. And even so, it maybe still meant nothing—nothing we could control, nothing we could use. There were budget priorities, resource issues. And then the Jade Sector was attacked and, well, you know the rest.

Your arm's bleeding again. Let me look at it. Don't give me that scowl. Here, we have a little healing ointment left. No, I'm fine, I swear. I don't need it.

It's cold. Let me build up the fire.

Yeah, that story you're holding? That's a good one. That's one of my favorites.

Academy Hijinks/High School Alternate Universe (AU)

The fanwriters like to reimagine our story as set in their own version of the Academy, usually in something called "high school." They do this with all their favorite stories. There's so much silly drama in these fics! But it isn't that different from what really happened, is it?

Okay, it is. We didn't throw nearly as many parties. I never saw you break curfew or get drunk in the dorms. We've never played spin-the-bottle or strip poker—never mind what that is—and Jin never pranked Master Ahn like that

—can you even imagine? Although of course he would have wanted to. It's classic Jin.

In real life, we didn't have much time for hijinks and personal drama; we were all studying and working so hard. It's funny to think now of how stressed we were. Of how Ratha had stomachaches all second-year and Tal lost weight and even Jin was retching from nerves during the Gateway Exams. We saw each exam and project as a matter of life and death, even when they weren't.

Although to be fair, a good number were.

We should have slacked off more, though. Blown off a reading or two, thrown parties. Gone all in on Jin's proposed escapades. Spent an afternoon just sitting in the Academy gardens, soaking in the sun's warmth and watching the light move on the sea below.

We were all together then. We didn't understand what that meant. Tal and Angel and Ratha and Jin and you and me. The rest of the Eighty-Eighth-Generation Worlds Guardian class. We were together and whole, for the very last time, and none of us had any idea of what that meant.

I'm sorry, I . . . It's just dust in my eyes, that's all. Some residual death dust from the last ghost battle. It's nothing.

Ha, remember how much you disliked me then? How insanely competitive we were? You really did hate my guts that first year. I don't blame you; I was an obnoxious prick who thought he knew everything. I was flippant and rude and not even half as funny as Jin. I didn't know anything at all.

Bakery Shop AU

This is like the high school AU, in that we're all together, and it's funny and sweet and very low stakes. In this one, you and I and Ratha and Tal are all working at a bakery when Angel and Jin open a rival shop across the road. Angel bakes the most heavenly of cupcakes: there's one with strawberry puree and buttercream frosting, and a fantastic lemon one, and a decadent one with caramel chunks and caramel drizzle frosting. Naturally, customers flock to the new shop, and we become obsessed with besting the new bakery while also eating their cupcakes. Masters Ahn and Neru are repeat customers to both shops and regularly lecture us all. Prince Ko appears, too, but he's not a traitor, just an earnest young man who loves sweets. No one betrays anyone; no one stabs or kills or imprisons anyone; no one even loses their job. Angel and Jin keep making their cupcakes, and to compete, our own shop adds a lunch menu and serves sandwiches with artisanal bread. Tal gets up her courage and finally asks Angel out.

It's cute. It's all so cute. The writer even gave me some of the best lines in the story.

It's so much better than what really happened.

Angst

Some of the stories aren't funny and cute. Some adhere closely to the *Secret Guardians* series, which in turn reflects our real universe and timeline.

I hate the *Secret Guardians*.

It does have its badass moments. There was so much I missed out on during my solo assignments, so much I didn't see or understand about the rest of the team's work. But in the *Secret Guardians*, I've seen those missing moments in their full-color glory. Like when Tal stole the key to the Cinnabar Gate and made her way to the fallen planet of Azith-i-thar to rescue Angel all on her own. And how she did it, and how those two blasted their way out of the Iron Palace like two angels from hell, fire streaming in their wake like wings, the ancient walls of iron folding and melting behind them. Or that moment when Ratha finally stood up to his father and literally spit in the Lis-Usurper's face. Or when Jin was caught by Dark agents in Silver Sector Five, and how he bluffed his way out so perfectly, how he even turned the tables and extracted information from *them*.

And you, Jenna. All the intelligence-gathering missions you've led. The worlds you've infiltrated, the knowledge you've brought back. Your skill in balancing the time-threads, calculating what's needed to tip a world away from Darkness. There's no one better. There's no one better in theory *and* execution, and the *Secret Guardians* captured it all.

I wish I'd been with you on some of those missions, if only to watch you in action. I wish I'd been there in the Tigoth Throne Room when you tore off your disguise to reveal your identity and laughed in the Witch Queen's face. I wish I'd been there when you subtly brokered the peace deal on Lazar-an-nan, which brought that world out from a path leading toward Darkness. I wish I'd fought by your side at Broken Tooth Mountain.

I wish I'd been there for you when your home world was lost.

I hate the story unfolding in the comic books now. When I left the little world that calls itself "Earth," the series had just reached the point where the entire Ruby Sector was lost, and Ratha was maimed and tortured by his own brother. Jin was hurt, too, but still alive.

The rest of our old group was still alive. And incredibly, I still had hope.

On Earth, I tracked down the woman behind the comic. She lives in a place called Toledo, Ohio, on a continent known as North America. She does both the writing and illustrations for the series, and there's nothing remarkable about her at all. She self-published two graphic novels before *Secret Guardians*. She has graying hair and a soft laugh and a crinkle-eyed smile; she lives quietly with her husband and two spoiled cats, and whenever she's alone, her mind fills with images from different worlds.

Our story has bled through to her. We don't know what it means.

Secret Guardians isn't well-known, but its fan base is loyal and obsessed, even if it's small. I started reading the fanfiction on Master Neru's suggestion. The original work had no useful content for us. As I said, it lags cycles behind our timeline, it only shows what we already know, and the writer has been getting slower as time goes on. Neru wondered if some of the fanfiction—these strange echoes, the bleed-throughs of a bleed-through—might somehow reflect real alternate timelines. True threads not detected by other means. We wondered whether at least one fic might provide clues or guidance toward a hopeful future we could steer ourselves toward.

A crazy idea, I know. The whole project was crazy.

Anyway, you're right: Focusing on the more canon-compliant fics does seem a reasonable place to start. But there was nothing there, and they hurt to read.

Did you know that there are fanwriters who set their stories in our universe but make things even worse?

The orphanage we saved on Karaph burns down after all, and the children's souls are harvested for the Dark Lord. Tal is exiled from the Guardians for stealing a gate key when she rescued Angel. Angel is lost to the Iron Palace. Ratha breaks under torture. Jin never returns from Silver Sector Five. A desperate last message is never delivered, and someone dies without knowing what they meant to another. I will never understand the writers who do this. These stories are just indulgent, angst-ridden fantasies.

And there are stories that don't alter the basic events but still revel in angst. They linger on the things that the comic series glosses over, that I myself try to forget. The nightmares and sleepless nights after the O-shoran Disaster, the faces of all those we couldn't save. The traumas and wounds that each one of us hold. The despair as we've watched world after world fall to the Darkness. The helpless rage of seeing what we once loved destroyed. There are fics that are just thousands and thousands of words that are only there to depict us all sobbing, in grief and in pain.

What the *fuck*, Jenna. Why do they want to hurt us this way? The canonical *Secret Guardians* is better; it skims past all this to get to the plot, the action. Moving forward. That's what our Masters taught us at the Academy: to swallow pain down, get a temporary mind-erasure if needed. To keep going.

***

Crack Fics

The wind and wolf howls have stopped. It's so quiet.

There's only the snow falling outside . . .

Prince Ko must know where we are by now, don't you think? Word must have reached him. We should check the defenses again; he'll be here by morning . . .

No, I'm fine, I told you. I'm not feverish. Well, I don't feel feverish.

Honestly, I've inhaled death dust before, and this scratch on my chest is nothing. I've been exposed to so much death dust on this world that I'm probably immune; my titers are sky high. The doctors can make a study of me when we get back.

What were we talking about again?

Oh, my report. Those papers you found. The fanfics.

There are "crack" fanfics that are wild, Jenna. Cross-over AUs where they put us in worlds where ponies talk and have magical adventures, where robots disguise themselves as ground transport vehicles, where there are unicorns and mafia battles and terrifying cephalopods from space. There were fics I couldn't understand at all and ones so disturbing I wished for a mind-erase after. None of these fics were relevant, and I soon learned to filter them out.

So many different fics, Jenna. I made a list, sorted them into categories. Most of them mean nothing at all.

But people are thinking of us. Some of their thoughts are truly depraved. But . . . they're thinking of us. A woman wrote down our story, and people read it. They want more.

***

Fix-it Fics

These are my favorites.

These are the fics where the bad things never happened. Where the story still takes place in our universe, but the universe took a different turn.

Where Ratha's father wasn't trash, where he didn't turn to the Darkness and try to force his son to do the same. Where Ratha wasn't maimed by his own brother, hurt by his own family. Because he grew up in a completely different family, even though they bore the same name. And he came to us at the Academy still sweet-faced and shy but with a sense of self-worth, an inner steadiness, which he never possessed in real life.

There are fics where none of us have been hurt. Where all of us have known only kindness. Where the time-threads run backward, and the very fabric of the universe bends. There's a fic where Master Ahn builds a time travel machine (impossible, of course), and a me-from-the-future warns us all of the attack on the Luminous Pearl, and so that beautiful world—the Academy's home, our sector's heart—is not lost. Millions never die in the attack, and millions more aren't lost during the frantic evacuation. All our teachers are alive, and all the students who came behind us. The original Academy still stands where it did for a thousand standard cycles: white and shining on the pearl-dusted cliffs above a dark blue sea.

There are fics where no world ever fell. Where the Darkness never returned; it was truly defeated eons ago, just as we'd thought. And we're still the guardians of ten thousand shining worlds, and there's still the lesser darkness of human hearts that can never be uprooted, but the threats we face are manageable. We keep the Gates open, we work to spread light and knowledge, we travel the worlds, and we're happy.

There's a fic where I visit your home-world with you. I once promised that I'd do so, and now it's too late. But nothing is too late in a fix-it fic. In this story, your parents and sisters are alive, and I meet them. I sit at your family table, and we eat the spiced stews and sweet fruits that you've boasted of. I pet your striped cat, whom you've had since you were a child. We wander through the famous outdoor markets, and you laugh as I clumsily bargain in your native tongue. It's a festival day, and everyone is wearing garlands of white flowers, so I buy garlands for us both. At sunset we take a sky-boat to the Floating City above, and we watch the cloud-towers glow crimson and gold, then fade to lavender and blue with the dusk.

Jenna, if I were the writer of a fix-it fic, we wouldn't be here now. We wouldn't be shivering in this outpost at the end of the world. Maybe we'd be on your home world, or on mine. Somewhere warm, without winter.

If this were a fix-it fic, I would have seen into Prince Ko's deceptions. I wouldn't have relied so heavily on reports; I should have known there was a way to circumvent our truth tests. I would have looked past his pretty face. He reminds me of Jin, you know? That irreverence and humor and charm, with that seeming earnestness beneath. Is that why I was caught off guard?

In a fix-it fic, Jin's still alive. He didn't die trying to reach his doomed world. And Ratha never gave in to despair; he's alive and safe, too. Tal and Angel didn't die alongside Masters Neru and Ahn and half our other colleagues, defending the Jade Sector.

They're all alive, everyone we ever loved and countless more as well. The Darkness is not growing. It is not overthrowing human hearts and swallowing star systems whole. And you and I are not in charge of the barely trained kids sleeping in the back room because those kids are still in school studying at the original Academy and maybe playing innocent pranks and throwing the occasional underground party.

In a fix-it fic, there aren't even any such things as ghost-wolves. This planet's Dark Lord shouldn't be able to raise an army of the dead; I thought we'd eliminated that trick *long ago*. What the hell?

In a fix-it fic, I would have done so many things differently. I would fix so much.

One Time, It Was Canon

I'm rambling. You used to hate it when I rambled like this: you always wanted me to get to the point. You've always been one to go straight to the heart . . .

Why did it take us so long to meet up again, Jenna? How did we let so much time pass?

Maybe I'm a little feverish from the death dust after all. But I metabolize it quickly; I'll be okay. Don't worry.

Don't worry. *Please.*

You're right: I should get some rest now. And so should you.

But there's something I have to say first. There's a question I haven't answered. It's a question that I know you've had since you first found that stack of fics. And I've been circling around it and babbling because I'm a coward and a fool. And you've let me.

Jenna, let me tell you one last thing about the fanfics I've read.

On Earth, it's common for fanfiction writers to "ship" characters. That means to write them into romantic relationships, no matter what their relationships are in canon. So, you'll get wild ships between characters who barely know each other, or who would never in all the potential timelines of any universe ever think of one another like that.

And sometimes you'll get ships between characters who maybe do think of each other like that.

On Earth's digital forums, the characters of *Secret Guardians* have been shipped together in every possible combination, in pairs and in threesomes and more. Jin gets shipped with everyone. So does Ratha. Tal and Angel as a pair are especially popular; they're a canon couple, after all. They've been so since our Academy days.

You and I are a popular ship, too.

I didn't write the stories you found. But there's a reason I kept them. There's a seed of truth in each one.

I love you, Jenna. It's canon.

It's canon, and I'm a coward for taking this long to say it. All the cycles that have passed between us—more than twenty standard cycles in all. Enough for several generations of Academy students to graduate. Knowing each other at school, then coming together again for training and missions, the occasional holiday. Parting each time. Losing touch. But I always thought of you, I swear, even when I went a cycle in silence.

I think I haven't stopped thinking of you since the day we met long ago. I think I loved you then at first sight: this thin, wild-haired girl with the impatient air and intense gaze. The girl who knew all the answers in class before anyone else, who wasn't afraid to argue with the most intimidating of Masters. Whose stern look could melt suddenly into a smile that felt like the touch of sunlight itself. Even when you seemed to hate me, I wanted to see that smile. I wanted to hear your laugh.

I'm such a fool for not saying any of this earlier.

No, you don't have to say anything. Don't. I just had to tell you, that's all, because I don't want to be the version of myself in one of the worst angsty fics I read, who remained a coward to the end and died without saying anything, and let you die, too, without knowing. Because this might really be the end now. Prince Ko will be here in the morning with his ghost army. When they're done with us, he and his Dark Lord will move on to smash the Gate that's hidden here. And another world will fall to the Darkness.

Jenna, I don't know if this is the end of everything. All the universes may fall. There's a world in a far sector that's still free, but they're in danger, too. And they're telling our story there; they might be telling of this very moment in a cycle or two. I want them to tell the truth when they do. I want to get this part, at least, right.

I love you. I love you. You've made my life better. And it's worth everything—all the wasted time, all the heartache and horror and death dust and frostbite and all the ghosts and demons of this frozen world and every other world—to be with you again, here. To work with you one last time. To see you and just breathe the same air as you. To feel the touch of your hand.

Oh gods, you're crying. And I'm crying, too.

Jenna, it was worth living just to know you.

You don't have to feel the same; it's okay if we—

What?

Oh.

You do.

It's so dark and still. It feels like we're the only ones left on this world.

But the ghost-wolves are out there. Prince Ko will wait for them to fade away with the dawn. Only then will he move against us.

We still have several hours left. We'll check the defensive spells again. We'll harden them as much as we can. We'll rally the kids in the back room. We'll do what it takes to survive.

My fever is gone; I told you I metabolize dust quickly. Go ahead and take my bio-readings. I'm as clear-minded as I've ever been.

Jenna, I was fine with dying, but I'd rather live. I want to live with you.

Oh gods, your smile. It's been so long since I've seen you smile like this. Do you even know how beautiful you are?

If we get through this I promise: I'll never leave your side again. I don't care if it's the darkest of Dark Lords standing against us or all the Masters of the new Academy. I mean it.

I know that our chances are bad. Almost nil, probably. But in a distant world, someone is telling our story. I don't know what it means; I don't know if any of my research on bleed-throughs means a damn thing. But our story isn't over yet, and they're waiting for the next installment. Jenna, whatever happens when the sun rises—let's give them something to write about.

Once on a Midsummer's Night

A midsummer night, full moon overhead. Its golden light is ancient and worn. A breeze sighs through forest and over stone, bringing the echo of laughter. The song of a zither seems threaded in the wind. A boy stands outside a crumbling gate, and his face is of one lost in a dream. Slowly, he steps forward.

We have been waiting for him. For centuries, we've been waiting.

A sudden burst of scent—roses and jasmine and night-blooming lilies. Laughter again, and the sound of running water.

Behind the stone gate, life has returned to our garden.

The garden has a hundred names, and a thousand tales are told of it. The Dead Garden, the Ghost Garden, Winter's Home. The Ruined Place, the Haunted Place, Sorrow's Ground. For decades at a time, nothing grows here; nothing moves. "Ghost Garden" is a misnaming. Even ghosts do not stir in this bare, dead place.

Until now.

Now memories wake, and water runs again in ancient fountains and streambeds. Lotus ponds fill, and fat fish move beneath lush lotus leaves. Fireflies wink in the darkness. The earth smells of rain and life. The air is perfumed with freshly bloomed flowers, and white moths flutter among the damp petals.

The boy steps through the gate. He takes his first steps on the path.

Faintly, music plays—harp strings, a flute. He doesn't remember the tune.

We remember. We are made of almost nothing but memories.

Far from this garden—past this valley and the foot of these mountains—lies a great blasted plain. There, nothing grows, and nothing ever will. There, the rain never falls. Green ghost fires burn at night. Wind scatters the smell of ashes long gone.

Hell itself once opened up on that plain.

Fire, burning everything away. Endless screams echoing still. Tens of thousands of men killed in an instant.

Legends speak still of the one responsible. A cursed and vengeful lord, the king of hell itself. A demonic god without remorse.

The boy who wanders through our garden now knows nothing of this.

He's only a child, perhaps barely thirteen. A farmer's son, dressed in rough-woven hemp, straw sandals on his feet. He's never seen fountains or roses. Or smelled such an array of exotic blooms. His eyes are wide with wonder.

Music floats from the shadows. Unseen fingers dance over pipes and strings. Silvery bells chime. Notes shape themselves from throats without breath, and lyrics in a language long dead are sung again.

The boy stops, listening.

We listen, too, and remember summer nights under a young, white moon.

Lanterns strung up throughout the garden. Feet dancing lightly on grass. The swirl of silks under a pavilion. Wine cups set floating in a little stream, to be delivered directly to the hands of waiting guests.

A young lord and lady presiding over the festivities together.

They are the centerpiece of the scene—of every scene. The fairest flowers of the garden. Poets from afar sing of the curve of the lady's dark eyes, the arch of her brows, the grace of her figure. Painters dream of capturing the lord's noble lines, the bones of his face, his luminous gaze.

Hear their bright laughter and see how the crowd presses in on them: friends, family, officials, and guests from the valley and beyond. See the warmth of their smiles and gazes, the joy they take in their companions. But see also how they constantly turn toward one another, how their eyes meet, how her wrist brushes his side and his hand grazes her waist.

The lantern lights halo them, flatter them. See how the golden glow caresses cheek and shining black hair. See how the moon itself follows them.

They lead a toast, to cheerful shouts from all. They dance together under the pavilion. And it's as though they are dancing alone in the crowd. He stares at her as though she is the moon itself come down from the sky to sway in his arms. She gazes at him as though he is every light in the world.

Our lady and lord, married nearly a year and still struck with wonder in each other's presence.

Their court loves them. Their guests love them.

We loved them.

The boy crosses bridges arching over flowing streams and lakes. Lanterns blaze along the bridge railings. Lights shine in pavilions in the distance.

For this night, the garden is again alight.

The dust of ages is gone. Crumbling wood and stone, faded paint and tiles —all is restored, all gleams again. Bridges and galleries, arbors and pavilions and great palace halls—all stand proudly intact. Time has slipped.

The boy begins running. His footsteps thud in the night.

There are other footsteps, always just around the corner. Just out of sight. Voices speaking words he can't quite catch. Music that comes and goes, melodies drawn from the deepest of dreams.

He has been here so many times before.

But will he remember this time? Will he dare?

We have waited so long. Has it been long enough?

He's reached the first of three islands in the central lake. He turns and looks back at the way he's come.

***

From where the boy stands, he has a perfect view of the Bridge of Hopes. It crosses the lake's narrowest point, near the eastern shore. The soaring bridge's white stones are among the first to feel the touch of the rising sun.

We remember another boy who once stood on that bridge. And the girl who met him there.

***

We remember more than we should. More than living humans can bear.

We know the sprouting of the first seeds to grow in this earth. The first unfurling of stem and leaf. The spread of raindrops through soil, the shifting of dirt, the burrowing paths of ants and beetles and worms. The taste of sunlight in every season.

Long ago, a prince met a girl on this bridge. They were children, still looking at the world with fresh eyes. "Is it true, what they say?" our young lord said to our Lady. "That this garden has been here forever?"

She looked into his eyes and smiled.

***

In a tiny stone shrine, there sits a cup of hot tea. It is brewed only once in a lifetime. The boy of this present time finds it. He kneels down before it. The light of a red lantern shines on his innocent face, his large, black eyes.

He drinks.

***

We know the stories of the greater world. Even in our sleep, the wind visits and whispers and blows dead leaves over the garden walls. We feel the tread of human steps from miles away. And when we wake, rain brings stories of waterdrops' journeys from river to cloud and air.

The Demon Lord, people still mutter. *The Lord of Hell. The Accursed, the Annihilator.* A story told still in fear and dread, in wonder and awe.

We knew him before he bore any of those names.

His first full day here, a princeling arrived from the capital. A child waking before dawn, creeping from the guest quarters where his parents lay sleeping. He ran to the central lake, eager to see the truth of one of the many legends he'd heard.

The grass wet beneath his silk slippers. The world gray under the shadow of the high mountain peak and a slowly lightening sky.

He leaned over the bridge railing, staring, waiting. Color spilled over the hills and into the world, reds and golds spreading over water and sky. The lake was a flat sheet of fire. He squinted and shielded his eyes, and finally looked away. A flash. And then the sun was fully up, and the sky was blue and birds were singing, and white clouds floated in the water.

Something else was reflected in the water, too. "Did you see anything?" the girl beside him asked.

"No." He turned his head. He'd neither seen nor heard her coming. She was about his own age, around twelve or thirteen. She wore simple robes, and her hair was unbound, falling like a dark waterfall over her shoulders.

"Did *you* see anything?" he asked. "Why are we the only ones here? Doesn't anyone else come? Is it always like this? Is it true?"

"People don't like getting up early." She shrugged. "I thought that I saw something, but I'm not sure . . ." Her voice trailed off. They stared at one another.

Midsummer morn. One of the legends of the Eternal Garden: that if you watch from the Bridge of Hopes on this day, at the moment of sunrise, you might see your future reflected in the lake below.

A ripple in the water, from frog or fish. The lake stilled again. The children's reflections were also still, staring at each other.

The boy suddenly remembered his manners. He bowed, and she did the same. They introduced themselves: the visitor and the girl who lived here, who we already knew as our Lady.

He was not the only one to grieve. We missed her, too, and miss her still.

He is not the only one who would set the world aflame, who would tear and destroy and turn the earth to winter in reaction to pain.

But he was one of the few with the power to do so.

The boy in the shrine drinks his tea. We kneel alongside him and taste the bitterness on his tongue. We have been here so many times before.

A rush of memories. The child closes his eyes. We remember alongside him.

Happiness. Heartache. Then joy again.

Long ago, a child came to the Garden on a visit with his family. As relations and representatives of the King, they had business with many parts of the country. But of all the places he had seen and would see, the boy would love this place the most.

He was of royal blood and blessed with talent. But also of relatively little relevance in the great political schemes of his day. The youngest son of the youngest son of the King's third half brother. He was allowed to stay and study for a time with the teachers of the Garden. And though his family resisted at first, he was eventually allowed to marry into it—to give up his name and family for a home far from the capital and great centers of power. To marry the heir of a family with its own power, but also with its own closed traditions and loyalties and vows.

The Lady had to convince her own elders, too.

They had been separated for years when he returned to her on the cusp of summer. He had ridden ahead of the rest of the wedding party. It was late afternoon, the sun slanting low through the trees. She stood waiting for him just outside the gates. When he saw her smile, he caught his breath—and there was a moment in which he could not move at all.

The Garden tries to keep itself apart. But no walls can keep out the world forever.

War in the North. An internal rebellion, and then an invasion across borders. The fall of the capital city. Hundreds of thousands uprooted, fleeing for their lives. Bodies lay unburied in fields. Blood flowed into streams and rivers.

News came by rider and messenger birds. Our young lord opened the letters with trembling hands. He learned that most of his birth family was dead, his surviving brothers on the run.

Our Lady did not argue when he asked to be released from his vows. When he asked to leave our home in the mountains, this remote place of safety, to join his brothers in war.

We know every person who set foot on our grounds.

We knew the first to come after the gods touched this land, the heart of the valley. We welcomed those who came to gather root and herb and fruit and fish. Who stayed to plant and tend and build.

We knew those of power, both born to power and able to channel it. Those who could draw upon the elemental forces of the world and hear the spirits and gods most clearly. Teachers and masters, and lords and ladies who commanded from palace halls and slept on sheets of fine-woven silk. And we knew the ones who changed and washed those sheets.

We knew the craftsmen who built the bridges and fountains, the viewing platforms and courtyards and covered arcades. We knew those who dug and terraced and tilled. We know those who worked in the kitchens: the head chef dreaming of new recipes, the staff shelling beans, the strong-armed women pounding roots and kneading dough.

The woman who pruned the roses. The children throwing food to the fish and splashing in the ponds and lakes.

We knew the poets and artists and musicians. We knew the women sweeping the shrines. The people harvesting grain in the fields. The teachers of each new generation. We knew all who tended to life, who planted and planned and fed and cut and gathered, who grew and loved and cared.

We knew those who watched the borders, who set the wards, who tried to protect us.

A young boy staggers away from a tiny stone shrine, the bitterness of a rare tea still harsh on his tongue.

He has come to us for centuries now. Once in every lifetime.

He's come to us as a beggar in tattered rags. He's come as an old man leaning on his walking stick. He's come ill and feverish, covered in sores, crawling and near to death's door. He's come arrayed in finery, a man in the prime of life: a prosperous merchant, a celebrated philosopher, even a prince once again.

He's come as a young adventurer, and an explorer, curious about the dead garden in a remote mountain valley.

He's never come to us so young before.

As young as that other who once stepped through our gates.

For the first time in several centuries, we feel real hope.

The boy walks a familiar path through the heart of the Garden. He finds a second shrine and a second cup of tea. Midsummer Eve's moon is at its highest point.

There is power flowing freely tonight. Spirits awake and singing. Old promises humming in the air.

There are also other powers in the world. And darker gods than the ones we knew.

We watched our lord ride away, and the stories trickled back to us over the next half decade. Stories of the invaders' depravities, of fields and cities burned, of ruthless slaughter and oppression. Of a Kingdom torn apart and quarrels among its own shattered ranks. Stories of our lord's heroism, of how he was working with his family to unite the remnants of the North. Of how armies flocked to his banner, of how tireless he was, how determined and brilliant, how inspiring and brave and kind. Of how thousands shouted his name, of how the countryside rose up for him, of how his soldiers would gladly die for him.

The legends grew: that he had access to all the powers of the Eternal Garden and more besides. That he did not need to sleep, that he could not feel pain, that he could disappear from sight and reappear in two places at once. That he wreathed his army in an obscuring, protective fog as they marched, and silenced the sounds of footsteps and breath. That he was able to command weather, that he could direct lightning and wind, that he spoke to bird and beast and could send his voice across miles. That he was blessed by the gods, their favored son. That he spoke directly to them.

We saw the letters that he wrote to our Lady. She untied them from the feet of purring messenger birds. Interspersed between news of politics and war, he wrote of sunlight on red maples, mist on a river, far mountains that made him homesick for the mountains he knew. He wrote of strange plants and a rare orchid he'd seen, of how he wished he could bring it back to her. He wrote her love poems.

She wrote back, of course. She opened the doors to her room and played her zither at night, sending the music out to him on the wind. And when wind and moon and mind and heart were perfectly attuned, they heard each other's voice across the miles.

When they were only sixteen, years before marriage, they'd pledged their souls to one another. On the banks of a lake, they wove together green willow branches. Years later, when he left for war, she snapped off part of a fresh willow branch for him to take. He carried it against his heart, where it stayed fresh and green throughout the miles.

In a wooden shrine, a child's eyes go empty.

A cup drops from his hand.

In later years, people would revise the stories they'd once told of our lord. Some would say that early on, even during those first years of war, he must have already had dealings with darkness. That he must have already made demonic sacrifices and bargained away his soul for vengeance. How else did he rise from nearly nowhere, this callow, untested young man, to number among the great generals of the North? How else did he so easily win powerful allies to his side? He took back city after city, province after province. He led the push into the old capital itself.

On the road to the capital, he walked into a trap.

He lost half his army. He nearly died.

Some say this was when he made his secret bargain. While his body burned with fever from an infected wound, and his mind wandered the borderlands between life and death. He'd seen the enemies' might, the new weapons and power they'd attained. He saw that might displayed again and again in his dreams. He caught glimpses of a hopeless future, all the Kingdom crushed beneath the wheels of war engines and the iron hooves of giant war beasts. All flattened, all burned, all turned to ash. The old gods were silent. A dark god called out to him instead, and in his mind, he responded.

Others say that it was not until much later that he turned to Hell's powers. Not until the Southern realms were invaded. Not until the Garden itself was at risk.

Some say his decision was made when he woke from his wound fever, when he opened his eyes from nightmares. He was lying in a clean bed, bandaged, safe. Sunlight poured in through an open window. Our Lady was there, her eyes upon him tender and bright, her hand in his. He saw her face, and in that moment, he knew all that he had to lose.

We have lost so much, too.

We wake and relive our loss again and again.

We did not deserve this.

We are awake now, and we watch as a child leaves a wooden shrine, his drained cup still lying upturned on the floor. His shoulders are bowed, his steps heavy and slow. His eyes far older than the mortal years he's seen.

The Eternal Garden had survived the rise and fall of dynasties. It tried to keep itself apart from the rest of the world. Its leaders paid tribute to whoever held the title of King or Queen; they did what was necessary to stay at peace in the nation. The Garden's leaders—*our* leaders—did whatever they could to keep us safe.

The war roared on. A tide had turned, and now the front pushed ever southward. Ahead of the armies, ordinary people fled with nothing but the clothes on their skin and the children in their arms. Each day brought new tales of hunger and chaos, cruelty and despair. And rumors of the enemy's dark powers: the engines they rode, the sorceries they commanded, the foreign gods that gave them strength.

Stay safe, our lord wrote. In every letter to his beloved, said in a dozen different ways, and not all quite out loud: *Don't work too hard. Take care of yourself and our people. Keep the Garden and yourself well. Stay safe, and I can continue to live.*

On a moonlit night, a boy enters a third shrine on a third island on a still, shining lake. This last shrine is made of earth and dug into a small hillside. He can only just stand up within. A third cup of tea waits for him on the altar. He stares at it for a long time before touching it.

Our lord did change. Those stories are true. We saw it in his rare visits home. We saw it through our Lady's eyes.

His strength became ever greater, even as the enemy's power also increased. He learned to wield fire. With a sweep of his arm, he set enemy encampments ablaze. He exploded their own munitions from hundreds of yards away. He melted flesh and steel.

He had long ago learned to ignore human screams.

He had seen too much. Friends and comrades dying before him. The deaths of the last of his brothers. The mutilated corpses left by the enemy in ravaged towns and cities. The countless numbers that he himself had killed.

In dreams, he saw the bodies of his parents and brothers and sisters hanging from the gates of the lost capital in the North. That first great attack, which he never saw.

We saw our Lady's fear. Fear of the fire she saw eating him from within. The rage and pain beneath the coldness. The power that he had taken in, but which he could only just contain.

She played her zither and sang to him across the miles, seeking to soothe the flames.

The green willow branch that she'd given him was long gone, withered and dropped somewhere in the long miles between them.

Our Lady, too, was near breaking. We saw it when no one else did. War brought waves of refugees even into the Garden's valley, and our Lady did all she could to share our resources, to feed and house and protect us all. She spent hours in council with elders and leaders; she spent her power healing those injured in body and mind.

She prayed at the oldest shrines.

Power. So many different powers in the world: power of earth and wood and stone. Power of living things, growing things, and things that have died and feed new life.

She drew on all these and more.

Our Lady made plans to send our forces down from the mountains.

No, he said, but she was as stubborn as he. And he knew that she was right. The Garden could not always keep itself apart.

Our forces joined the war. They were there on that great plain when armies clashed.

Before battle, our Lady and lord walked through the Garden again, hand in hand. A tender calmness on both their faces. They lay together in a private spot under the willow trees. He ran his fingers through her silken hair. She caught his hand in hers. Afterward, she sang to him softly, her eyes still closed, resting against the rise and fall of his breath. They breathed in together. Under the dancing leaf shadows, their hearts were at peace.

They raised a great mist before they left. A thick, obscuring fog over the mountains, over the valley, hiding the Garden. One last defense, in case they never came back. One last attempt at protection for those of us left behind.

It is Midsummer Eve's night, and with a last cup of tea, a boy faces his final memories.

What he never told her, what he never told anyone: that he knew he could lose control. That he knew what he could be: a weapon greater than any seen in his lifetime. A weapon without discrimination. He could become fire itself: the heat of the sun, the force of the lightning. An explosion ten thousand times greater than anything the enemy could achieve with all their sorceries and firepowder. He could burn down the world. All he had to do was lose control, to give himself up to a hungry god. All he had to do was lose all mercy, all humanity, to give up his soul itself.

As a soft dusk fell, a messenger bird came to the Garden with news: a temporary truce on the battlefield. Heavy casualties on both sides, but more damage taken by the enemy. A pause to exchange captives and care for the dead.

Seconds later came the second message, written in fire in the sky.

The truth of that day is still known only in fragments. Even to the boy in the shrine tonight. We watch him shudder with memories.

A few last messages sent from the battlefield. A handful of witnesses from the field itself. The few who stood closest to our Lady and lord, who were protected by the instinctive shield that he raised up around them before the blast.

Minutes before: our Lady and lord walking with others to the parley. The arrow from high above. The arrow that came from above and behind, from our lord's own army fortifications. From within his own ranks. A streak of shadow, a missile of ice metal, shaped and targeted to our fire lord himself.

She sensed it even as the archer took aim. With inhuman speed, she pushed her beloved aside and reached out with all her power to deflect—

He fell, then rose to his feet. He ran. He knelt over her, keening. The ruin of her chest. The blood soaking his hands, his clothes, as he held her. The black ice arrow, a metal whose shaping was known only to the enemy.

On the walls above, fellow soldiers had already seized hold of the traitor assassin.

Silence below, save for the sound of our lord's sobbing. Those closest to them frozen in shock. A moment in which time seemed suspended.

And then everything exploded.

We saw the fire in the sky. We felt the earth shake.

And then our lord came to us with our Lady in his arms, the mist defenses of the Garden torn away, useless. He flew to us on wings of fire. He took her to the center of the Garden and knelt with her there.

And then he brought the cold.

He did not know what he was doing. He was lost to grief and rage.

But he still killed us.

He knelt over her body, and the fire around them dwindled and failed. Now it was cold that spread out from them. Cold from where his knees touched the earth. Cold that seeped deep, deep into the soil, freezing it and all the air pockets between; cold that found and froze each root and root hair, that stilled the hearts of the tiny creatures that wriggle and dig through the earth.

Cold that spread above ground as well.

Within halls and houses, people started as floors froze underfoot. As the air suddenly sharpened like knives. A child playing in the lotus pond yelped, jerking her foot from the water just as it turned to ice. There was the sound of shattering as iced tree branches began to break, as pipes and fountains burst. The cold spread and birds lifted into the sky, seeking escape. At the edges of the Garden, people, too, tried to run, the blood already slowing in their veins .

. .

The lakes froze solid, from bottom to top. No living thing moved. A deathly stillness. And now mist began to steam from the iced ponds and lakes, pools and streams, as the frozen water evaporated directly into the air. And the air itself dried out, all moisture gone. The ponds and lakes were emptied. The trees all bare. The Garden a frozen desert, squeezed of all life, hard as stone.

In the center of it all, as everything died: our Lady and lord, so pale and still. Our Lady already dead, and our lord dying inside. The ice arrow still in her chest. Her blood splashed red on his chest and arms, the only color in a colorless world. His grief mixing with known and unknown sorceries and powers, killing us all.

We froze and dried and died along with them. We crumbled and blew away like autumn leaves.

It has been a thousand years.

We have watched our lord come back in lifetime after lifetime. Cycle after cycle, another attempt to expiate his sins, to understand and atone.

To work through his fate.

We are revived each time, his silent witnesses.

We are still angry after a thousand years.

He swore to defend us. He vowed never to leave us, to always protect us. He left with our Lady's blessings. But he was not released from the other half of his vow.

It is midsummer night, and he weeps now in a dark, earthen shrine. He's a child again but bent to the ground with the weight of sins from another life-time. His shoulders shake silently, and his anguish bleeds into the night.

The last cup of tea is gone. But this night is not over.

After a while, he crawls from the shrine, compelled to finish his journey. He gets to his feet and sways. We catch him. His lips move, his eyes unseeing. We hold him and give him the last memories he'll have for this night.

Our own.

We are the spirits of the garden. We were born when the gods touched this land. We were here when the first seeds sprouted, when the lakes first filled, when the first people came to shape and tend us.

We remember everything.

We remember the boy who came to our Garden, a stranger. We remember the first time he stepped through our gates, his parents beside him. His eyes so bright and curious, his smile like sunlight. His heart an open field.

And we remember our Lady. He loved her, but we loved her first. We knew her first. We knew her from birth, just as we knew her parents before her, and their parents before them, and all her family and line. We knew her as a child learning to walk, falling and giggling in the grass. Picking flowers and sneaking cakes from the kitchen before supper. Slowly learning to hear the heartbeat of the land, the pulse of sap, the song of water and wind in the trees. Slowly learning to hear *us*. We rejoiced as she grew stronger, as she reached out to us. We were there for all the small triumphs and rebellions of her childhood, her pranks and quarrels with teachers and family. Her friendships and joys. Her loneliness as an orphan whose parents died when she could barely remember them. Her loneliness as heir to the leadership of the Garden. We watched her grow up. We watched her fall in love.

We were there when he wasn't. We saw her leading her people confidently by day, hiding her vulnerability and fear. We saw her in her bedchamber at night, wiping away tears. Grieving and afraid for herself, and her beloved, and the world.

She, too, was our sunlight and water.

And we loved all the children of the Garden, all that we knew. Those born with power and those without. Those who could hear and speak with us, and those who heard only faintly. The noble-born children, and the cook's son sneaking cakes with our Lady in the kitchen. The woman pruning roses. The girl weaving in her room. The toddler chasing ducks by the lake. The boy sweeping marble steps, and composing in his mind a song for his love.

The ones who left for war. The ones who stayed to guard us.

The last residents of the Garden. The last generation.

The boy with us tonight knew them, too, but we show them again to him through our eyes. Everything that he missed while he was away. Everything that he missed even while he was here. The lives he knew only in passing. Scenes known only to a few, or to none at all. The multitude of lives that no human could know in full. We knew them—each private story, each struggle and heartache and triumph and joy.

We are the Garden, and each life here has left us an echo of its soul. We know them in full. We carry them all: the memories, the soul imprints, of all our children.

Save for two.

Far from this garden—past the forests, past the valley and the foot of these mountains—lies a great plain. It, too, is a desert.

A thousand years ago, hell itself erupted on a battlefield. Nearby towns and villages were turned to dust. A river evaporated. Ashes rained down for days.

Two armies burned alive. A hundred thousand dead, including innocents miles from the battlefield. The worse fate was for those who didn't instantly die.

Some of the dead were ours.

Their hearts melted in fire. Against their hearts, each had worn some memento from the Garden. A garland of jasmine flowers. A single orchid. A bundle of sweet herbs. A frond of willow leaves.

The moon is sinking toward the horizon.

Our lord has fallen to his knees yet again.

Remember, we whisper to him. *Remember.*

For once, let him accept the weight of all he did. For once, let it be enough for the gods.

The day that he first left us for war, our Lady gave him a branch of willow leaves. An old custom of the Garden.

The day that our army left our gates for the last time, the willows near the Bridge of Hopes were visibly shorn on one side. So many willow branches had been broken off, given as gifts of farewell.

All has changed in the outer world. But they still tell his story.

The nation we knew has broken and reformed, again and again, as war sweeps the land. States join and dissolve; empires fall. The name of a lost, ancient kingdom is spoken in strange accents and tongues.

He was a prince possessed by a demon god, some say. *He lost control.*

Others say: *He himself was a demon god in disguise, come to earth to punish and destroy.*

In the most common telling, it was he who broke the truce, who came to parley with dishonorable intent. He gambled with dark powers to win a war. He killed his own people and lost his soul.

Only among some is a different tale told. A minor variation, told in the mountains of the South. *It started as a love story*, this other tale says.

He did, indeed, give up his soul.

But she had pledged her soul to his. Their souls were joined. From the moment they met, and then again and again, as they consciously promised themselves to one another. The weaving of two willow branches into a single wreath. Two hearts singing each to each. Our Lady's prayers.

His soul is mine, our Lady declared to the God of Death when she met Him. *I cannot go on to the afterlife, nor be reborn on Earth, without him.*

The great Gods of Death and Life met and looked at her, and conferred.

So be it, they agreed.

In every lifetime, he finds his way to us. He has been given a chance to redeem his soul and, with it, hers as well.

Three times he drinks the tea that restores the memories of past lives. He makes a circuit of the oldest shrines of the Garden.

He remembers his past life. And then he's asked to remember more.

He's on the ground now, hands over his ears as though to block out screams. His eyes are closed, and he moans.

The weight of all the lives that he took in one day. All those memories, all that hope and fear and pain. A burden that doesn't even include the lives of those we didn't know, the enemies and strangers who also died.

It is too much for one person. Too much, even for our great Hero Prince, the Uniter of the Nation, the Savior of the Kingdom, the Demon Lord, the Cursed One, the Lord of Hell.

Too much, too much, and yet it must be borne—

We have been bearing it. All these long years.

Our lord sits up. He jolts to his feet.

There is one last cup at the end of this path, just where it connects to the final bridge. There, a hooded figure in the gray raiment of the Underworld stands and holds that last cup in their hands.

A cup of clear liquor to take away all memory again.

The boy starts toward this figure, trembling. The moon has nearly set. The sun will soon rise.

If only we can stop him. If only we could ever stop him. If he could only hold on a bit longer until the sun rises—

We are angry. The rage of all our memories scream.

The weaver girl breaking a willow branch for her beloved. The cook's son grown and walking with his love beneath wisteria blooms. A mother keening in her room, bent double in grief for lost children. A boy standing frozen on marble steps, the broom dropped from his hand, holding a letter announcing the death of his lover in war.

Our lord was not the only one to lose his beloved. He was not the only one to love fiercely, with all his heart. He was not the only one who would have set the world on fire, who would have turned the Earth to winter in response to loss.

He was merely the only one with the power to do so.

We loved her. We loved her. And we loved him, too.

An hour to dawn. No sound but the sobbing gasps of a child stumbling blindly forward so that he might forget again.

No, we cry to him. *Stay with us. Remember with us.*

Stay.

Stay this one time, if you can.

He stops. He turns his head.

There was another voice that called when we called. Another voice that was somehow also part of us, added to us.

We carry the echoes of all the souls who ever lived in the Garden. Their thoughts, memories, feelings. But now we feel the true souls returning.

Souls who knew both our lord and Lady. Souls who loved them both and died.

The aunts and uncles who cared for our Lady and who took our lord under their care when he arrived as a child. The teachers who saw their blazing talents and encouraged and helped shape what they saw. Their elders and mentors. Their peers and playmates and friends. The people they taught and mentored in turn, the people our Lady healed from injury or illness. The councilors, the guards, the people of their household, the ones who worked with them day in and day out. And those who knew them only from afar but saw their essential decency and goodness and rejoiced in the light that followed them both.

Those souls are here now.

And something shifts in the burden we carry.

Our lord stands frozen on the path, tears slipping down his cheeks.

Lost souls have returned. And the weight we bear lessens.

In a thousand years, all can change.

Stories are rewritten. Minor gods and spirits rise and fall, along with mortal kingdoms. Things of beauty and light are destroyed. And the descendants of those we called our enemy, and the descendants of those who fought against them, live peacefully together, bloodlines inextricably entwined.

Over a thousand years, the last souls of the Garden have all been on their own journeys through rebirth or through the Afterlife beyond.

They are here now, warming and lightening the night.

Our children are here again. We see and hear and feel them. And our lord does, as well.

We see him through their eyes, and we see him again through our own. The innocent child he once was. The broken man he became. The soul who has come to us again and again, struggling and learning with each lifetime.

The boy who came with his parents for a visit and whose heart never left. Who *heard* us. Who stood in a sunlit clearing, eyes closed, reaching out to us. Who sat in our shrines, letting our songs fill his heart.

Who loved our Lady. The two of them laughing and then hushing each other during lessons. Running through the Garden, hand in hand. Whirling dizzily in a field of tulips and then falling silent, listening to us together.

The souls of our other children are here with us now, remembering with us. Reminding us.

He loved us. He loved us all. He risked everything to protect us.

He failed.

There are promises that were broken. Suffering that cannot be redeemed. Horror and pain and betrayal. But there are also promises that may yet be fulfilled.

In the distance, music plays from lit pavilions. The sound of a zither seems threaded in the wind. A yellow moon is falling.

Is this forgiveness? We think of our Lady. We reach out to him, our lost child. And we also let go. Finally, we let go of our bitterness. We hold him, as we hold our other children and as they also hold us. Together, we all bear what can't be borne.

The sun is rising. There is one soul we haven't yet met. The figure standing near the bridge tips back her hood. The test has been passed. She is released, too. And as light in the east flashes, we see for a moment her face. Then the Greater Gods speak, and time dissolves and reforms, and all the world is changed, and we, too, are changed and reborn—

Midsummer morning. Two children stand on an ancient bridge. They are perhaps twelve or thirteen, dressed in the casual clothes of this age. They're both staring into the lake below. The hills around them are green, and the earth smells of fresh rain. By the northern shore, willows sway in a gentle breeze.

"Did you see anything?" the girl asks.

"No." The boy turns to her in surprise. "Did you?"

"I thought that I saw something, but I'm not sure . . ."

They stand a moment in silence, looking again at the water, and then at each other.

"Are you from the village?" the girl asks. She gestures to the west, beyond the crumbling old gates.

The boy nods. "You're not." It's plain enough in her accent. She's not from anywhere in the valley. "Are you with the, the archaeologists?" He pronounces the last word carefully. Curiosity is alight in his large, black eyes.

She grins. "My parents are working on the restoration, yes. Though they're both more gardeners. Landscape designers."

The boy nods, distracted only a little by the way her face flashes with light when she smiles.

"Do you believe it?" she continues. "That if you look at the lake from here at the right time, you can see your future?"

Does he? He's known that legend for as long as he can remember. One of many legends of this ancient place, these ruins that are only now being restored.

"I don't know." He looks again at the water, where the reflections of both of them float dimly. Something about the moment tugs oddly at his memory. He's never known anyone to actually see anything at the midsummer sunrise. Why did he come here, dragging himself so early from bed?

He looks again at the strange girl before him, standing on a bridge in the Eternal Garden, dressed in a plain T-shirt and shorts. Her hair spills over her shoulders like a dark waterfall. Her eyes look into his, waiting for his next words. Suddenly, he feels as though he could tell her anything. Suddenly, he feels as though a door has opened, as though the cover of a new storybook has just been turned, as though something new has begun.

"I don't know if I'd want to see my future in a lake, after all," he says. "I think I'd rather find it out on my own."

An Address to the Newest Disciples of the Lost Words

You are here because you ignored the words of your parents and elders, your more sensible peers. You have thrown away promising careers in sheepherding or law, trade or civil administration. You bribed your way here; you stole money for your passage; you broke promises and made new ones that you never meant to keep. You've sailed rivers and oceans, crossed mountains and plains, and now here you are at the edge of the desert, on the outskirts of a dead city, at the very edge of our known world.

You studied and practiced till your eyes nearly bled. You passed the entrance exam. You sent your last letters home, and now you're robed in your new disciples' clothes, and you think you know what it means to commit.

You think that you'll master the Lost Words.

The Twelfth Word
Anchor: The Wind

One of the easier Words for new disciples to learn. The gestures involved must be fluid and graceful, yet require no special strength or flexibility. The sounds can be reasonably approximated by a standard human voice.

This Word is inherently appealing to many of you.

A flutter of eyelids. A hand pressed to the heart then flung wide. The whisper of the first syllables slowly rising in volume and pitch.

I was a boy of twelve when I first saw/heard/felt this Word. There was a woman at the night market of my hometown, performing Words by the river for free.

The anchor for this Word is wind.

This Word is restlessness coiled deep in the heart. It is a longing without a voice.

It is restlessness gusting aimlessly inside your chest, trapped. It is a gray autumn day, and brown leaves spinning in circles before you. It is treading the same paths from home to school and work, over and over; the same chores, the same tasks, the hammering of hot iron or scrubbing of pots or scratching of notes for your father's account books—all while a wind stirs uneasily in your heart, swirling through your limbs, setting your feet to tapping and threatening to spill out your skin. This Word is what you felt when you kept quiet by the fire as your parents planned out your future, as they spoke of what trade you should follow or who you should marry. This Word is all the stories you ever caught of far-off lands—the tales from traveling merchants, the poet in the square, the old soldier drunk at the inn. It's the horse you saw tied up next door, whinnying and pawing at the ground. It's the sound of geese flying south for the winter. It's music half heard, and an exotic perfume. It's the small voice inside that told you there was more to your life than what others said. This Word is the wind moving over bare hills and fields and into your soul.

I knew this Word before I ever heard it. You did, too.

The woman at the night market performed it beautifully. I stood, enraptured, as she spoke the Word again and again. The crowd around us swelled and shrank; the night grew old. I stood there until my brothers took me by the arms and pulled me away.

On Choosing Your Words

Saint Helabora uncovered eighty-eight Lost Words from the desert. Over the centuries, thirteen more have been added. It is expected that you will attain a basic understanding of them all.

But to master even one may take a lifetime. It may take more: It may be forever beyond your grasp.

I advise you to focus wisely.

It is smart to choose Words that align with your natural talents. For instance, Words Forty through Fifty are particularly suited for those skilled in hand gestures and the graceful movement of arms, while Word Fifty-Three is known for its demanding footwork. A number of Words require vocalization range and techniques beyond the reach of many of you. Some of the middle Words are good for those with naturally tranquil minds and decent breath control.

Choosing a Word beyond your ability only leads to heartbreak.

Even when you focus on a Word within your range, you must be careful. Ambition has destroyed many a disciple. You may know the story of Varas, who fell in love with Word Forty-Four and, determined to improve his technique, attached weights to his fingers and engaged in bending and stretching exercises that destroyed his own hands. Or the tale of Yi La, who dared a dangerous operation to restructure her vocal cords, the better to sing Word Eighty-Seven, and lost her voice.

Innovation and daring are valued, of course. We owe nothing but gratitude to Master Ruel, who invented a series of string instruments to better approximate the sounds required for some higher Words. These instruments brought us closer to the True Speaking, and allowed those Words to be said by those with no inherent vocal ability at all. But Ruel became obsessed with approaching ever closer to perfection and died mad.

Remember to drink water. It's dry here in the desert; those of you from elsewhere often forget. It's so easy to get parched.

On Choosing Your Words: Addendum

You will fall in love with Words, of course, even those far outside your ability to speak. You are already in love with them. That's why you're here.

The Sixteenth Word
Anchor: The Door

The years ahead will be grueling. There will be many times that you wish to give up.

It helps to remember why you came. What Word it was that brought you here. For that, you were willing to leave family and home. For that, you turned away from easier paths. Perhaps you defied a father who, seeing your talent in scholarship and ordinary words, dreamed of how he might use you to increase your family's status and wealth. My own father, a shopkeeper, hoped to install me as a high-ranking agent in our local merchants' guild, or perhaps in service to our provincial governor. He did not expect me to run off to the desert.

But I could not forget the woman speaking the Word that is sometimes known as Wind. And I felt in my being another Lost Word.

The anchor for that other Lost Word is door.

It is a physical door, opening into a hidden room. It is a gate swinging into a secret garden. It is the sensation of a door opening in your heart.

It's what you felt when you first realized that marks on paper could translate to sounds and meaning, to words in your own native tongue. It is the first written word that you recognized. It's the first map you ever saw—all those cities and countries and rivers and mountains, spread out in ink before you. It's the first book you were ever given.

It's the great court astronomer of Hu, Ren Aja, and what he felt when he turned his farseeing lenses to the heavens for the first time and saw stars and planets, and moons around planets, that had never before been seen by mortal man.

It's a key turning in a heavy oak door.

It's a beam of light sliding through curtains into a darkened room.

It's your first understanding that the world—the universe—is so much bigger than you ever imagined.

And with the proper stress and tones, it's a door opening slowly rather than swinging wide all at once. Creaking forward, bit by bit. An agonized journey. The slow, arduous work of mastering your first written script. Of memorizing all eight-thousand characters of the Classical Script. Of slowly mapping a foreign terrain.

I saw a master of Lost Words performing at the night market of my old hometown, and it was a door swinging wide all at once for me. She spoke the word that we refer to as "Wind" in our standard shorthand. But she herself was the "Door."

On Words of Pain

There are Words rarely spoken aloud for an audience. Words that crowds do not clamor for.

There are Words of such pain that no human has spoken them in full, although we have the instructions for doing so. There are Words that would kill with their grief, should any person say them perfectly enough.

Nevertheless, Saint Helabora taught us that all Lost Words are holy, and we seek to comprehend them all.

There are some Words that are gentler in their pain, and these can offer a strange comfort at times. The Words that speak of homesickness, disappointment, melancholy. Calmness after great sorrow. The reminder that all is transient in this mortal world, that all things pass. The Words known by their anchors as: Bare Trees; The Empty, Rain-washed Sky; Shattered Stones; Vanishing Morning Dew.

There were times that I sang Empty, Rain-washed Sky to myself again and again, falling asleep to its images each night. I never came close to mastering this Word. But just repeating its rhythms in my mind brought me comfort. I knew there was a Word for what I felt at that time, that encapsulated all my emotions.

On the Finding of Lost Words

Three centuries ago, Saint Helabora entered the Forbidden City of the Kar Desert. She roamed its underground vaults and penetrated even into the heart of the Labyrinth. She discovered the bronze steles and tablets with their ancient inscriptions.

She studied the scrolls of the buried libraries; she cross-checked their writing with the tablets and steles. And slowly, slowly, she came to understand the written notations and glosses. She learned to read a writing system more complicated than even our Classical Script. And from that she learned, finally, to speak the first of the Lost Words.

It is assumed that divine inspiration also played a role.

We are gathered here in the desert so as to be close to the Ancients, close to where Saint Helabora uncovered miracles. You are welcome to follow her lead and descend into the Forbidden City whenever you wish. You may walk through the libraries, trace her marked steps through the Labyrinth, and even run your fingers over the inscriptions of the First Stele.

Breathe in the inspiration from these physical objects and landmarks. Breathe in their power. You will need it during these first years of training.

Some of you are more inclined to scholarship and research than active speaking. You hope to follow in the footsteps of famous scholars, to expound on novel interpretations of Words. You long to comb through the archives for yourself, and perhaps, in your secret hearts, you even dream of stumbling upon the written instructions for some new Lost Word in a forgotten volume or scroll. You remember our founding saint's words: that in the Ancients' Lost Language, there is a Word for everything in the universe.

I believe this. Though I fear that some Words are indeed forever lost.

You are welcome to prove me wrong.

On Leaving the School of Lost Words

You will leave.

You may not wish to go. But this school cannot keep you all here forever.

Some of you will be lucky enough to find good patrons. Great princes will take you into their courts; they will shower you with silver and praise. Wealthy audiences will clap and cheer for your Words.

Others of you will speak Words for thrown coins at market fairs.

Some of you will try to teach, to pass on the art of Lost Words to others. There are other schools throughout this world, though none as prestigious as this one.

You will struggle to keep the Lost Words alive in your heart. In many places, we're still seen as a strange and possibly blasphemous cult. You will be met with suspicion and misunderstanding, indifference and worship and fear.

I first left the desert thirty-eight years ago. I rejoined the outer world. I did not go happily.

On Failing Your Words

You will fail. You will fail. You will fail.

You will not achieve as much as you want. You will never master all the Words you wish, or in as great a depth as you hope.

The Ninety-First Word
Anchor: Broken Strings

This Word is a musical instrument that cannot play. A harp with broken strings. A flute without breath. Master Rael's greatest creations, all rendered mute.

It's Yi La's beautiful voice, so lovely it was said to surprise the sun and call birds down from the sky—strangled and dead in her throat.

This Word is silence.

It is the wind that once blew through your soul—now thickened into a smothering weight in your chest.

It is a once-sparkling stream that's been damned, that now collects as a black, stagnant pool.

It is a dull ache without relief, a stilled passion with no outlet, a flowing current that's been stopped, a river drained.

This Word is the lost ability to speak Lost Words.

It happens to so many of us. There is no single cause. There is no ready cure.

I spent years in this state. Under its spell, I could not even speak the Lost Word to describe it.

On Finding Your Words Again

If you lose your Words, you will find them again. I promise you this.

Over the course of your years here, you will hone yourself as an instrument. You will learn to speak with sound and gesture, breath and mind.

But your most important instrument is your heart.

Speak each Word with all your heart, and the Lost Words will sink into you. They will take root and become part of you. You can never truly lose them.

As with everything else, this is a technique you must master—ultimately —on your own.

I was once lost for a long time. I did not quite finish the last step of my training. Somehow, the Words had dried up for me. And then I came home to my small market town by the river; I came to pay my respects to a dying father. On the journey I rehearsed in my mind, again and again, what I might say to him. I wondered at how I might play, at last, the role of a dutiful son.

When I arrived, he was already dead.

Our small business was gone. High grain prices, business debts. One of my brothers had done what our father had hoped: He'd studied hard, done well on our country's civil service exams, and taken a position with the local governor. He lost everything when the political winds shifted and the governor was deposed. He killed himself.

My other brother was a gambling drunk. Our mother was near to selling her home for debts.

I found a job as a low-level clerk with the merchant's guild. I worked my way up. I paid off our family debt.

I struggled to revive the Lost Words in my heart. I practiced for myself, late at night. But somehow, somewhere, I had lost them.

But I've already told you: you can never truly lose them. They come back.

. . .

<u>The Ninety-Second Word</u>
Anchor: The Flowing Spring

The anchoring image for this Word is a spring as it emerges from the ground, nearly hidden among rocks and bracken. A tiny bubbling spring, easily overlooked in the forest. But its waters are clear, and its source is true, and even if you don't see it, it's there: flowing, flowing, flowing.

One day, I felt this Word in my chest. I felt that tiny spring flowing again.

I was married by then, with three children. We were living comfortably on my merchant guild salary. I had responsibilities. Yet I took the time to call to mind old rhythms and tones. Slowly, clumsily, I moved my hands in ancient gestures.

Our youngest son was around four at the time. One night, he could not stop crying. He'd had a fight with his sister, been thwarted in some childish wish by his mother; he was overtired. It was deep winter, and he'd spent too many days inside; I knew he longed to run outside, free.

I spoke for him a modified version of the Wind.

Instantly, he stopped crying. His eyes widened in wonder.

His little hands came up; his fingers spread and moved in an echo of my own. A childish echo of The Wind.

<u>On Keeping Your Words</u>

This school will teach you all it can, and then send you back into the world. Let the world then be your teacher. Learn whatever you can from it.

You will struggle. But you do not need to perform in a prince's court. You do not need to teach in a prestigious school. You do not need to make astonishing new interpretations or discoveries.

You might become a tired parent soothing your children with Words. You might share your Words with family and friends. You might be the one in your community who knows the right Words for different occasions, who visits those in mourning with Empty, Rain-washed Sky, who visits the dying with the Seventh Word. Who knows the right Words to say for celebrations of joy.

You might teach those who care to learn: curious children, those who chance to hear you speak, those who've heard the rumor of your presence.

When the fancy strikes you, perhaps you even go to the market on a warm summer night and speak Lost Words of meaning to strangers for free.

Perhaps you continue to practice, and learn, and speak, only for yourself.

<u>On Coming Back to the School of Lost Words</u>

You can come back.

You cannot stay here forever, but maybe—just maybe—you might return.

I spoke Words in my community. I taught those who would listen; I continued to learn. I achieved a small bit of local fame. But one thing nagged at me slightly: I'd never quite finished the last part of my training here. I had a conditional degree.

In my sixty-third year, I returned to finish it.

My wife, my love, granted me leave to part with her for a time. Our children are full grown, with children of their own. They love Words, but not enough to devote their lives to it.

And so here I am before you, an old man just graduating as you are beginning your journey. An old man who has been student and teacher and student again. One who was asked to speak a few words from his experience to you today and whose discursive ramblings you've so kindly indulged.

The Truth of Lost Words

This is the terrible truth: No matter how hard you practice, how inspired you are, you will never speak any Word perfectly. Perhaps Saint Helabora was able to do it in the end. But she was a saint, and long gone.

We—we ordinary people, with our frail human bodies and hearts and minds—for us, everything we say is only an approximation. All of it is only translation. Imperfect translations of a language that is ultimately beyond us, a language of saints and angels and gods. A language that speaks of all things, even though we cannot. We have only fragments of this lost language left, and no understanding of its grammar at all.

This is another truth: We will not stop trying.

We will not stop reaching for perfection, even as we know its impossibility. We will not stop seeking the divine.

We will try to say, again and again, the Words beyond our saying.

The Tenth Word
Anchor: Catching the Sea

The anchoring image of this Word: a great ocean, fathomless, endless. A small, frail boat on its surface; a small, frail human inside.

This Word is you on the surface of this great sea, trying to collect what you can of it in a cracked cup. All around you, the waves swell; you are gently lifted and lowered. The water runs through your cup, over your hands; you will never catch more than a thimble's amount, and never for more than a few seconds. And yet you persist, and the song in your heart is both joyous and sad.

The House of Illusionists

Boys always stay up later than they're told, of course. I walk past their rooms and hear their whispered voices. If I open a door and walk in, I'll see their shadowed bodies huddled together and catch the spark and glow of illusions in the dark. If I focus, I might see a pirate ship sailing toward the moon, a silver tree with shining leaves that chime like bells in the wind, or a flight of dragons across a stormy sea. My mouth might water at the scent of a rich stew or meat pie, crisp and bubbling from a non-existent oven. I've told the students so many times that food illusions only leave you hungrier, but some never learn. It's been weeks since any of us have tasted meat.

I don't step into any of their rooms. I walk past, toward my own room at the end of the hall. Above me, Nala might be making her own round of the girls' hall. Or she's asleep with her daughter, or burning precious lamp oil as she pores over a book. So often these days, Nala and I slip past one another like ghosts.

If I climb to the roof of this house, I might see lights high in the hills surrounding the city. The flare of artillery fire. If I could climb higher—if I were to take the steps to the top floor of the Great Library or the Academy's bell tower—I would be able to see over the city's western walls to the plain directly below. I might see the army camped outside our walls, the glow of enemy campfires. Here and there, spots of light burning in the night.

Should we leave? This is what we murmured in teahouses during the months that Gan's army advanced. We asked it of each other over private dinners, over strolls in the park, and in private rooms. To ask the question too loudly, too openly, might be seen as an expression of faithlessness in the Emperor's might.

For Academy scholars and staff, there were consequences to leaving. There were consequences for anyone. And how many of us had the means and a place to flee toward?

All roads held danger. And then the available paths narrowed until there were none left at all. The city gates are closed. No one enters or leaves without Imperial permission. Corpses hanging from the trees on Traitors' Lane discourage those who would try.

Nala and I never spoke of leaving. I don't know if she even thought of it. And what would we have done with our students, the youngest of the Academy illusionists? These boys and girls from all over the Empire, from distant towns and provinces? The students staying in this house have no family in the city and no way to get home. Some may no longer have a home. Leth and Kiset weep over accounts of pillage in the North, the terrifying rumors of massacre and worse. Neither have heard from their families.

We have little news from outside the city. The papers print only what the Palace wants. We are trapped behind our walls.

A dull roar of artillery like distant thunder. The sound of Gan's rockets exploding against and over the walls.

"Focus," I tell my students.

We are recreating The Hunt in the Grove. The famous scene where Prince Kithwa pursues the Fire Bird through a forest of silver birch trees. Wounded in one wing, the bird skims over the trees, landing frequently among the silver branches. The Prince whistles. He hopes to ensnare the bird with the Four Note Song, which the old Hermit of Thorn Mountain has taught him.

Elis, my most senior student, directs the scene. Under her lead, the students weave together strands of light and sound, touch and smell. Wind in the trees. A breeze across the face. The Prince's whistled notes, piercing, and the flash of red and gold as the bird slips above . . .

A thunderclap splits the scene. The ground shakes—the real ground beneath our feet—and the illusion is ripped, shredded. We're all thrown out of the vision. Window panes in the classroom are rattling. We stare at one another and our true surroundings; I see Elis' eyes wide, her mouth open, our hearts thudding hard.

A rocket has fallen somewhere in the outer districts. Something closer and louder than ever before.

But nothing in immediate sight is burning. The city has not fallen; no enemy hordes fill the streets. Outside the windows, a clear blue day.

A few moments of shaky conversation, reassurances. One of the boys cracks a bad joke; there's laughter.

"Master Taz?" Elis asks, and I nod. She retraces the illusion's outlines, and I help. The grove returns. We begin again.

What is Gan's army, that it can afford to shoot so many rockets over our walls, merely to terrorize the citizens within? What are the Haaks, these people north of the plains, with their weapons that can reach so far? They wield metal tubes that shoot white flame and hand-held cannons that fire projectiles more accurately than anything we have.

I tell my students what we've all been told: that Gan's rockets can't reach us here in the Academy district, that we're too far back from the western walls. That our stone walls have stood five hundred years, and that even the greatest of the Haaks' siege cannons will not bring them down. But I don't know this. I know nothing of what they are capable of.

Aki would have known. He studied these matters; he left us to develop weapons of our own for the Empire. He loved the illusion arts, but his true gift was in the physical and engineering sciences.

But Aki's not here. Nala still wears a widow's gray robes of mourning. But she doesn't speak much of him anymore. When she's not teaching or caring for her daughter, she's withdrawn into her books and papers, studying furiously and crafting illusions alone.

A moment today: the house quiet, the students gone across campus for their lessons in other fields—history at this hour, I think, or perhaps rhetoric. Sunlight in the parlor. Through the windows, a view of the green hills. I stand at the windows, and Nala steps up beside me. I see her thin, strained face, her dark curling hair spilling out from her gray hood. She looks past me to the world outside, but she slips her hand into mine. I squeeze her hand back gently. We don't say anything. We just stand there, looking out at the hills.

It's spring. The scent of lilacs in the air when I walk out the door. Everything blooming or dressed in new green.

And in any other year, people would be flocking to the hills. Countless little streams have been loosed from winter: They're rushing downward, foaming over rocks, making a constant, light music. The purple crocuses are blooming, along with primroses, violets, the rare golden orchid, and flowers whose names I never learned. People should be hiring out carriages for the spring blossom-viewing parties. Servants should be packing baskets of food: hard-boiled eggs, meat or cheese pies, breads stuffed with roast pork or sweet jam, and steamed cakes light as clouds.

Last year Nala and I took a class of students into the hills to celebrate spring. Everyone had new clothes for the occasion; the girls wore red ribbons in their hair. Aki was there. He held his daughter's hand. Little Migu wanted to stop at every flower, each new bird or plant or beetle: "Look, look!" she kept saying. Our students went ahead, and I lingered behind with Nala and Aki and their daughter, we adults speaking easily of art and history as we walked. We talked of politics and music and weather, of nothing and everything, while light shone through the tender green leaves. The trees thinned; we came to a meadow of bright crocuses, and the sky overhead was a river of light.

"I want to see Lahar and Kithwa," Migu says.

We're gathered in the parlor at the end of day, trying to distract ourselves from worry and hunger. The porridge and bread at dinner were bland, but we all would have welcomed more. Rations for the Academy kitchens are tightening.

Smiles appear at Migu's request. She always wants to see the Cycle of Lahar and Kithwa. At six, she's only starting to learn it. Spring is the season for these tales; all around the city, selections from the cycle are performed. The crowning piece is performed each year before the Emperor himself during the Festival of Reunion by the finest of the Academy's illusionists.

We all know these pieces; the students have been practicing portions of them daily for weeks. But no one can begrudge Migu for wanting to see one again.

Nala leads the illusion. It's only in the past few months that she's started performing for us again. She can't resist her daughter's pleas.

A clear, cool night opens around us. A crescent moon hangs in the sky. There's laughter and the sound of lute music. A brightly lit pavilion. A lake, and lanterns in the trees, and a garden of peonies . . .

A sudden fall of moonlight, like snow, to the earth. From the moonbeams step four beautiful women. It's Lahar Star-Maiden and her sisters. They laugh mischievously, for they've come from Heaven in disguise to enjoy this evening party thrown by a mortal king. As they make their way to the lit pavilion, moonlight glints off their white gowns and the white jewels in their hair. Unknown to them, Prince Kithwa and his friend have also stolen secretly into this party. Even now, Kithwa strums a golden lute in the pavilion. Lahar and Kithwa will meet there and fall in love over a game of poems . . .

The students, tired after a day of lessons, drift in and out of support roles in the illusion; there's a loose, improvisatory feel to the piece. Nothing like the structured, high level of an official performance. But even with this spare support, Nala creates magic. The purity of the visuals, the gleam of light on the lake . . . And I'm there to reinforce her, to strengthen the visuals and interweave sound, the two of us stepping together in a dance we know well.

It's just Nala and me, and fifteen junior students, the youngest of the Academy illusionists. One six-year-old child who adds her own hesitant strength. But together, we can create something beautiful.

I feel Migu withdrawing and just watching the illusion now, experiencing it. I peek out and see her eyes shining, face rapt.

I melt back into the moonlit garden. Together, for this hour, we escape.

"Your illusions are stupid," my father always told me. I remember the sneer in his voice, on his face. "When will you care about what's real?"

It's impossible to deny reality for long. Yet we all try; we're all pretending. Teahouses in the city stay open, even though there are no cakes or pastries to serve with the watered-down tea. Shop merchants open their stalls at market, even when their shelves are nearly bare. The scholars of the Academy are still teaching, researching, writing dissertations and articles in their respective fields. Junior students study as though end-of-term exams will still take place. We all act as though the war is but a temporary thing.

One gate to the city remains open to the world. Gan's army has taken the riverbank and western hills, but our forces still control the northern hills and roads and access to the North Gate. Through that single gate comes all the food and supplies we have.

The Emperor proclaims that the Festival of Reunion will take place this spring as always. He predicts that it will be the greatest celebration of his reign. The best artists of the Academy practice their dances, musical pieces, and illusions.

The students of this Academy House are too young to perform for the Emperor. But we study these pieces so that they may properly appreciate the performances. I run the students through standard practice pieces; I try to instill some sense of discipline and care. When Leth breaks down, crying, during a demanding lesson, I quietly let her leave. When other students lose a thread—when they drift off, distracted—I gently try to guide them back.

We're almost used to the sound of cannon fire and distant blasts.

Our youngest boy, Chiho, joins with Migu in making food illusions after dinner. Kiset snaps at them for it; Migu cries, and Chiho turns red with anger. Nala is in the room, and she scoops Migu into her lap. Quickly, Nala sets an illusion of golden frogs hopping across the floor, tall blue hats on their heads and diamond scepters held in their mouths. Migu's tears turn to laughter. Elis jumps in; the frogs grow wings and fly about the room, croaking . . .

We laugh until we're sick. We laugh and laugh, until we cry.

Afterward, I lecture Chiho again about the proper use of illusions. Not even the most skilled artist can make an illusion real. Even the most sumptuous and detailed of illusory feasts will never fill your belly. I remind him to set a good example for Migu. The people of this house and city are hungry. Using illusions to try to sate real needs is dangerous.

I don't tell him of the consequences I've seen.

A lull in the fighting. We tell each other that the Haaks are running out of ammunition. We say that they, too, are getting hungry and tired. We say that help will come soon from the eastern provinces, that the Haaks' supply lines are under attack, that our allies will soon ride to our aid.

Warming days and lingering twilights. I see the first butterflies in the kitchen garden. Nala's found something in the notebooks she's studying. I see it in her eyes—some connection, some discovery that she's made. She's turning something over in her head. She begins to meet me more regularly for tea in the parlor between classes. We talk at night, after the students and Migu are in bed.

We talk about the war and the future. We talk about immediate things—the price of grain at the market, a merchant who is rumored to be hoarding a stash of fine orchid tea. The Emperor's latest mad proclamation. How to keep two of our quarreling students from tearing each other apart.

But more often, she wants to talk about philosophical questions. The history and theory of our craft. The spark of old arguments is revived; as we debate, her face and voice grow animated and warm. We find ourselves slipping back to an earlier time, before war and any hint of political strife, when staying up late and discussing the performance notes of an obscure but beautiful illusion piece seemed the most important thing in the world.

"Do you remember the way we used to argue in Master Kha's class?" she interrupts me one night, smiling.

I laugh, for how could I forget?

"Did you ever believe it?" And her eyes are intense now, no longer laughing. "The Marilaird Heresy?"

I look away. There's pain in that phrase. But for a moment, I also feel the lightness of those student days. That rush of excitement—Master Kha, renowned scholar back from a sabbatical in the East, talking of his new findings to us, waving his arms in his enthusiasm, illusions sparking casually from his mind. My own mind spinning with new ideas. I was a naïve boy from the southern coast, still new to the capital. It was my first real introduction to the theory of my craft, and how stunning that Master Kha should open his lectures to everyone, even junior students like me. Arguing with Nala and Aki in teahouses afterward. The three of us giddy at the sound of our own words. Aki spinning his complex geometries of logic, only to have Nala bring them down with a single, devastatingly honed point. We tossed ideas back and forth like a child's ball. And underneath the playfulness, a seductive question: What if the Marilaird Heresy were real? What if illusions really could become truth?

It was but a small part of Kha's lectures. A revival of a historical argument long suppressed and nearly lost. But it was the part of his course that captured every student's imagination.

Of course, I wanted to believe. We all did, even as we took turns debating both sides.

"No," I tell Nala now, meeting her eyes. I've never been good at lying. I never believed in it, despite my excitement. It's as I told Chiho. Illusions are only that: illusions.

White butterflies in my mother's garden. Brown lizards scampering up the sun-warmed walls. And me playing with my younger brother and sister, crafting illusions to entertain them. My father's footsteps, his curt words as he walked briskly through our illusion-play. His growing impatience. I tried to hide my illusion crafting, then, to focus on practical matters. To be a good son.

The blow to my face. The warm blood filling my mouth. My father stood there and winced, rubbing his hand from the pain that his own blow had given him.

Artillery fire again, a constant thunder. Refugees from more of the outer districts crowd our streets. A growing hysteria in the air.

Reinforcements have come, but they are reinforcements for Gan's army. A new division of Haaks from the west. There's fighting for the northern hill forts and access to the North Gate. It's rumored that any day now, our defenses there will fail.

The Academy closes. There is no Imperial announcement; the Emperor has said no word—but His Majesty's Royal Academy of Science, Knowledge, and Art is suspended. End-of-term exams canceled. No one has been paid in weeks, and paper, ink, and other supplies are so dear. *Go home*, the Academy officials tell us. *Take care of your families. Take care of yourselves.*

Nala and I are both far from home. Anyone who lives in an Academy House is.

We confer with our cook before she leaves our service; grimly, we inventory the storeroom shelves. There will be no more food supplies from the Academy. We're on our own.

We still practice illusions each day with our students. We're still working through the Cycle of Lahar and Kithwa. There's little else to do.

"Focus," Nala says.

Prince Kithwa and Lahar Star-Maiden have fallen in love. They played a game of poems in the Moon Pavilion, and at the first touch of dawn, Lahar vanished, even as Kithwa was reaching for a final rhyme.

But then Kithwa captured the Fire Bird of the Silver Grove with the help of the Hermit of Thorn Mountain. Now he commands the Fire Bird to take him to his beloved. The bird calls upon her kin, and a flock of flame-plumaged birds carries the Prince to Heaven . . .

The wind of their passage. A canopy of fire. The Prince lies in a silken hammock suspended on strings from the Fire Birds' beaks. He stares upward at their beating wings.

We fly him through a brightening dawn. In the distance, a mountain swathed in purple clouds. A city on the mountain peak, and Lahar's castle shining within it: a brilliant star.

"Marilaird," Nala says, and I don't have the heart to argue.

Marilaird is a legend, a myth. A story brought back by a deluded old man. The basis of a heresy buttressed by even more obscure tales. A footnote in the *Chronicles of the Twin Empires*. A few lines in the *Annals of the Grand Illusions*. The subject of an unfinished monograph by one Master Kha.

Marilaird is the story of an illusion that became real.

Illusions aren't real. Even children know that, for even a small child can see right through one. We illusionists can spin visions of shimmering light; we build palaces from air and pluck stars from the sky. We conjure dragons and the songs of dead poets.

If I wanted, I could lay out a feast for this starving city that would best anything at the Emperor's table. Platters of roast meats and fowl, grilled fish from the Sapphire Sea. Dozens of kinds of breads and dumplings, saffron-scented rice from the Valley of Ahn, and tea from the fields of Lash. Delicacies from every corner of the Empire. Lush fruit from the far South where snow never falls. Figs and oranges from my own home on the southern coast. The crisp flatbreads we bake there, the sweet cakes drenched in lemon syrup.

But as I've told my students, that feast would satiate no one. In the end, it would only sharpen hunger.

Only the gods can make their visions real.

We humans believe, while we're weaving our illusions. For a time, we can make others believe. But the audience has to *want* to believe.

This is why Father called me a fool, and worse. Why I never returned home after enrolling in the illusion division of the Academy. Anyone can see through illusions if they wish; anyone can refuse to believe, can recognize an illusion for what it is. *Lies,* my father spat, and the spray of his spittle touched my face. *Children's tricks, stupid, useless*—! If he could, he would have physically dragged me from my Academy House. But at sixteen, I was as tall as he, and no longer so weak. He shouted in rage until he was incoherent, but he did not hit me. And though my voice shook, I did not change my mind. I did not switch my studies to more practical matters. I took a sword to his heart, my mother later wrote me. I betrayed my parents' trust. They sent me to the capital for the prestige of having an Academy-trained son. They'd meant me to study law so that I might help advise my father's business; perhaps I might even become a judge or enter the Imperial administration. I was not meant to indulge in pretty illusions. I, the eldest son of an ambitious merchant.

Lies. Tricks. Useless.

The Haaks have taken the northern hills and roads. They shoot rockets at us from our own hill forts. The city is surrounded, the North Gate blocked. The siege is now complete.

"I want to see Lahar and Kithwa," Migu says, and we answer her together. We continue the story.

Kithwa has landed in Heaven. He wears a cloak of fiery feathers, given him by the chief Fire Bird herself. At the First Gate, he dances in his new finery and the gatekeeper applauds and lets him through. At the Second Gate, he sings and strums his golden lute, and the second gatekeeper is so enchanted that she tries to keep him for her own. He escapes and answers three riddles at the Third Gate . . .

On and on, until he reaches Lahar's palace and finally her throne room. She has heard of his coming. She and her three sisters greet him in disguise; they all wear the faces of old women, and it's all the same face. But he goes to Lahar without hesitation and speaks to her the poem he was unable to complete before. He tells her the final rhyme.

The great wedding in Heaven. The rain of rose petals, the perfume of the gardens. The song of the Fire Birds flying overhead.

When I peek out of the illusion, I see the light of Heaven reflected in Migu's eyes.

It's dangerous to fall too deeply into your own illusions. Cautionary tales abound. Once, I thought them all apocryphal. Then I walked into Master Kha's bedroom. He lay in his bed, eyes open and staring at a world only he could see. His pale lips were parted. He spoke no word. He would never speak again. They tried to feed him with a spoon, but he would not swallow. He died last spring, a month after Aki went off to war.

―――――

The heavy scent of funeral incense. Once. Twice. Again and again in this city. So many dressed in the gray of mourning.

―――――

We are hoarding water and food. We are trying to figure out how to survive.

If the Haaks take this city, they will loot every house and building they see. They will kill citizens they find on the streets. The stories of their cruelties— and particularly those under General Gan's command—have swept before them. Weeks of pillage in the ivory city of Lan. The razing of fair Tirelis in the North. Men and male children used for target practice, tortured and killed for sport. As for what was done to the women and girls . . . Not even little Migu is safe from that. The troops took both elderly grandmothers and tiny girl-children. They killed those who resisted and often killed them afterward anyway.

Is there any hope in hiding until the worst is past? Hunkering down in cellars and locked rooms? Rumors fly about the city like panicked birds. Some say that even after the customary pillage and chaos, there will be no hope. They say that Gan has vowed to coldly kill every male he finds and enslave every woman and girl.

Rockets over the northern walls. Houses aflame in our own district. Rumors that the Haaks are digging and mining tunnels under the walls. Our own troops hiding in their fortifications within, unable to confront them on the field.

We have a hidden room in the cellar, behind the storeroom. We drag blankets there, food, lamp oil, water. Our house once belonged to a rich trading merchant, and it's been long supposed that he was also a smuggler, storing illicit goods in this hidden room.

Water. Walking again and again to the public pump on our street to fill whatever containers we can find. Our house has its own courtyard fountain and tap, but the pipes were disrupted days ago.

Kiset rages at the city's plight and flees us to join the Imperial garrison. Months ago, after his home in the North was destroyed, the military turned him away, seeing him as a scrawny, untrained child, a soft Academy artist who would only be another mouth to feed. But this time, they've accepted him, along with anyone else they can find.

I think that I should join him; I should be there on the walls with him. I could at least die feeling a little useful, my corpse perhaps plugging a hole in the wall, slowing a Haak down for just a moment.

I think of Aki, who joined the corps of military engineers. He walked away from his gift in illusions to devote himself to something real. He rode away from us to join his colleagues at the secret Jassen Foundry, to supervise the casting of new cannons for the Emperor, based on Haak designs. He was killed there in a surprise attack, mere weeks after arriving.

Useless. My father's word for me. Ringing in my head.

I'm in the kitchen, staring at the row of knives. They're all we have for weapons. We have no hand cannons. No fire lances. We don't even have a sword ...

"Taz." Nala calls me by name. Her hand warm on mine. Her eyes, large and dark. "Help me."

I give in. I join in her illusion.

Marilaird is the story of an illusion that became real. A fabled castle in the East. The site where a miracle happened.

A Queen summoned the most talented illusionists in the world. It was spring, and she wanted to pay tribute to the immortal lovers, Lahar and Kithwa. She gathered her court, guests, and performers to celebrate the Festival of Reunion at her mountain retreat, the beautiful Marilaird. In a heroic feat of stamina, the illusionists performed the entire cycle, start to finish, over the course of three days.

And it's said that the illusion became truth.

It's said that the gods blessed the gathering at Marilaird, and the illusionists received the power to make their visions real. Lahar and Kithwa walked the earth again. Fire Birds sang. Heavenly flowers bloomed. Ancient battles raged, and the Gate to Paradise opened.

There were servants passing in and out of the audience hall, catching glimpses. But when they came back to clear the room, they found no one there. The Queen and all her court and guests had vanished, along with the performers. It was said that they had all passed through the door Lahar opened. They were never seen again.

"We can do it," Nala insists. "Master Kha was alone. We're not. We have each other."

We never knew exactly what Master Kha had done. Only that he had disappeared, somehow, into his own mind. Nala was the one who found him.

She was his only student that term. She was working with him for her post-graduate research.

She shows me again his notebooks, the text copied from archives in the East. Performance directions discovered in an old library. Biographical notes on Marilaird's lead illusionists. There are other legends collected in Master Kha's handwriting: The story of a woman who used illusion to create a great jewel, a warrior who used illusion to summon a mythical sword. But the legend of Marilaird has the most historical support. There is even an account of Kha's travel to the ancient ruins; his description of the faded mosaics and tiled fountains, the cracked arches and columns open to the sky.

"If we work together," Nala says. "If we believe."

And it's absurd to think of: two of the most junior faculty in all the Academy working with the youngest of students to recreate a performance of legend. But what is there to lose in the attempt? We've been practicing all along.

I almost laugh, for no one else in the Academy would even try. The Marilaird Heresy—true to its name—was always controversial, and after Master Kha's death, it came under new clouds. Numerous faculty advised Nala that it would be best for her to choose a different line of research. It's likely the reason why she's still teaching junior students, why she hasn't been promoted —why, despite her talent, she was put in charge of this youngest Academy House with me.

She was always stubborn.

I grasp her hand.

Grace. The unearned gift of the gods. She's identified it as a thread binding Marilaird with similar tales. Can you ask the gods for grace? Can you anticipate it? Or, as some of our theologians say, can you only open yourself up to its possibility?

If she could truly bring any illusion into being, what would she choose? What did Master Kha try to do by himself? Was there some private illusion he desperately wanted to make real? Did he die believing that he'd achieved it?

Someone is screaming in the streets outside.

"Yes," I tell her.

As the city falls, we huddle in our cellar and spin illusions.

Lahar and Kithwa meet on a lilac-scented night. Kithwa follows her to Heaven, passes the tests laid out for him, and wins her heart. After their wedding, they depart for his earthly kingdom.

But their bliss does not last.

For envy is stirred in the heart of Kithwa's eldest cousin. An old rivalry between family branches is renewed. The King of Demons sees a chance to make mischief and walks in disguise through human courts, whispering rumors into willing ears. Kithwa bests his cousin at a public game of archery and the resentment grows.

The death of Kithwa's father, the King. Then open rebellion. A kingdom torn. Neighboring kingdoms are drawn into the conflict. The world is ablaze.

Lahar heals Kithwa's soldiers on the battlefield with a Heaven-grown herb. She advises him on military strategy. Their forces are winning. But then she is lured to Heaven under false pretenses, and her family attempts to hold her there.

The Demon King raises a mighty mountain range. Jagged peaks which scrape the sky. Sheer cliffs of rock. Lahar escapes Heaven, but the mountains block her return to Kithwa's kingdom. Her husband and children are now on the other side of a wall of stone.

This is the part of the story that always makes Migu cry. Her eyes well up, and she begs us to hurry through this section or to skip it altogether.

But we can't.

We have to stay with Kithwa as his forces crumble. As his people die. As he and his children—a boy and a girl, twins no older than Migu—flee into the wilderness. They run into the foothills birthed beside the great mountain range.

The Fire Birds have vanished. In their stead, Lahar sends ravens as messengers to her family. But none can find them.

She vows not to give up.

We finish the scene and darkness returns. No light in the cellar.

Above our heads, sharp blasts from hand cannons. Shouts and running feet. The sound of breaking glass. Our soldiers and the enemy, fighting in the streets.

"Take care of them for me." It was the last thing Aki said to me. The clink of cups and cutlery, the buzz of voices in the teahouse. His crooked smile. He tried to keep his voice light. We were always trying to keep our tone light. Even when he was leaving for war and asking me to care for his wife and child.

He touched my shoulder. I covered his hand there with my own. He squeezed lightly, and I saw him swallow. And then he smiled again.

"Take care of them for me," he repeated, and walked quickly away. I dropped my eyes, unable to watch him go.

"Again," Nala tells us. "Again."

We shape the final scene together, the most critical one. Again and again.

Each time we withdraw from our shared illusion, each time we return to the cellar—the world feels a little less real.

There is a place our teachers warn us of. A place where illusion and reality blur. A moment when the illusionist loses control, and the illusion takes over.

I don't know how long we've been in the cellar. No one asks. Our water is running low, and our food is long gone. But those concerns are distant. I scarcely feel the thirst or hunger now. No one complains.

The illusion continues. Students drift in and out as they need a break, but someone is always there to maintain it. Nala is always there. She's brilliant, and I'm with her, and we work together as one, as though we know the other's mind and heart, and I know this is the best work of my life.

Is this what it means to be blessed by the gods? Heavenly wind scatters the purple clouds hiding Lahar's star castle, and it's more real than anything I've ever known.

I fall asleep, I think, and there is no separation between dreams and waking. The illusion continues, and I'm Prince Kithwa borne aloft by a flock of Fire Birds. I'm Kithwa's best friend—the one who went with him to the fated garden party, who sat beside him as he rhymed in the Moon Pavilion— falling beside him in battle. I'm Lahar, desperate to save her children, and I'm a child running from the Demon King's army . . .

A pounding noise. Deep voices, laughing. They speak in the language of the Haaks.

With a start, I'm back in the cellar, sitting bolt upright, heart pounding. The Haaks are here. They're broken through our compound's gate. They're ramming down the front door.

In the darkness, I grope for Migu, my students, anyone. I cry a warning. In our carelessness, we've left the door to our hidden room open, and some have been resting in the outer storeroom, seeking to escape the close quarters and accompanying stench of the smaller, hidden cellar room.

We grab up all evidence of our existence, blankets and buckets of human waste, and seal them and ourselves in the inner room, just as we hear the Haaks enter the house.

We hear them moving through the parlor and kitchen. Their voices— loud, jovial, excited; they might as well be men making merry at a liquor house. They're pulling down furniture, jerking open cabinets, stomping up and down stairs.

My heart goes still as they pound at the cellar door.

Nala and Migu and Elis and Leth, Chiho and Aran and Kel, and the rest .. . My boys and my girls. Kiset, who is probably dead. I hold the ones I have left. We're all motionless, silent, together in the dark.

What do you miss most? Nala asked us. *What do you love most? What would you see in Paradise?*

It's the famous last scene of the Cycle of Lahar and Kithwa. But it's also incomplete, for no illusionist depicts the opening of the Gate to Paradise. Paradise is beyond description, even for a Heavenly being like Lahar and her kin. True Paradise is a place beyond visible Heaven, unreachable by Fire Birds, and far beyond the mortal realm.

"It is a field," the poet Kalis says, "beyond gods and demons, beyond our ideas of suffering and joy."

Lahar opens the Gate to Paradise, and this is told in words, not illusion. To try to depict it with illusion—to project a vision for others of what cannot be seen with living eyes—is sacrilegious. No one can envision Paradise. There is a reason that an idea inspired by a legendary performance is called the Marilaird Heresy.

Many would say that Nala is asking us all to commit blasphemy. But is it blasphemy if we summon the Gate in truth?

What would you see? Nala asked us one by one, and over days of practice we've shown her. She's paid close attention and shown our visions back to us. Back and forth, adjusting, subtly changing, incorporating new details each time.

But she hasn't yet fit those visions into the final act. The sacrilege hasn't been formally committed.

Now, as we press tight together in the hidden cellar room, she brings up the first image of the last act, exactly as it's laid out in official performance notes. As one, we jump in to reinforce the illusion. Constant practice enables us—even Migu—to snap instantly into a scene.

Kithwa and his followers are stumbling through the wilderness. His numbers have been so reduced by hunger and wolves and demons that only he and his children are left.

On the other side of the mountain range, Lahar is still calling and searching. She has not given up. She has sacrificed her immortality and youth. She has sought the aid of the Hermit of Thorn Mountain. She has spent years in silent meditation and endured painful rites of purification to do what she needs to do.

She will create a path through the mountain range where none existed before. She will find and rescue her family.

Somewhere far from this mountainside, a cellar door splinters and gives. I hear it break. Faintly, at the edge of my consciousness, I hear the Haak soldiers stomp down the stairs. Their rough voices—grumbling, disappointed—at the lack of food on the storeroom shelves.

But the sounds are distant, from another world. They catch my attention only for a second. I sink deeper into the illusion.

I feel something in myself give way. Some submerged barrier that was always holding me back. Some fear that is now gone.

The illusion arts are important. I know this now. They've always been important, and what we are creating together is *real*.

Lahar sings a song of piercing grief and strength and longing. The mountain shakes. The mountain cracks. A rift opens through a core of solid rock, and a new valley is created.

Up this valley, slowly, climb Kithwa and their two children, now grown.

Lahar waits for them at the top. She is not allowed to go to them. She is no longer quite of their world; nor is she of Heaven. She's caught between.

If they are to be with her, they will have to leave their world as well.

They near, and she prepares to open the Gate to Paradise. The only place where they can now be together. The only way to escape their enemies of Heaven and Earth and Hell.

And this is where the Cycle of Lahar and Kithwa should end. Here the director of the performance should stop and describe the last events in words alone. The actual Gate to Paradise is never seen.

But we see it now, and it's opening for us. A fair country glimpsed through an archway. A field of golden grain. A cold and rocky seashore in the North. The seaside hills of my own home province: the dry grass turned to gold in the summer sun and the ocean shimmering below, a deep, vivid blue-green that I've seen nowhere else in my life. There is the smell of lemons, of citrus, of jasmine from my mother's garden. And then I see the green hills of my adopted city. It's spring. The hills are blooming with purple crocuses, with primroses and violets and orchids. Master Kha is waving to us from the meadow. Kiset stands next to him, grinning. My younger brother and sister, who I've missed for so long, are there, too, happily eating lemon cakes and jam. It is the day of the Festival of Reunion. And it doesn't matter if we leave our bodies behind, if none of this is physically real, if the Haak soldiers have found our hidden cellar room and are even now dragging us out—or if they've opened the door to find no one at all. My young students are screaming in joy, running through the gate. Nala is crying. Aki is smiling at us all, and Migu throws herself into her father's arms, shrieking, as Nala and I run to keep up.

Acknowledgments

"Wild Ones," *Bracken*, January 2018.
"Traces of Us," *GigaNotoSaurus*, March 2018. Reprinted in *The Best Science Fiction of the Year: Volume 4*, 2019.
"Taiya," *The Future Fire*, September 2017.
"The Wave," *The Future Fire*, June 2016.
"The Young God," *Kaleidotrope*, June 2018.
"The Message," *The Future Fire*, February 2019.
"The Things That They Will Never Say," *Daily Science Fiction*, May 2018.
"The Breaking," *Mithila Review*, March 2020.
"All the Souls Like Candle Flames," *Luna Station Quarterly*, December 2016.
"Of Milk and Blood," *Unsung Stories*, December 2016.
"Between Sea and Shore," *GigaNotoSaurus*, August 2014.
"Wings," *Translunar Travelers Lounge*, August 2019.
"Fanfiction for a Grimdark Universe," *Translunar Travelers Lounge*, February 2021.
"The House of Illusionists," *Liminal Stories*, August 2018.
"An Address to the Newest Disciples of the Lost Words," *Lightspeed Magazine*, January 2022.
"Once on a Midsummer's Night," *GigaNotoSaurus*, February 2022.
"Sweetest" is original to this collection.

Author's Note

This book would not exist as it is without the help and encouragement of many people. There are far too many to thank by name, but I will attempt to thank some of them here.

First, my thanks to Oghenechovwe Donald Ekpeki for plucking this collection out of the slush pile as a guest editor for Interstellar Flight Press. My thanks to all the staff at Interstellar Flight Press who were involved in shepherding this book to completion. Special thanks to Holly Lyn Walrath, publisher and editor extraordinaire, for her thorough and thoughtful edits, her beautiful cover design, and all the additional work she's put into bringing this book to life.

Most of these stories were first published in speculative fiction magazines. Thank you to all the editors, publishers, and staff at these venues. You gave my stories their first homes, you gave a new writer her first taste of real encouragement, and your work keeps the speculative short fiction scene alive and thriving. Thank you for all the work that you do, for me and for so many other writers and readers.

Thank you to the larger community of fantasy and science fiction writers and readers I've met. Thank you to that first little critique group at Critters. Thank you to those I've met later, online and elsewhere. If we have ever exchanged beta-reads, if you have ever read and boosted my work, if we have ever simply gushed online together about a book or story we loved—thank you, thank you. The community, support, encouragement, and camaraderie helps me keep going.

Not least of all, thank you to my family. Thank you to my daughters, Willow and Rowan, who are also lovers of other worlds. You two have been, at various times, inspirations, muses, first readers, and fellow writers. I hope you like this collection.

Thank you to my husband, George. You bought me the fancy office chair, gave up the office to me, cook me focaccia and curry, and listen to me ramble and rant about writing. You support me and our girls in all ways. Thank you.

A final thanks to you, the reader, holding this book in your hands.

About the Author

Vanessa Fogg dreams of selkies, dragons, and gritty cyberpunk futures from her home in western Michigan. She spent years as a research scientist in molecular cell biology and now works as a freelance medical/science writer and editor. Her fiction has appeared in *Lightspeed, Podcastle, GigaNotoSaurus, The Deadlands*, Neil Clarke's *The Best Science Fiction of the Year: Vol 4*, and more. For a complete bibliography, visit her website at vanessafogg.com.

Interstellar Flight Press

Interstellar Flight Press is an indie speculative publishing house. We feature innovative works from the best new writers in science fiction and fantasy. In the words of Ursula K. Le Guin, we need "writers who can see alternatives to how we live now, can see through our fear-stricken society and its obsessive technologies to other ways of being, and even imagine real grounds for hope."

Find us online at www.interstellarflightpress.com.

facebook.com/interstellarflightpress
x.com/intflightpress
instagram.com/interstellarflightpress
patreon.com/interstellarflightpress
bsky.app/profile/interstellarflight.bsky.social